Roaming Holiday

ROAMING HOLIDAY

MARINA HILL

For
those of you who feel unseen
or like a ghost in your own life.

You are seen and loved.

CHAPTER ONE
NINA

I don't want to die today.

My fingers ache from drumming them against my thighs for the past ten minutes. I narrow my focus on my tired muscles. If I stop, I think. If I think, every deadly scenario will force its way—

"Stop," Maia says, covering my hand with hers.

I inhale and crane my neck to see how many more people are behind us. At least thirty. I study their faces because they might be the last ones I'll see.

"Is it hot in here? I'm hot," I say, fanning myself after rolling up my sleeves. I refuse to remove my jacket because I'll have to put it back on before sitting down so my bare skin doesn't touch the airplane seat. The thought sends a shiver through me. I exhale.

Calm down, Nina.

"No, you're just freaking out," my sister says with annoyance edging her tone. She scrolls through her airplane playlist. "Did you download your music so you can listen during the flight?"

I gather my hair to twist into an updo. "Yes, of course."

While my fear is the very concept of airplanes, Maia's is having no music to listen to for nine hours. I tie off my bun, and she silently fixes stray curls for me. Still addled from my anxiety, I text my best friend.

I'm panicking.

Even though she's busy moving her stuff into her boyfriend's apartment, her answer buzzes back quickly.

RAVEN

What's wrong? Is the flight delayed?

No, but I'd like to delay getting on a flying death trap.

Aw :(Deep breaths! Take the trazodone as soon as you sit down and you'll wake up in paradise!

I snort a laugh, shifting the heavy bag over my shoulder.

That sounds like a threat.

Shit, you're right.

Zafir says to challenge yourself to not feel stress.

That's awful advice.

I know, but he's a football player. Everything is a competition to him.

You got this. I'll be waiting for your text when you land! Love you!!!!

She attaches a slew of emojis, and I send a heart before

locking my phone. I don't feel better, but now I focus on how at least one of us is making strides in life. Raven is a year and a half younger than me and on a better track than I am. Even though we both graduated with honors this year, she's starting the well-paid internship she'd always dreamed about and is moving in with her annoyingly perfect boyfriend. For god's sake, he nearly lost the interest of the NFL because he delayed a game just to tell Raven how he felt about her.

Me?

Within the last month, I moved back in with my parents after graduation, I dumped my cheating boyfriend of eight months, and I accepted a mid-paying job because I'm too scared to dream bigger.

Rather than panicking about being thousands of feet in the air with nothing between me and the hard ground, I'm panicking about my life path that has absolutely no traces of light.

"Teach me some Maldanian," Ruby says as she packs her phone away.

"Oh!" I squeal, reigning in my thoughts. My stepmom may not have given birth to me, but she knows when I need a distraction from anxiety.

I tamp down my bubbling excitement; talking about a language is the quickest way to calm me. I can't wait to be completely immersed in the Maldanian language. I repeat plenty of basic phrases and give her tips on remembering them. Maia slides off her headphones to practice with us.

I avoid falling into a lesson about the foundations of Maldanian because then I'd lose both completely. "Okay, let's try a conversation," I say to Ruby. "Ciao, bueninera. Cómi stara?"

She clears her throat. "Stari bueni, gracea. Ke tu?"

"Bueni, gracea. Tu fimare?"

Ruby opens her mouth, but no words come out. Her gaze wanders as she tries to form a reply. "What does fimare mean again?"

"'Tu fimare' asks if you're hungry."

She huffs. "This is the extent of my knowledge."

"That's okay!" I exclaim. "To help with your accent, remember that it's almost a perfect blend between Italian and Spanish, with a dash of Greek elements." The line moves slowly along the jetway, and I eventually drop my duffle on the ground to nudge it ahead. I roll my aching shoulder.

Maia snorts. "Step one of learning Maldanian: master three other languages."

"You took Spanish in high school," Dad says to her. "Some of it should come easy to you."

"Why even try, though? I have a translator right here." She jabs her thumb in my direction. Languages have always frustrated her to the point of tears. A jetway isn't the place to lecture my younger sister about her own brilliance. She's a genius in her own right and doesn't give herself enough credit. I don't tell her this. I've said it so often that it has less value with each utterance.

I sling an arm around her shoulders. "And *I* have a botanist to tell me all about the flora in Maldana. Which fruit is edible, which isn't..."

Dad beams with pride at us. "I'm so proud of you girls." He releases a sharp breath. "Twenty-four with a master's in linguistics and twenty-one with a bachelor's in botany. Wow. I'm the luckiest father."

"Plant biology," Maia corrects, blushing, "but I get the sentiment."

I wouldn't call it lucky that our combined debt is over

200,000 dollars. And if not for scholarships and financial aid, it would have been much worse. My five-year program lasted six, but stretching it out was worth it.

I look over at Maia and her button nose and high cheeks and remember the weekend she'd visited and demanded I cut my workload. The stress would have killed me; she saw it before I did. Gratitude swells in my chest. I spent my whole life taking care of her, and it feels good to know she takes care of me, too.

"You have your inflatable thing for your back, right?" I ask her.

"Psh, of course. I checked five times before we left." The vacation would start off horribly if her chronic back pain flared because she didn't have her proper support. I would have given her my neck pillow and then *I* would be miserable.

At this point, we reach the plane entrance and step onto the winged tube of death. Maia notices my discomfort. She removes the headphones from her neck and places them over my ears. With a couple of swipes and clicks on her phone, soothing ocean and seagull sounds fill my ears and block out the world. My sister smiles at me, and my anxiety dims.

CHAPTER TWO
WESLEY
KOSITA, MALDANA

"Why don't you just stay with me for the summer?"

"Because you have enough on your plate," I say, folding an arm behind my head. To prove my point, Joey begins crying, and Peanut barks in the background.

Cora huffs and yells off-screen. "Babe!"

I hear John's distant *"I got it,"* as my sister focuses on me again.

"Told you," I say, situating my hand around my phone so I don't drop it.

"Wes, you're never a bother. Me and Mom are worried. You should be with family right now." Her concerned blue gaze melts my heart a little, so I look away. I spot a fly on my open window and hear a nasally *beep-beep* from a motorbike on the street.

"It was just a job," I say. "I have more than enough money saved to last me until I get another one."

"I'm not worried about the money or the job. I'm worried about my little brother."

I open my mouth to speak; no words come out. It's hard

to tell her not to worry about me when I'd be just as concerned if I were in her place.

Questions and concerns are a constant when your brother pops up out of the blue after years of radio silence. But there was no purpose for me in the underground anymore and I'm skeptical of my purpose in my family's life, too. If I tell Cora that, she'll panic, and she's too good to worry about me. Guilt shreds my gut. I don't know how to get rid of feeling useless if I'm not hunting or eliminating my targets. It solidifies my identity as a ghost.

"If you're not killing men for me, then what are you good for?"

I don't resent Santiago for saying that. For six years, that was my duty.

I glance around my dingy room. The French doors leading to the kitchen have hand-cut sheets nailed above the glass to give me some hint of privacy. Not that my roommate ever leaves his cave.

Before I can convince Cora of something I'm struggling to convince myself, John shouts, *"Babe! Where are my keys?"*

My sister looks off-screen. "Where are you going?"

"To get ice cream."

"I haven't cooked dinner yet!"

"Well, then when's dinner?" John asks.

She scoffs. "You know, you can cook, too. If you—" She cuts herself off with a groan. "Wes, I gotta go."

Thank god.

"All right."

"Love you. *Call Mom*," she insists.

"Love you, too. I will."

Cora hangs up FaceTime, but I still catch her saying to John, "You never help—"

I chuckle and toss my phone across my bed as another

call comes in. My stomach clenches at the name. *Jack Costas.*

Police sirens erupt from the street below, and my heart lurches from the sudden sound. Memories begin to surface, ones I'd prefer to forget.

But I can't decline this call.

With a sigh, I answer. "Jack."

"I half expected you to send me to voicemail," he says in Maldanian.

I switch languages to reply. "It's rude to ignore the man who saved my ass. What can I do for you?"

"Got a job for you. It's temporary, but it could help you out."

"I'll take anything," I admit. "What is it?" I glance at my door to ensure it's shut when my roommate lets out a string of curses at his video game.

"Can't speak of it over the phone. Gotta come in."

I sit up. "All right. Where should we meet?" I don't have expectations for this job. Expectations cost money, but I don't anticipate Jack's reply.

"The royal palace."

I stride down the palace's elegant corridors with two security guards flanking me.

It's not the royal palace that intimidates me; it's the fact that Jack seemingly found a job here despite what happened a couple of months ago.

When reaching a secretary's desk, the straight-nosed older woman behind it goes over the required confidentiality paperwork before I can meet with Jack. I sign several contracts and hand over my phone for her to put into a safe. Everything spoken inside the palace is under complete secrecy. I cannot share that I even attended this meeting. The security guards search me for any wires or other listening devices. The secretary points and instructs me to wait in this chair. No, *that* one.

I sit in the correct chair, twiddling my thumbs before chiding myself to stop. Shoulders squared, I brace my hands on my knees. Awkwardness isn't becoming. El Revalté was deadly and quiet. Military Beck was confident, sure of himself. Civilian Beck is nervous. Desperate, even. I need Military Beck to return and El Revalté to stay in the shadows for good.

Perhaps I could be Wesley at some point and shed the past entirely.

"Beck." Jack opens his office door with a pleasant expression.

I rise. "Jack. You're working at the palace now?"

It hasn't been long since I last saw him, but I didn't think I'd ever see him again. We hug swiftly and pat each other on the back. "Head of royal security," he says. "It's a good gig."

"The big boss, huh?"

He shrugs. "Head of *palace* security. Not the royal guard or anything. Come on in. How's the hand?"

I hold up my unwrapped burn wound as we step into his office. "Better. Doesn't hurt as much."

Inside, another man waits. Middle-aged. Slicked-back thinning hair that reaches his chin. When he rises from his seat, I notice he's at least six feet tall—still a few inches shorter than me.

"You must be Mr. Troutbeck." He reaches out. "My name's Andrew Elias."

"Beck is fine." I shake his hand, watching him curiously. "Elias? As in—"

"The royal family, yes," Andrew confirms. "Princess Beverly is my wife."

Before I can react, Jack guides us over to a seating area. "Let's cut to the chase," he says, gesturing for me to sit in the chair. "What do you know about the royal family?" The men lower onto the couch.

"Other than the queen dying from cancer twenty years ago, little to nothing."

"Good," Andrew says.

"Good?"

Andrew nods slowly.

My childhood in Maldana was restricted to summers and Christmases. I remember the parades and memorials after the queen's death. As far as I know, the royals weren't interesting enough for the media to exploit, and their importance diminishes each year. By the time I moved here full-time, I focused solely on the military.

"Indeed, she died about twenty years ago," Andrew begins. "However, it's not public knowledge that Queen Ophelia had abandoned her role six years prior to her death."

I cinch my brows. "How is that possible?"

"As you might know, Maldanian royals were hardly in the public eye to begin with. When she abandoned her role, we released a statement citing prolonged illness about why Princess Beverly would take her place. The plan was to eventually convince Ophelia to return."

"Why did she leave?"

"She fell in love with an American and wanted a normal life with him. They had two daughters together." Andrew reaches across the coffee table to hand me a file.

"Maia Laffley, the younger one. And Nina Laffley, the older one."

I open the manila folder. "Do they know about their mother being queen?"

Elbows on his knees, he laces his fingers. "No. Queen Ophelia didn't die from cancer, either. She died in a car crash when Nina was five and Maia was two. Their father, Pierce Laffley, raised them in a Massachusetts suburb where they knew nothing of who their mother really was. Pierce remarried when the girls were teenagers to a Ruby Conner."

"What does it say on their birth certificates? How did they never find out?"

"Pierce was adamant they didn't know the truth so they could have normal childhoods. However he avoided the topic, that's for him to say. We kept tabs on the girls throughout their lives."

I look down to see a scanned college ID from Wilton University. Nina Laffley. The princess of Maldana is beautiful. Sharp jaw, knowing eyes, a cloud of curls around her head and down her chest. Her brown skin tells me Pierce is Black.

"We want the girls to take on their birthrights as princesses and for Nina to eventually become queen. From our research, we see both are very educated and kind. Not to mention beautiful. We believe they would make excellent royals."

The following documents include transcripts from Nina's college and grade schools, letters of recommendation, pictures of her childhood home in Massachusetts, her playing volleyball in high school, and anything and everything about her life.

"So, what's the job for me, then?"

Jack clears his throat. "The royal family and their advisors will spend the summer convincing them to take the crown. Although their identities will be kept tightly under wraps, there's always a risk of a leak. We want to assign you to Nina as her bodyguard until—or if—she goes public."

They need a security detail—and they called *me*? I tilt my head and admit, "I don't have the experience."

"You were on our radar because of Jack, yes. But after researching you, the rest of the security team believes you're more than qualified. You've been an outstanding soldier for over a decade and single-handedly took down a subversive organization responsible for the deaths of many Maldanian citizens. Jack tells me you know the city like the back of your hand. Is that true?"

I nod once. "I know it well, yes."

"Then you're qualified. The only question now is whether you'll accept the job. Housing in the palace guest quarters is included."

A summer of following around a suburban American. There are worse ways to make money, and I'm indeed desperate enough for something to do. I inhale a breath.

"Okay. I'm in."

CHAPTER THREE
NINA

Once the plane is high in the air, I flick on my favorite movie: *Roman Holiday*.

I bite back my excitement the moment I spot Audrey Hepburn on the back of a moped. I thought it would bore me considering I've seen it a dozen times. But it's been years and I'm as invested in the film as if it's my first time. Even now, Audrey's elegance inspires me.

Roman Holiday tames my anxiety and builds excitement for the trip ahead. Dad sprung this vacation on us a month ago, declaring everything had already been planned and booked. Being in the throes of finishing school, I couldn't prepare the way I wanted. I need a few more months to be fluent enough in Maldanian!

Rather than stressing over integrating, I try to emanate Audrey's grace. I can do what my heart desires and eat copious gelato and french fries. If I'm lucky, I'll meet a hot Maldanian guy to show me around.

Yes, this is supposed to be a family vacation, but I'm reeling from a bad breakup and would *cherish* a distraction.

By the time Gregory Peck finishes walking down the

never-ending corridor away from Princess Ann, I take my trazodone and snore my way through the free meals and snacks. Maia wakes me up when we start descending.

"How's your back?" I ask, rubbing the sleep out of my eyes before holding my nose and blowing for my ears to pop.

"Not bad. Would've been worse if not for the pills." She twists her spine, and I hear a few cracks. "I'm going to meditate for a bit."

With her headphones on, she closes her eyes and takes steady, slow breaths. It took days to convince her to take pain pills for the flight; she prefers holistic and alternative medicine.

The overnight flight and time change puts us in Maldana's late afternoon, and the fresh breeze is a relief after breathing in recycled air for nine hours. We deplane and walk outside with our luggage in tow. Up ahead, I spot a man in a suit holding a sign that says *Laffley*.

I stop in my tracks. "Dad, why—?"

He smiles. "Nothing but the best for my girls on this trip."

Maia cackles and runs to the man, handing over her bags without hesitation.

"It's best not to argue," Ruby says, nudging my arm. It's good she mentions it because I have dozens of comments bubbling. How can he afford a professional car service? I expected us to be doing things the cheaper, smarter way: the metro, walking, stocking up at the grocery store, et cetera.

"Dad...," I drawl.

"Neen, don't," he scolds lightheartedly as if I'm a kid again. "Don't question it. Don't argue it. Just smile, say thank you, and have the time of your life. You spent the last six years working your ass off."

I sigh and quell my arguments; I've worked my ass off my entire life. My childhood consisted of telling him we couldn't afford everything. He gets ahead of himself, and I'm always left picking up the pieces. I took care of him—of our family—more than he did.

Everything he's done for us, he did because I reminded him.

Once the driver takes my luggage and I thank him, I unbraid my hair to distract myself from thoughts of the past. I'm no longer a child and I don't have to look after anyone. I'm here in Maldana—a stunning country.

My gaze sticks to the outside as we're driven through the condensed roads surrounding the airport. Palm trees line the streets and mountains curve against the horizon. The signs along the highway have more pictures than words, and the views are unremarkably beautiful. The trees and fields are run-of-the-mill by European standards, but I appreciate that I'm not in America. I lean my head on the window and try not to fall asleep. My eyes droop and exhaustion creeps in until the car jerks and my head thumps against the window.

"I avoid roadkill," the driver says, his English broken and accent thick. "Sorry."

I suppress a groan and rub the sore spot on my fore-head. A few minutes later, the trees turn into buildings and the pavement turns into cobblestones. We pass under a sign that reads *Kosita*. I roll my window down for fresh air, only to get smacked in the face by the stench of cigarettes. I grimace and roll it back up. When approaching a round-about, I perk at the statue in the center.

"Oh—Maia!" I blurt.

"What'd I do?" my sister asks.

I chuckle. "No, the statue. I did some reading on the culture, and that's the Maldanian goddess of love. Her name is Maia."

There's very little I know about the history and culture of the country—a downfall of this trip being sprung on me while I was stressed over graduation, my ending internship, and my ending relationship.

My sister scoots closer to lean out the window. "Oooh, I'm named after a goddess?"

"Wanna know what's weird? There's a goddess called Antonia, too. Goddess of fertility or something."

"So—*my* first name is Maia. *Your* middle name is Antonia. Both of whom are goddesses in Maldanian lore?"

"Yup."

She looks at Dad seated in front of us. "Was our birth mom from here or something?"

My chest tightens at the blunt question. Even Dad tenses. Our birth mother has always been a taboo topic. I don't remember her. To me, my mother is a blurry figure buried deep in my memories and a dark cloud that has haunted my father for two decades. My sister and I have always been scared to bring her up; we didn't want to make him angry or sad. Then I got too busy taking care of him and Maia to be curious.

Dad doesn't answer as awkward silence fills the expensive car. Ruby reaches over and takes his hand. Maia and I glance at one another, brows pulled.

"Ask him that tomorrow," Ruby says. "He can give you an answer then."

"What's the—?" Maia cuts herself off, both of us too tired from the flight to argue. I want to laugh at such an ambiguous reply. It's been twenty years.

At the hotel, I freeze in the lobby, my jaw slack. This is much too charming and expensive to be ours—and my sister and I have our *own room*. The receptionists greet us with mimosas and tora di pomke—slices of Maldanian-style apple pie. Its crust is flaky like a croissant and the inside is warm apple. I suppress a moan at the divine flavor.

"Welcome to your home away from home," Ruby says, pushing open my bedroom door with her butt as she cradles a plate of dessert.

My eyes widen at the spacious room. "I..."

"Here, eat." She pushes a whole tora di pomke into my mouth, knowing I want to argue her and Dad's decisions. My words are muffled and filled with soft apples I can't help devouring. While Maia's balcony faces the front to overlook the city, mine faces the back to overlook the hills leading to the ocean—a perk of the country's capital sitting on the coast. I stand on my balcony and let my concerns about costs slip away.

It's Dad's choice, and I don't have to clean up his messes anymore.

After a hot shower, I put on a halter top covered with blue flowers and pair it with white linen pants. Thankfully my period ended the other day.

"Neen!" Maia calls.

"It's open!"

My sister enters the bathroom as I gather my curls into a loose ponytail. Through the oval mirror lined with gilded designs, I notice her hair is wet and in a ballerina bun.

"You washed your hair?"

She grunts. "I had to. It was so knotty."

I tsk. "That's why you gotta braid it for flights."

"Yeah, yeah, whatever." She hops on the counter and

surveys my outfit. "That's cute. Are you almost ready? Ruby and Dad are downstairs waiting."

I pull a few curls down to frame my face. "Yeah, just about. I was thinking we'd go to this place that's near the town center. Only a ten-minute walk from here."

Maia looks over her shoulder at her reflection. She fluffs up her eyelashes. "Dad actually said we're going to a place called Dominik or something."

"What?" I squeak. "What is *up* with him? He's never planned anything in his life. Or at least as long as I've been alive."

She slips off the counter and follows me into the bedroom. "I know, right? I don't understand why he's going all out for this trip."

I pick up my blue cardigan. "You won't be cold in that tonight?" I ask. Her green skirt reaches the floor and her tube top hugs her chest. "You can take one of my jackets."

She lights up. "The green one?"

I shoot her a glare—she knows that's my favorite one. My gaze rakes over her three necklaces and hands full of rings. "Fine. Just don't let your jewelry get caught in it."

A grin spreads across her face. "I promise!"

CHAPTER FOUR

WESLEY

The onboarding process is quick.

After two hours of paperwork and protocol review, I'm sent to retrieve my things from home. My roommate, Noah, is furious that I'm leaving without warning. I offer to pay another month's rent just to shut him up.

It's past dinnertime when Jack leads me to my condo in the guest wing. The only time I was near anything royal-related was at age thirteen. My summer camp took us on a tour of the botanical gardens, but I only remember being so focused on getting Anastasia Rosso's attention. We ended up kissing in a gazebo.

Jack stops in front of the door and holds up a single key. "There's a map of the palace on the kitchen counter. Be in the east wing Antonia room at eight tomorrow morning." He steps closer. "Andrew was being nice. I stuck my neck out to get you this job. Don't screw it up."

My stomach sinks. My skills don't speak for themselves after all. I take the key. "Yes, sir."

He gives my single duffle bag a long glance before walking off.

Inside is a fancy efficiency with a king-size bed and a kitchen blocked off by a breakfast bar. The bathroom is enormous and there's even a balcony overlooking the garden. To my surprise, the refrigerator and cupboards are stocked with foods like fresh fruit, protein bars, and canned goods. Even the linen closet is a mini drugstore.

I plop on the end of the bed with a huff as dizziness overtakes me. Twelve weeks ago, crime bosses fought over who I got to kill for. Ten weeks ago, I made my first good decision in years. Six weeks ago, that decision nearly cost me my life. Thanks to Jack, it only cost my job instead. This morning, I was roommates with a guy allergic to showers.

Now, I'm in the fucking royal palace to be a security detail for a princess the country doesn't know it has.

I take a hot shower and trim my beard before studying the file about my client—Nina. She's won plenty of academic awards and even took her high school volleyball team to the championship her senior year. Every Instagram photo and Facebook post she's ever put out there is included. Pulling up her Instagram now, I see it's private with fewer posts than on file.

I note the frequency and content of her pictures. Very few of her face in high school—mostly with her friends or sister. Nina doesn't post or wear anything remotely revealing, but her volleyball uniform hugs her curves. There are a few photos with two different boyfriends, and whoever researched her concluded that her recent breakup was because he cheated. Who could cheat on her? She's perfect —at least on paper.

The file depicts the tension between her and her father. After a second glance, I notice she's posted nothing including him until her college years.

Under a section solely about her father, it states he

worked as an architect manager for thirty years, had frequent alcohol purchases, and attended AA on and off. He was a man grieving his wife, no doubt. Nina likely had to grow up fast, creating distance between her and Pierce.

I examine the information hours into the night. It's the first time since my life imploded that the night is dead silent. I stare at the ceiling, knowing that nightmares will haunt me when I fall asleep.

In the morning, I text Mom with hesitant fingers, explaining that I have a new job and will get in touch when I can. Memories slit my chest open every time I talk to my family. Our final interaction years ago was ugly; they saw a hint of the person I had become, and I knew it was better to leave before they saw the rest.

I arrive early to the meeting. Relief washes over me when spotting an Antonia statue marking the room. I walk past the Maldanian goddess to find others already waiting. Jack introduces me to Mason Antoni, a retired military soldier assigned to Maia. He's around six-one of a similar build to my own. His hair is more gray than brown, and a beard clouds his unsmiling face. There are two others—Gregory and Silas—whose appearances I instinctively memorize.

Jack flicks on a projector at one end of the conference table. "Now, we were given the itinerary, but Mr. Laffley stressed that this news will likely throw it out the window," he explains.

Still, we review the blueprints and environment of listed and unlisted locations before discussing Mineté and its known gangs. Even though it's unsafe, many tourists will visit because it's the city's oldest neighborhood. As Nina learns about the country, there's a possibility she'll visit. Her safety risk increases even without public knowledge of her lineage. She's beautiful—both sisters are. Dangerous men in those neighborhoods will notice that.

And Maldanian men are notorious for wanting to make themselves known.

Possibly because we're so forgotten on the world stage. Maldana is a low-threat, low-risk country. Most of us cherish that, some of us resent it. We want to be taken seriously.

Working with Santiago, I was.

I was feared as his soldier. Trakas was ready to make me a millionaire because of it. But I was loyal to Santiago—to a fault. Despite the darkness rapidly growing inside of me, I had everything I wanted. I will never be brought to justice for any of it. I caress the burn scar on the back of my left hand, its soft, raised flesh still tender.

"Beck," Jack says.

I blink. "Sir."

I clench and unclench my wounded hand as he slides over a work phone. I push down my near-constant self-deprecating thoughts and study the iPhone. It has the appropriate numbers saved, and the case has a built-in, scan-protected wallet with proof of employment and a credit card.

The only times I'll be off duty are when Nina is on private palace grounds and when the night team—Gregory and Silas—starts monitoring the princesses once they go to bed. Cameras line the hallways of their hotel.

Jack instructs us of safety points and their code names if we're separated or compromised even though many of these preparations will never be used. A thrill jumps down my spine while we take time to study the blueprints of the hotel. Regardless of how unlikely an attack is, planning for it requires well-rounded considerations that never cease to interest me. It's a single puzzle piece with many different outcomes. My dexterity in preparation helped me succeed —except I used it for the wrong people for years.

After the long day of meetings and briefings, I flop into bed at seven p.m. Once the Laffleys arrive in the country tomorrow, I'll sleep even less than I do now. Jack instructed Mason and me to dine at a nearby table during dinner and monitor from a distance until they return to their hotel.

My fear of the inevitable nightmares usually keeps me from falling asleep. Tonight, it's the anticipation for the future. The money from this contract will last me at least another year. What happens after that, I don't know. I have to become someone entirely new. Do I want my family to be part of that?

I lie back, staring at the ceiling.

Years ago, I became El Revalté, the Ghost. He was known for his deadly silence, for creating ghosts without a trace.

Santiago gave me that name, thinking I would be thrilled. And it stuck. Underground, I was known solely as El Revalté. Above ground, I was Beck, never Wesley.

El Revalté will never die—he's already dead. He's a stain on my soul that I'm forced to carry into every room. Mom, Cora, John, and Joey deserve a family member without such darkness.

I shut my eyes.

Just try.

CHAPTER FIVE
NINA

Maia and I stay arm-in-arm on the short walk to Dominik. The uneven stones trip us up every so often while the evening sun cuts right into my vision. We walk up exterior winding steps that resemble a castle. But it's Europe; it very well could be. I inhale crisp evening air, reveling in the distant sounds of acoustic guitars and clinking glasses.

The steps reveal a huge restaurant patio with dozens of tables and a hostess who smiles and greets us in Maldanian.

Glass panels line the patio, and our table is along the edge with an umbrella angled perfectly to block the sun. Down below, the ancient buildings of a neighborhood protrude from the cliff. The people in the narrow streets look small, showing me how high up we are.

I shiver and have Maia sit at the edge instead.

"Was it hard to get such a good reservation like this?" I ask, marveling at the ocean view.

"I made them early enough," Dad says with a smile.

A waitress brings us water and English menus. I stick to

the Maldanian one for as long as possible, but it doesn't take much to decipher that the dishes are *thirty* euros a piece. Early reservations? An expensive restaurant? I bristle at this newfound side of him.

"They serve *veal?*" Maia blurts, making a disgusted sound.

"Oh, stop it," Dad chides as Ruby seems to search for the veal listing.

"No," she insists. "It's a *baby*."

"Then don't get it," he says, his voice sharpening.

She shakes her head and drops the menu in front of her. "I can't eat at this table if anyone gets veal. I'm sorry."

"No one's getting veal," I say, covering Maia's hand with mine. "So that won't be a problem."

I don't look at Dad or Ruby to confirm. Although my sister's reactions are pretty fiery, I don't disagree with her.

I spot two men at the table diagonal from us only because the grey-haired man with his back to me is rigid, while the man across from him is the opposite. He relaxes, slumped in a chair he's too big for. His dark hair and trimmed beard send a spark through my stomach, so I look away. Even with sunglasses on, he's still fine as hell. But I shouldn't jump on the first man I see.

After the deliciously expensive dinner, we wander the neighborhood below within the cliffside, which is a leg workout with all the hills and stairs. The uneven street is about four or five people wide, yet motorbikes still honk and rev their way through fast enough to frighten me. Maldanians don't care. If we're not perusing the stores, we're looking over our shoulders for passing bikes.

I fall behind the group to stop at a jewelry stand until the owner lights up a cigarette. The stench drives me away. All too quickly, I step without a glance behind me, and the vibrating engine and *beep-beep* of a moped sends my heart into my throat. A person walking in my direction lurches and pulls me from the bike's path, his hands on either of my bare arms.

"Prosítentto," the man says and continues his walk without another word. I double-take as he strides off, for his soft hair and scruff match that of the man I saw at the restaurant. What are the chances? It's not until he's long gone that I realize what he said in Maldanian. *Be careful.* I shake off the whole incident and rush to catch up with my family.

I roll over in bed, huffing at the time: 7:32 a.m. For once, can my body let me sleep in?

I lay cuddled in the surprisingly soft comforter. The fabric feels expensive; its pristine fibers brush my skin. I drift in and out of sleep for at least another hour, dreaming of peaceful bliss, until Maia sneaks into my room and leaps onto me.

"*Good morning!*" she yells. Her minty breath and glowing cheeks greet me. She's a breath of fresh air, cutting into my sleep so brusquely. "How'd you sleep?"

I shut my eyes and push her face away. "No."

"Hey," she squawks, swatting my hand. "Oh, come on. These beds are so comfortable, aren't they?"

I flip sides.

"Dad and Ruby are waiting for us for breakfast."

I groan, pulling the pillow over my face. "Too many words."

Maia huffs, yanks the pillow, and crashes into my back.

"Get *up*," she says, leaning in and singing, "There's french toast."

My eyes pop open to find her sly grin. "Really?"

She nods, and I haul ass out of bed.

Maia and I walk downstairs, clad in our robes, to find a woman serving Dad and Ruby in the back garden. Dad introduces us to Theodora—Dora for short—who will be our caterer for our stay.

"Our caterer?" I echo. She's not much older than I am! It's uncomfortable to be served by someone I could be friends with. She's short and curvy with tanned skin and loose brown curls.

Nonetheless, I order french toast while my sister asks for pancakes. When the two of us gather fruit from the buffet, Maia leans in and mutters, *"Dora's got a donk."*

I snort, clamping my hand over my mouth. It's funnier because I noticed Dora's big ass, too. Not in a bad way, though. I'm envious, and Maia's scrawny ass *definitely* is, too.

After eating breakfast in the back garden illuminated by the abundant flora, Dad lays out the day ahead: a history museum, a vegetarian restaurant he found, and then a private tour of the palace. Maia and I look at each other but don't say anything. We both know that Dad isn't a palace type of guy. He'd prefer to bar-hop and explore local neighborhoods. But he and Ruby seem excited, so we go with it, no questions asked.

It's a hot, cloudless day, so I step into a spaghetti-strap dress that reaches my calves. The sun-yellow fabric hugs my body just enough to keep airflow. I twist my curls into a messy claw clip and slide in daisy stud earrings to match my simplistic gold pendant. James bought me this necklace, and I fight the stinging reminder. He's already taken my confidence; I won't let him take my favorite necklace.

The word *stunning* cannot adequately describe the royal palace.

We pass through decadent ballrooms and abandoned bedrooms of historical kings and queens. The tour guide is so attentive and personable it's almost unusual; it's as if he's hanging out with friends.

"Do people still use this?" Maia asks, her neck tilted to look at the detailed paintings on the ceiling.

"Yes," our tour guide Andrew says. "This wing of the library is just for the museum."

"Those are from the thirteenth century," I tell my sister, looking at the paintings with her. "It took the artist, Sacco Andreas, five years to complete."

"That's correct," Andrew says to me. "You've studied our history. I'm impressed."

I blush. I don't tell him that my "studying" was a Google search on the drive over.

"*Wow.*" A hint of awe covers Maia's tone. Her neck is still craned back and it looks almost comical. "It's incredible how it still looks so pristine."

"Come on," Dad interjects, "we still have a lot to see."

"But—"

"Let's go, girls," Ruby says, beckoning us forward with a manicured hand.

We pout, wanting to bask in our love of academia for a few moments longer. With our arms still linked, my sister and I begrudgingly follow Andrew and our parents through a gargantuan set of doors.

"Gracea," I say to the two men who opened the doors for us. A look of gratitude passes their otherwise deadpan faces. I want to use every chance I get to practice Maldanian, even if it's to thank a couple of museum employees.

The room we enter doesn't appear to be a showroom, but a sitting one. The tall windows and French doors to my right allow the late-afternoon sun to paint everything in a yellow hue, emboldening the already golden decor. Between two couches is a coffee table, and farther back is a fireplace. Above it, a large, classical-looking painting of a pale woman in an elegant dress and bejeweled sash. A woman I've seen before. My stomach tingles. It can't be.

"Maia." I stop walking, which forces her to stop, too.

"What?" She follows my gaze, then smothers a gasp. "Is that...?"

"Our birth mother? Definitely."

ROAMING HOLIDAY

CHAPTER SIX

NINA

Maia bristles. "No. That's impossible."

But I've seen a picture of her before. Eleven-year-old Nina sneaked into Dad's room and rifled through his nightstand because he avoided all conversations of my real mom. He refused to talk about her and I wanted answers. I found a single picture of her—of *them*. They were smiling together. It was only her side profile, but I returned to that picture dozens of times in the following years. Maia, too. I know that profile. I know that face.

"Welcome! I hope your flight was smooth."

I flinch at the new voice. A woman greets Dad with a hug before shaking Ruby's hand. I don't hear their introductions to one another; I stare at her striking similarities to the painted woman above the fireplace. Same dark hair, pale skin, and sharp cheekbones. She walks over to Maia and me with an outstretched hand to shake, her heels a subtle *clack* over the marble floors.

"Nina, Maia. It's lovely to meet you two at last." Her professional tone and demeanor belie the growing sadness in her glassy eyes. "My name is Beverly."

"At last?" Maia repeats.

Beverly gestures to the seating area, and we only move when Dad and Ruby do. The three of them sit across from us.

"What's going on?" I ask, craning my neck toward the painting above. "Why does that look like—"

"She is," Dad says, and my entire body tingles—down to my toes. My heart thunders. This can't be happening.

"Ophelia Jolie Elias," Beverly says, enunciating each syllable. "My older sister."

"Ophelia Jolie Elias," I whisper. My shoulders tense.

"Wait—that's our mom?" Maia asks, glancing back and forth between the portrait and our father. I spot her swishing earrings from the corner of my eye. "What the hell is this, Dad?"

"I'm giving you answers," he replies. As with every mention of Mom, he sounds defeated.

"And we needed to be in a palace to do that? What's with these theatrics?" Unlike her, I don't feel angry. I'm confused. Wary.

"They're not theatrics," Beverly says calmly. "We are telling you here because this is a complicated—"

"Who is *we*?" Maia interjects. "And if you're my aunt, where were *you* our whole lives?"

The older woman flinches. My stomach twinges—not out of pity, but of how noticeable her relation to Ophelia is. *Ophelia Jolie Elias.* Those three words echo in my head. *Ophelia Jolie Elias.* Her full name remained a mystery my entire life. Until today.

My sister's questions are valid, but I want to know more about Ophelia Jolie Elias. Anything. I want to understand why they think this is complicated, why there's a painting of Ophelia Jolie Elias inside the palace, and why Dad had to fly us to the Mediterranean to say it.

"Let's hear them out," I say quietly. Maia huffs but doesn't argue.

Beverly clears her throat with a glance at Dad before she begins. "My sister became the queen of Maldana twenty-six years ago—after our father died. While on a private holiday in Rome, she met an American man who had been studying abroad there, and they fell in love. Ophie loved this country, but she loved him more. So... she left."

Dad's head lowers and Ruby squeezes his hand.

"They moved to the United States and had two daughters—Nina and Maia—before she died."

Ophelia Jolie Elias gave birth to me. She was Queen of Maldana. *The* queen. Crown and all.

"My mom was a queen?" Maia exclaims, her anger dissipating. "Holy *shit*."

Roman Holiday is the extent of my knowledge of monarchs. Audrey Hepburn's character, Princess Ann, felt suffocated in her role. She wanted freedom—and found Joe.

Just like Ophelia found Dad.

Ruby cuts a glare at my sister, and Beverly bristles from the foul language. Dad doesn't care; he squeezes his eyes shut to fight his tears. For a moment, I look at him and see twenty years of complicated silence. How do you tell your children their mother wore an actual crown? He never spoke of her. Our mother remained a mystery because of his pain and her origin. I expect him to say it's a joke, but it makes sense. He poured *everything* into this trip. Because he wants us to feel close to the woman who gave us life.

"All this time," I say to him. "That's why you didn't talk about her?"

"I wanted to wait until you were old enough—until you were ready."

"Ready for what?" Desperation slips through the crack in my voice. When is a child not ready to hear about her own mother?

He reaches toward a folder on the coffee table between us. "The letter. Your mother wrote a letter to Beverly."

Beverly perks and takes out a sheet of paper. "Oh, yes. This letter should explain it better than we are. The original is in Maldanian, so I translated it for you."

Hope sparks in my stomach. I almost ask for the original—to read her unfiltered words. My mother is a distant, faded memory. I'll never speak to her again, but to read her thoughts... It might bring her back to me. Maia and I hold the letter to read.

Beverly,

It's been too long. You're my sister and I love you. We shouldn't stay angry at one another. Like I said, this isn't forever. Pierce and I want to return once the kids are old enough. All we want is a normal life. We deserve that. The institution is no place to raise a child.

At the time of writing this, I can tell you that baby number two is a girl! We haven't picked a name out, but I'll write the moment we do.

Nina is a little blessing. She's such a bright star with so much personality! She's far smarter than a two-year-old should be and she and Jace would be inseparable! I want to visit. I want *you* to visit. I want us to be a family the way Mom and Dad couldn't.

We both said hurtful things. I regret leaving us like that and I'm so sorry. I love you, Bev. <u>I'm not abandoning Maldana.</u> It's my home! My girls will grow with Maldana in their blood. I will raise them to love our world and then, when they're old enough, they'll decide if they want to be princesses. Nina will only become queen if she wants it. I won't take that choice from her the way it was me.

Becoming queen was your dream. Now you get to do that. I know how you are about tradition, and my girls deserve the option of their birthright, so we'll be back. I don't want to lose you in the meantime.

Love,

Ophelia

I read the letter twice. Judging by my sister's silence, she does the same.

Nina is a little blessing.

Nina will only become queen if she wants it.

"You brought us here," I whisper, "to be princesses of a country?"

"I-If you want," Dad replies.

Beverly reaches for the large book on the coffee table. "I

put this together for you." She opens the cover to reveal a baby picture. Under it reads *Ophelia Jolie Elias* along with her birth date. "It's all about Ophie's childhood and life."

Ophie. This woman I've never met before is calling my mother *Ophie.* I want to be defensive, but she knows more about Mom than I do.

Questions about Mom plagued me for years. Now that I have answers, I expect relief and joy to fill me to the brim.

I've never felt emptier.

Beverly is a stranger. Ophelia too. This book won't bring us closer; her being white makes it worse. I look *nothing* like my mother or the woman in front of me.

How can I be queen of a place I feel I don't belong?

"I know this is a lot," Dad says.

"*Understatement,*" Maia mutters. It comforts me that she doesn't reach for the book, either. She's as hesitant as I am.

"But that's why we—"

"Stop," I snap, my voice echoing. "Just—*stop* with this. I'm not old enough to run for president and you're asking me to be queen."

"Princess," Beverly corrects, "until your coronation."

"I'm not the princess of anything! *Or* a queen!" I look at Dad. "You let us build our lives only for this to come tearing it down. We—we have dreams and goals and you encouraged us to follow them *knowing* this enormous decision would come our way."

"I wanted you two to have a normal life! That's what your mom and I worked so hard to give you. I wouldn't defy her wish by doing the opposite."

"So your outcome was to bury her memory?" Maia whispers, knocking through the tension instantly. Dad's defenses crumble. As always.

"I... It wasn't easy. I didn't know what to do."

"Anything," I press. "Instead, you did nothing. She wanted us raised with this culture, and you did *nothing.*"

Ruby's eyes pop with surprise and Dad's head flicks up. His eyes flash with warning as his voice deepens. "Watch it. I did the best I could with what I had."

Fear slithers into my stomach as it does every time he raises his voice in his authoritative manner, but my anger is stronger than my fear today.

"You made my own mother a stranger to me. Not the grief, *you*. What did you think would happen? That I'd suddenly forget you emotionally abandoned us our whole lives? That I'd be okay with being asked to take care of a country when I grew up taking care of you and Maia instead of enjoying my childhood?"

I don't wait to see his reaction. With an anguished huff, I get up and head for the French doors behind me. They're a clear exit to the garden outside, and the height of the day's heat assaults my skin instantly. I walk through the pristine paths lined with colorful flowers. The gardeners give me a nod of acknowledgment. Trellises with crawling vines surround me. I want to take it in, but my entire body is thrown off kilter from jet lag and this staggering news. How could Dad keep this from me?

I walk into an empty gazebo and collapse onto the bench, fighting to hold in tears. I want to forgive his emotional absence during my childhood, but seeing more of the life I should've had makes it that much harder. Mom says in the letter that it's my choice, but I know what's expected of me. Taking care of people is what I do.

Even though Ruby entered my life during high school, she didn't truly become part of the family and help with Dad until I went to college. Before then, I made sure Maia did her homework, kept curfew, stayed out of trouble, had good grades, did extracurriculars, and ate breakfast, lunch, and dinner. I made sure Dad woke up on time, packed a lunch, got to work, didn't drink, cleaned him up when he did, and attended AA. He loved bragging about my academics, so I worked harder. I did my best in hopes it would inspire him to be better; it never did. I drove myself into the ground by being an impeccable sister, mother, waitress, athlete, academic, and daughter. When can I be Nina?

I spent my life being something for someone and nothing for me.

And now I'm expected to take care of an entire country.

CHAPTER SEVEN

WESLEY

Jack sends me to trail after my client, who's slumped on a bench in the same gazebo I kissed Anastasia Rosso in. Nina flinches when she sees me, her eyes wide and glassy with unshed tears.

"Madam," I say with a nod.

"You," she says, studying my beard and hair. She doesn't rise from the bench.

I extend a hand that goes untouched. "Wesley Troutbeck. Everyone calls me Beck."

"Why are you following me? And I don't just mean today."

I close my hand and drop my arm. Clearly, they didn't let her know a strange man would be following her around all summer. "I'm your security detail during your holiday in Maldana."

Nina recoils, considering my words before saying, "I don't need a bodyguard."

"We cannot guarantee your identities won't be leaked to the public. We want to take precautions."

"You're Maia's bodyguard, too?"

"No. Mr. Mason Antoni has been assigned to her."

She hesitates, swiping her manicured fingers under her eyes. "Is that why you were stalking me last night?"

I clench my jaw to crush a sigh. "I was monitoring you from a distance."

"I noticed you at the restaurant," she deadpans. "You're pretty awful at being undercover."

"Preserving my identity wasn't a priority. Your safety was."

She rises to her feet. The yellow fabric of her dress is just tight enough for a taste of her curves. My sunglasses block my curious gaze caressing her smooth neck. I'm no stranger to beautiful women, but the file doesn't do her justice.

Nina walks closer to me. "Do you drive me places, too?"

"Yes, we have a town car. Where to?"

"My hotel."

Before leading her to the car, she finds Maia and meets Mason. The girls speak in low voices with each other. I scan the area to give them some semblance of privacy, as the risk of threat in the public sector of the palace is low.

I survey the city crowds during the drive. Everyday life has been a faraway world for years, and the weeks I've dealt with it weren't good. I spent the better part of them reading in my room. It's not my favorite pastime, but anything is better than adjusting to civilian life full-time instead of short increments like I'm used to. I know best how to be a soldier, a hunter. A figure more than a person. While I can't be more different than my client in the back seat, I can sympathize. She's being asked to give up everything she's spent years working toward.

At the hotel, I hear Nina turn on the shower. Not long afterward, a busboy—Christopher Doukas, born and raised in Kosita to a single mom—rolls a room service cart down the hall.

I stand aside as he knocks on the door and rolls inside once she opens it. I stand in the threshold during the exchange and notice Nina in a robe, her hair wet. I want to admonish her for answering the door while damn near naked. I stare at Doukas, prepared for any wandering eyes. When he rolls the empty cart out of the room, Nina looks at me.

"Are you going to stand out there all night doing nothing?" she asks.

"A night team will take over once you go to sleep."

Her gaze falls to my shoes. "Your legs won't hurt standing for so long?"

I almost react to her perceptive question, but without my sunglasses, my face is easier to read. "No. But I have a chair."

She perks. "Wait—does this mean I can send you to get me french fries? They don't have any here."

"No, but I will accompany you whenever you wish to go." I nod toward the door, hinting it's time for her to close it. "Enjoy your meal."

CHAPTER EIGHT
NINA

After my room service is delivered and I change into pajamas, I plop at the table and unlock my phone with three words in mind: *Ophelia Jolie Elias.* I start typing the name into the search bar until a notification pops up.

> **RAVEN**
>
> So how's the trip??? I haven't gotten any pics!!

I click her message, my fingers hovering the keyboard. Should I tell her? We didn't sign any non-disclosure agreements. I trust Raven, but I'm not ready to talk to anyone other than Maia about this.

> It's… eventful. It turns out my mom was from here. A lot of emotions I'm not ready to talk about, but I'll let you know when I am! Love you.

I add three red hearts before heading back to Google. Her reply dings a second later, but I slide it away without

41

reading. I sprinkle some pepper over my fettuccine alfredo as I click my mother's Wikipedia page.

Ophelia Elias, Former Queen of Maldana

A name.

That's all Dad had to give me. I knew my birth mother's name was Ophelia, but I never knew her maiden one. Searching Ophelia Elias tells me *everything* I ever wanted to know about her. Height, favorite color, what she was like as a daughter and sister. But nothing of what she was like as a mother. Maia and I don't exist in the recounts of her life. The Ophelia Elias biographies believe she died childless and of cancer. It makes me feel disconnected from her all over again.

When I come across a biography that says she used to paint, I leap from the table and shove my feet into slippers, eager to share this with my sister. I swing open the door only to see Maia dashing down the hall, too.

"Did you know she played volleyball?" she asks, phone in hand.

"Oh my god, really?" I squeal. "I was coming to tell you she used to paint!"

She gasps. "No way!" She takes my wrist to look at my screen as I do the same to her.

"Come on, I ordered extra room service," I say, urging her through the threshold. Beck continues standing at attention without ever saying a word. With a curious glance at his profile, I disappear into my room. What type of experience does one need to be a bodyguard? I would go crazy having to stand in one spot for hours at a time and then follow someone around.

Maia and I spend the next hour eating and sharing random facts we're discovering about Mom. A knock at the door cuts into our conversation.

"It's just me," Ruby says, her voice muffled. "Can I come in?"

We exchange glances. The last hour was the first today that this news about our family felt good. I shrug and say hesitantly, "Come in."

Ruby inches into the room wearing the same linen pants and blouse as earlier, but she wiped her brown skin clean of makeup, and her pressed hair is twisted into a bun. "I just wanted to see how you girls are doing."

"So you can report back to Dad," Maia says, curled up on the divan with a pillow.

"No," my stepmom replies firmly. She lowers onto the edge of the bed. "What you tell me stays between us. Ask me anything and I'll tell you what I know."

I'm sick of asking questions. My college years consisted of figuring out what I would do once graduation came around. Would I find a good job? Would I have to move back home? Would James and I stay together? I found answers. Yes, no, and no. I may not like this job for a language app I'm starting in a couple of months, but it was good enough to take care of myself. Now I have a whole new list of questions and a blurry future.

"How long have you known?" I ask.

"He told me right before I moved in."

"Why didn't he tell us sooner?"

Ruby inhales. "I don't know. He always said he would do what Ophelia wanted."

A dozen arguments fill my mouth, but I swallow them. Ophelia didn't know she would die when I was five years old. "Still," I say, "do you think he should've waited this long?"

"I think he did the best—"

"That's not what I asked."

"I didn't lose my spouse when my children were toddlers. There's no way I can say what he did was right or wrong."

She has an opinion—the way she does about everything. But she's always made a strong effort to stay out of my relationship with Dad. I don't know if I respect or resent her for it.

"No one said this was an easy thing to digest," she continues. "Your father knows that."

I rise from the table and start gathering the dishes to load into the dumbwaiter. "My anger goes beyond what happened today."

"He *lied* to us," Maia says.

"Your stay here isn't about him. It's about the two of you learning more about your mom. Your dad anticipated you'd need time to process, so he says there's no pressure to spend the next few days or however long with him."

Ah, the real reason she came. I lock the dumbwaiter door and turn to her, arms crossed. "Duly noted."

CHAPTER NINE
WESLEY

I know it's a dream, but I can't shake the feeling that it's real.

The gun is heavy in my hand, its roughness scraping against my aching fingers. Dust clings to my lungs. Each moment arrives with repeated precision, and not a damn thing changes. My limbs are stuck. No matter how much effort I pour into moving my body, I remain still as gunfire pops off around me. The blown-up car provides enough protection for me, but not for the little boy standing frozen with fear in the line of fire.

I get to him in time. I know I do.

But here, I don't. My eyes snap shut after the first bullet strikes his body. His screams of agony cut into my mind, followed by Santiago's rough voice.

"Clean this up. Find Revalté and bring him to me."

What I think is fury and anticipation building in my chest turns out to be my face dug into my pillow, blocking airflow. Instead of a gun clenched in my fist, a comforter. I flip from my stomach to my back and inhale fresh, crisp air into my lungs. If I know it's a dream, why can't I escape it?

I glance around my new apartment. Moonlight streams through the curtains.

3:22 a.m.

All hope of sleep is lost. The brightness of my personal phone blinds me, and when I turn it down, I notice at least ten texts from Cora. Half of them are life updates and the other half are questions about my new job. She would worry if I respond now, so I shut my phone off and take a shower. The hot water eases my muscles, but the sound of the boy's frightened scream makes me tense instantly. My hair isn't dirty, but I wash it anyway.

A new part of my life began and I'm trying to see the improvements. It's a relief to not be surrounded by a death roster, but mirrors stand at every turn now. I scrub the conditioner into my scalp, hoping that each scrape will rip out the memories.

By the time I'm done, it's four in the morning, and after a few minutes of sitting on the edge of the bed bouncing my knee, I drop to the floor for push-ups. Each rep gives me something to focus on. If I have nothing to focus on, I'll drift back to self-loathing and ruminating on the past.

And I hate letting that control me.

CHAPTER TEN
NINA

I don't realize how tired I am until after Maia and Ruby leave my room. My body sinks so deep into sleep that I forget where I am in the morning.

Memories of yesterday rush back, and I push them aside. This is supposed to be a *vacation*.

I perch on my elbows and study the room around me. The bathroom is straight ahead from the bed. To my right is a sitting area with elegant furniture—tufted seats and sofas made of silk and trimmed with gold designs. In the right corner, a loveseat with a similar style. In the left corner, a bureau. And in the middle of the bed, a frustrated woman. I fall back with a groan, covering my face.

My phone buzzes from the nightstand.

MAIA

You up?

Yup

I'm surprised she doesn't come bouncing in without

warning like before, but I'm not complaining. Seconds later, she leaps onto me.

"Oh jeez," I huff.

"They have *really* good coffee at this hotel. You should try it. I'll order you some." Before she can settle, she crawls over to the phone to order coffee from room service.

"How long have you been awake?" I croak.

"Couple hours," she says to me, then exclaims into the phone loud enough for me to flinch. "Ciao, buenimara! It's me again! I'd like to order more coffee, this time to my sister's room." She briefly looks over her shoulder. "What's your room number? 302? To 302, please! Just one? Ummm—"

"Yes, just one," I interject. "No more coffee for you."

She smacks her lips. "Yes, just one coffee, please. Gracea! Ciao." Once she hangs up, she turns and settles beside me. Maia's morning energy is more than enough caffeine for me. She lets silence join us as she leans her head against my shoulder. "It's just us today. What do you want to do?"

I sigh. We had an itinerary to cram as much as we could into two weeks. Are we even still leaving on our return flight? Do we even *have* a return flight?

"Anything. We can wander, go shopping, go to museums..."

Maia smiles. "Let's do all of it. I, for one, want to learn more about this goddess I'm named after."

We hit the streets to explore.

While my sister dresses in her usual hippie attire, I opt

for high-waist denim shorts with a sun embroidered on the back pocket and pair it with a simple white tank top.

Beck and Mason trail us from the hotel, and I'm not sure the best way to handle having bodyguards. I keep wondering if they need to stop to use the bathroom or get something to eat. Maia routinely sneaks a glance back, and I'm seconds away from insisting they walk in step with us. What if I have a wedgie?

Both men are handsome as hell; I can't decide if that's a good or bad thing. Mason rocks the silver fox look with at least twenty or twenty-five years on me.

Beck is a whole other story.

Tall. Broad shoulders. Dark hair. Stubble. My goddamn weakness. It helps that he's a man of very few words.

These men we just met match our every footstep, and it makes me painfully aware of all my movements. I shake off that worry and focus on walking through the streets both wide and narrow. The summer heat quickly exhausts us, so we seek a gelato stand for relief. The man behind the counter is impressed with my Maldanian as I order vanilla for myself and lemon for Maia.

"Sto bueni," he says, thick brows raised. *Very good.* He's at least two decades older than me, but I'd give him my number. Needless to say, the men in this country are delightful to look at. His smile fades once I ask Beck and Mason if they want anything. Mason looks like he could be our father, but Beck looks like one of our boyfriends.

Hopefully they don't ruin every chance at finding a Maldanian distraction from this staggering princess news and my cheating ex.

My sister and I stroll to more souvenir shops. While I distance myself from being an everyday tourist, I can't help drifting to the trinkets and perusing the jewelry, wallets, and other cheaply made items. When I look at Maia to show her a bracelet, she's already making googly eyes with a Maldanian man standing with a group of friends.

I scoff at who she deemed worthy of her time. He has a stud earring, a partially shaved eyebrow, a tattoo on his neck, and cigarette in hand. I open my mouth to protest, but Mason shifts into view between us ever so subtly. His movement makes it clear that he's with us, and the Maldanian's smile falls as he and his friends walk away. I take a scoop of gelato to hide my laugh. Our bodyguards scared off two men already.

Maia groans loudly, stomps over to him, and throws an arm around his shoulders. "All right. Listen, Mason. I know you're doing good and protecting me and all, but you're getting a bit in my way. I'm trying to slut it up this summer. Just a little, though."

I nearly choke on my gelato. *"Maia."*

She has a habit of being a bit too raw; she doesn't hold back, which is both a blessing and a curse. Mason clears his throat awkwardly before saying, "I've no interest in getting... in the way of that, but—"

"Great!" She pats his arm. Her gaze lands on my bewildered one, and she giggles. "Don't look at me like that."

"He had a gang tattoo," Beck says suddenly, and all attention swings to him. "The ink on his neck was from the Cranéos gang. They're guilty of dozens of crimes including rape, murder, and assault."

Maia looks at Mason for confirmation, and he nods. My sister inches closer to him. "Well, that's good to know."

Sheesh. Maybe it's good to have a bodyguard after all.

We continue to stroll and shop for bracelets, shot

glasses, men, and mugs. Every crowded street includes women who can't stop staring at Beck. He has a steady presence even if he says very little and has virtually no facial expressions. Every time I scan my gaze over my shoulder in the following hours, I can spot him in the crowd quickly, his height a dead giveaway. He's a moving shadow that can't quite be described as stealthy. He's being discreet, yet his size and handsome face—even with sunglasses on—garners all attention.

Even though I may not want a bodyguard, I don't like the scrutiny he gets. He's not here for them to stare at.

An old man with a bulbous nose plays the accordion on a narrow road we pass through. Souvenir and clothing shops flank us. The street is filled with minimal chatter and soothing tunes from the instrument. Maia takes my hands and twirls our way into a dance, and I tap into a faraway dream of being a ballerina and spin with attempted poise. While giggling, I toss a few euros into the performer's hat.

"Wait, wait, wait," my sister blurts, taking out her phone. "This is a cute background. Neen, let me take a picture of you."

"Of *me*? Oh, no, no. I'm good."

It helps that there are few people around, but there's no way I'm getting my picture taken with Beck and Mason watching. Anxiety stacks inside my stomach. Maia tries to encourage me, but I'm insistent enough I'm almost mean.

"All right, all right, fine," she mumbles. "Jeez."

The moment Maia spots a restaurant with a sign showing off that they have vegetarian burgers, she insists we eat there. Our bodyguards sit at the table next to us, and it's getting harder to ignore them. They sit too close for us to talk about them, but it would feel like I'm being stalked if they sit far away. I don't know how people function like this.

Most of the day is spent in the many museums of Kosita. Maldanians love to cherish their history; historical plaques decorate every other block, and a museum or exhibit pops up in random pockets of neighborhoods. When we pass a vine-infested archway with a sign reading *art museum*, I tug on Maia's arm.

"Look at this!"

Since she loves art, we spend the longest time here. There are exhibits dedicated to each Maldanian deity, and we start with the goddess Maia for obvious reasons. The paintings depict the goddess as blonde with porcelain skin, not at all like my sister, but I wonder why Mom gave this name to her.

My birth mother is the only person I want to ask questions to. Not Beverly, not Dad—only her. Why did she leave her country? Would she truly want us to become princesses? She left. She wanted a different life. Why would I come back to the life she ran from? Neither Maia nor I brought back the scrapbooks that Beverly gave us depicting Ophelia's life. It's too much too fast.

Beck stays far behind, near the entrance of each room we enter. The crowd isn't too big, but it's still possible to get lost in. When Maia and I wander apart, I toss a glance behind me to check if he's still there. On one hand, I hope he's gone. On the other, I'm irritated to see a young woman talking to him. She looks more like the goddess Maia than my sister does, and she finds something hilariously touch-able about his arm. But what has jealousy twinging in me isn't from what she's doing; it's from what *he* does. They stay engaged in conversation and a chuckling smile even breaks across his face.

No, I don't want a bodyguard.

Yes, I want him gone.

But he's here. And while he's here, his attention is supposed to be on *me*. I use the crowd to slip away to the bathroom. If he's serious about his job, he'll leave her to follow me, and I feel deliciously petty because of it.

In the bathroom, I use a damp towel to refresh the sweaty parts of my face before reapplying tinted sunscreen. I'm careful not to ruin the perfect messiness of my bun and wait another few minutes to leave.

Beck leans against a wall ten feet away, his arms crossed. His sunglasses are folded over the neckline of his white dress shirt. "Trying to get rid of me?"

I mimic his pose. "I'm surprised you were able to find me."

"Surprised?"

"You were rather preoccupied." I slide sunglasses over my face with a smug grin. "To answer your question, no. That was only a test."

He's the type of person who's good at masking their emotions. Even the smallest bodily movements are calculated. He gives a quirk of his brow and looks away to tell me he's annoyed. He clears his throat, and my own tightens when his eyes land on mine and he lowers his chin.

How can someone's eyes be so damn sparkly?

"Did I pass?" he asks.

I square my shoulders, hoping I emanate some form of confidence. I shrug and walk off. "I'm still deciding."

Maia and I haven't spoken of the princess thing all day. Even now, the car ride to the hotel is silent. It's only four p.m., but we need an hour or two of rest before we go out for dinner. The summer heat wiped us out.

"I don't want Dad to join us tonight," she blurts.

I inhale. "All right..."

"How could he just keep this from us? And *never* talk about Mom? We're just starting our adult lives and making commitments. You have your new job in a couple months and I have my fellowship—the one he *helped* me apply to."

I don't tell her I hate this new job I'm taking. Yes, it's working with languages, something I love, but it's an administrative role. I was too scared to be without a job, so I accepted the first offer. But I still have a life plan. Both of us do.

"He did it for himself," I explain. "He didn't want to talk about Mom so he waited until the last possible moment and still had someone else tell us."

Because he's a coward.

I keep that to myself no matter how badly I want to say it. Maia scoffs, and silent contemplation falls over us. We've asked about our birth mother for years. We ached to know more about her, and Dad dropped her entire life on us without warning.

"I wish I remembered her," I say quietly. I might have remembered her in some form—filled in fractured memories if Dad kept pictures or talked about her. But she was taken from us twice over.

Maia takes my hand. "Forget Dad. This is about us and our mom. Our *real* mom. Maybe this princess thing can bring us closer to her."

I snort. "We shouldn't inherit an entire country just to heal our mommy issues."

"Then we do what Beverly said." She breathes in deep.

"We enjoy our vacation and see if we fall in love with the country."

I squeeze her hand with a smile. A summer in Maldana—riding mopeds, eating gelato, and trying not to twist my ankle on cobblestone roads. Regardless of the outcome, this summer is going to change my life. Giddiness blossoms in my chest.

CHAPTER ELEVEN

WESLEY

I'm no stranger to long, uneventful hours. Many of my targets led rather boring lives, lives I studied for days—sometimes weeks—before taking.

But witnessing Nina's joy throughout the day was invigorating. She found joy in spotting her name on personalized bracelets. She bought one, then a different one two blocks away because she liked the print better. Whenever there was a dog or cat, she and her sister did their best to pet it. She lets her guard down whenever she asks a stranger to pet their dog, trying to appear as unalarming as possible. It creates a window for someone to strike.

Fear pierces my gut. Nina is my client—*not my target*. I shouldn't fixate on her the same way. I just met her, but the thought of hurting her sets my stomach on fire. That's not who I want to be.

When I work, my guard is up and my muscles are on edge. Everything was too calm today. I can shy my way through civilian life, but putting my work mode in a civilian setting is an obstacle I wasn't prepared for. Too many people stared today. Too many questioning eyes glued to me because I couldn't blend in. I tried to be normal at one of the museums; I engaged in a brief, friendly conversation with a woman, but Nina didn't like that. I deciphered her plan to get rid of me before she stormed off. She wears her emotions like a skimpy bikini—impossible not to look at.

I can't be annoyed she did that; countless men either attempted or considered approaching her today, and a glare from me stopped them. I can tell myself it's because they looked dangerous or I didn't like their shoes, but I know I would've listed possible ways to kill them if they spoke a single word to her. I've worked mostly with men over the past decade, which makes walking behind a woman with an ass I'd love to fill my hands with that much harder.

When I pull in front of the hotel, Nina says, "I want to get some french fries."

"Oh, okay," Maia says. "Do you want to look for a place to walk to?"

I park the car and wait for them to decide. Nina clears her throat. "Um, no. I wanted to... go alone. I just don't want to be around Dad right now. I'll be back before we go to dinner, though."

Her sister and Mason leave the car after a few hesitant seconds.

"Where to?" I ask.

Nina clicks off her seatbelt and pops up to my right, leaning against the center console. "Hmm. Do you know a place where I could get some good french fries and watch the sunset?"

I pause to consider. "Yes, both, but the sun won't set for another few hours."

"I don't care. Take me there, please." She suddenly climbs over the console to the front passenger seat.

"What are you—?" I narrowly miss getting knocked out

by her hips swinging by my head. I swallow the agitation and smother a huff. Her flowery scent infects my nose. She plops in the seat and buckles in.

"Is there a reason for this?" I ask, keeping my voice monotone in hopes she won't start a conversation.

"I figured if you're gonna be my paid stalker, I might as well get to know you," she says, kicking her feet onto the dashboard.

"Security detail," I correct, shifting the gear and nodding toward her legs. "And feet off the dash."

She clucks her tongue and puts her feet down as I drive off. My hand tightens around the steering wheel. How am I supposed to act around her? Curt enough that she doesn't want to be my friend, or open enough so she trusts my judgment in case of an emergency?

"Where are we going?" Nina asks—and her light, sweet voice spikes my nerves.

"A restaurant in Monitta."

"What's Monitta?"

"A small mountain town. Ten minutes outside of the city." It has less than five thousand inhabitants, but plenty of restaurants and bars that tourists frequent because of the unobstructed views of the city and sea. Moritzi is a low-key restaurant on the side of the road and the one place I know of that has a good old-fashioned hamburger and fries. There are few things I miss about the U.S., and an American burger is one of them.

A few moments of silence pass before she asks, "So why'd you leave the military? A man named Jack called me last night and asked if I wanted any adjustments to my security. When I said you were fine so far, he told me you *used* to be a soldier, but you don't look old enough to retire."

Hm. Perceptive. I clear my throat but don't answer. The car rolls to a stop at the traffic light.

"Why do they call you Beck?" she continues. "I mean, why not Wesley? Wesley is better than Beck."

I lift a brow and look at her slowly.

"That was rude," she says with a nervous hike in her voice. As she speaks, my gaze drifts down to her bare legs. "I don't know why I said it. Ignore me. As you already are."

Her thighs flatten against the seat, and I bite my tongue at the thought of gripping and digging my fingers into them. Instead, I shift the gear with more force than necessary as the light turns green. I clear my throat again, this time to reply—if only to avoid indulging more possibilities.

"I didn't leave. I was forced out."

"Oh," Nina says, and thankfully that's *all* she says. The drive continues in blissful silence between us. She even turns on the radio at low volume. Commercials in Maldanian crackle through the speakers. I sense Nina's stillness and find her staring at the radio with a faraway look. I figure it's to decipher the Maldanian in the commercial, considering she's a linguist, but I'll be damned if her expression isn't cute and her determination isn't sexy at the same time.

"Are you from Maldana?" she asks.

I smother a sigh. "Yes."

"What part?"

"Kosita and Palfu."

"Then why do you sound American?"

So much for a quiet drive. The city fades as I drive through winding roads up the mountain.

"Mother from U.S., Father from here. School in America, summers and Christmases here."

"Why do you talk like that?" Nina asks. "You don't even

use pronouns or articles. Just *'Mother from U.S.'* instead of *'my mom's from the U.S.'.*"

"*The* fewer words, *the* better."

Her eyes widen, and she fights to hide a smile as she notices my annunciation of the article *the*. "At least give me facial expressions. I'm a linguist. I need something to read."

At my silence, she pokes my elbow. I grit my teeth. She pokes me again—a gentle press of her finger into my upper arm. *Please don't let this be a preview of what the summer will look like.* I give her a look, the corners of my lips pulled down. I expect a falter in her expression, a hint that I intimidate her somehow. But an amused smile spreads across her face as she reaches out to poke my cheek.

I catch her hand before the target can be reached. "Please don't touch me."

She pulls away from my gentle grip and situates herself to face me. "Why are you so grouchy?"

"I'm not grouchy."

"You are."

"I'm not—" I stop, shaking my head and closing my eyes briefly while at a red light. A mother pushes a stroller through the crosswalk. Trash litters the side of the roads, and I spot a stray orange cat digging for food.

"You're my bodyguard against my wishes," Nina declares. "I don't need you and I don't want you. All I *want* is to know more about the person driving and following me around."

I resist throwing my head back and rolling my eyes. A dozen responses come to mind, but I have to remember that Nina is more than a civilian. She's a sheltered suburban American who's never had so much as a school detention.

"What is it you'd like to know?" I eventually ask. She

won this time, but I still refuse to be anything but vague. I pull into the Moritzi parking lot and shut off the car.

"How old are you?"

"Thirty-four."

"Where were you born?"

"Kosita."

"Was Maldanian your first language?"

"Yes."

"Do you like being from here?"

"Yes."

"Why?"

"Beautiful city, beautiful country."

She rolls her eyes at my lack of article usage. "How is it beautiful?"

Instead of speaking, I point to the view in front of us. Golden hour falls upon the cityscape, blanketing the world in bright orange. I slide on my sunglasses.

Nina huffs. "You're impossible."

I unlock the door and get out of the car. "I'll get the food —the owner gives me a good deal. *Do not* go anywhere."

I take the keys with me just in case. I don't need to lose my client for the second time on my first day. As I head inside, a man stumbles—five-seven, dark hair, olive skin— and bumps his shoulder into mine.

"*Sorry—!*" he exclaims.

Instinctively, I snatch his arm in an iron grip. He winces as fear crosses his freckled face.

Not everyone is an enemy. I need to integrate.

I soften my hold and pat the same spot, offering an apologetic smile before walking away. He mumbles to his friends about how hard I grabbed him.

Is this the way I want to live? Stuck in trauma?

I can't cite my time as a soldier for being horrible at

socializing. I withdrew from my comrades more as I worked underground. How could I sit and joke with them over lunch when I poisoned a man six hours earlier? It became harder to face them until, at some point, I didn't at all. I spoke when spoken to—sometimes. I was hollow, knowing I didn't want this, not knowing how to stop myself, and questioning what I deserved. I killed a target because I already killed the last one; it was too late for me.

Was too late.

Stop.

That's not what I'm doing now. I may not be convinced that I'm a different person, but my current job is to protect the woman who ignored my instructions and got out of the car anyway. She gushes over a wiener dog, who jumps up and sniffs her face. She giggles as it licks her chin.

I bite back a groan and step inside. The Moritzi family is happy to see me, and I feign enthusiasm. It gets harder to slap on a fake smile, but I manage to get the deal and keep up appearances. Once I pay with Nina's designated credit card, I glance back to check on her, and both she and the wiener dog are nowhere to be found. But with a quick scan of the area, I spot her a few hundred feet down the hill, watching the sky.

"Is this going to be a normal thing? You, not listening?" I ask when getting close enough.

Nina looks over her shoulder, the backlight giving her a halo. The golden hour sun silhouettes her curls and profile, outlining her body with light. All I can think of is the word *angel*. She looks like an angel. I clench my jaw to crush the thought.

"Probably," she says without an ounce of sarcasm. When I stop beside her, she blurts, "I'm not a snob, you know."

I steal a look at her. I don't care about what she's saying. The light turns her brown skin into a radiant golden shade. It's all I want to pay attention to.

"I never said you were."

She snorts. "Right. I'm offered luxury, riches, a *country*. Who wouldn't want that?"

"It comes with a loss of freedom," I find myself saying. Despite struggling to adjust to and empathize with the issues involved in civilian life, there's something about Nina's contemplation that has a small part of me wanting to comfort her.

She folds her arms across her chest, and I'm keenly aware of the cleavage it gives her. She nods down the hill. "Enough people in that city down there would think a loss of freedom is a price worth paying."

I shrug, continuing to be impressed at her self-awareness. "You're right."

"I know," she replies, and a chuckle at her conceit escapes me before I can hide it. "So what does it say about me if I decline it?"

I don't want to lose what little faith I already have with her. If a deadly situation occurs, I need her to trust me. But my desire to get out of this conversation intensifies with her rumination of moral conflict. Morality and my lack of cost me my career and the life I knew.

"I, uh... I can't answer that," I say quietly, forcing myself to turn and leave her alone.

CHAPTER TWELVE
NINA

I wake up to a *memories* notification in my photos. It takes all my willpower not to throw my phone at the wall when a picture of James and me pops up.

I groan and bury my face in the pillow. One month. One month has passed of not waking up to a good morning text from him and two weeks since slinking onto his Instagram page. The mere thought of him ignites anger. I have nothing but animosity toward my ex-boyfriend, but that doesn't mean I don't wonder what his life is like now and whether it looks better than mine.

A boastful, vain streak runs up my spine at the thought of him learning I'm the heir to a royal throne. His inflated sense of self-importance would implode.

I pull the blanket over my head as shame pools in my stomach. This is why we broke up. I wanted a supportive partner while he wanted an obedient one whose goals would mold into whatever suited *his* path best.

Of course, also because he can't keep his dick in his pants.

Maia and I still don't plan on spending time with Dad, but we settle for having breakfast with him in the garden. It's filled with colorful flowers that I'm sure my sister could identify within seconds. Enough foliage and flora climb the trellises to block sight of the outside world. The only other people here are the few employees—no guests. Now I'm wondering if Beverly made it that way.

The awning above us provides enough shade for the morning heat. At home, I'm used to a bagel or bowl of cereal for breakfast. Here, Dora serves us yogurt, slices of baguettes, marmalade, fruit, and more. The nasal honks of mopeds remind us that we're not in the countryside. At some point, we'll venture deeper into the country, too.

Ruby and Maia do most of the talking this morning— about our museum visits and gelato-consuming the other day. No one loves ice cream like my little sister.

When I'm picking out my clothes for the day, Dad knocks on my door. I leave it open for him to follow me inside. I admit acting like he wasn't there during breakfast was weird. Maia will reluctantly talk to him, but she said she won't talk about the crown. Not with him.

It's just Dad.

Things shouldn't be awkward between us, but I'm finally angry enough to argue past his limits. My own mother became a ghost in more ways than one—and he's to blame. I hope he's not here to discuss her or the crown. It's too soon.

"I... wanted to ask what you girls have planned for the day," he says.

"Why?" I ask, unintentionally cold. He isn't afraid to confront my disrespect and I don't want to argue.

He doesn't ease into the space; he stays tense, his hands

knotted behind his back. "Your aunt Beverly would like you and Maia to join her at the palace for lunch so you can meet your cousins."

My aunt Beverly. It still doesn't feel right. "Okay. I'll call her."

Beverly has my number; she could've called herself, but Dad wants to test the water between us—and it's boiling. Tense silence falls between us, so I refocus on picking different outfits for the day.

I sneak a glance at him, and a small twinge in my core feels bad for icing him out. He's gone through a lot. His wife died. He was left to raise a five-year-old and a two-year-old while grieving. There's no right way to mourn and he's made a lot of mistakes. I'm trying to see his point of view, but almost twenty years have gone by and he's still working for his *own* ease, not ours.

My sister and I just found out that our mom was more than a picture we sneaked looks at while he was working or passed out drunk on the couch. He had two decades of mourning someone he knew; we had less than a week of even knowing her name.

"What, uh, what have you and Maia been doing?" he asks in a quiet voice.

"Exploring."

"What are you finding?"

I sigh. "A world I should've known about already."

Dad wants to say more; I can tell. He takes the hint and lowers his chin. "I should go."

Once he leaves, I settle for a white knitted dress with bold colors around the chest. The pattern forms a point to my throat before splitting to tie around my neck in a halter. I twist my gladiator sandals around my ankles but grab a pair of heels and peek my head out the door.

"Can we keep these in the car for later?" I ask Beck sweetly, considering that holding my shoes probably isn't part of his job description.

Instead of speaking, he nods and takes the heels, barely sparing me a glance. Am I that easy to ignore?

"Thank you!" I chirp, poking his cheek before dashing off to Maia's room. I don't look behind me to see if I got a reaction. One day, I will; he doesn't need to be so stoic all the time.

I find my sister in front of a big mirror, putting on an earring. "Hey," she says, glancing over her shoulder at me.

I flop on her bed and study her colorful harem pants paired with a crop top and chains decorating her stomach. Her long hair is in a bun atop her head. She fixes a stray curl before saying, "Our lovely auntie Beverly wants us to have lunch with her and our cousins."

"I know; Dad told me."

Her eyes widen. "You two talked?"

"Briefly," I say with a shrug, propping up on my elbows across the comforter. "I could tell he wanted to keep talking, but I just get this—I don't know. I can't help feeling—"

"Furious?"

I shake my head while searching for the right word. *"Grief."*

My answer surprises both of us. Maia sits in front of me on the foot bench at the end of the bed. "For what—Mom?"

"Yes and no. I keep thinking about all the possibilities we could've had if Dad had at least taught us about the culture growing up. We could've spent summers visiting Beverly. Grew up learning the language."

My sister tilts her head in consideration. "They wouldn't be able to keep the crown thing a secret for very long then."

I try to think of plans they could've come up with, but the what-ifs start to drive me crazy. I settle for shaking my head and saying, "It would've been better than what we had."

"Yeah…" She bites her lip as she contemplates. "Can I tell you something?"

I crease my brow. That's never been necessary to say; we share everything. "Of course."

"I know we've been here for, like, four days, but… I love it here. Like—I *really* love it."

A grin stretches across my face as I sit up. *"Me, too!"*

"Seriously?"

"Yes!"

We start squealing and flapping our hands together—and I suppose one of our squeals resembles a scream because we suddenly see both of our bodyguards in the doorway with menacing expressions.

"Is everything all right?" Mason asks.

"Oh my god, *Mason!*" Maia wails dramatically. "What if we were naked?"

I snort out a chuckle and slap my hand to my mouth. The two of them blanch and stammer.

"The door—," Beck says.

"—it was open," Mason finishes.

"I don't care! We're gossiping in here. Out." Maia shoos them away, nearly shoving them out the door before slamming it shut. She whirls around with a toss of her head and rolls her eyes. She flops back onto the bench. "Anyway, it's so vivid and alluring here. I feel like I'm in a daydream but at the same time I'm so grounded and spiritually connected to the life here."

I let a full-bellied laugh break free. That's such a Maia

thing to say. "Well—let's stop talking about it and go experience more of it."

The streets are crowded beneath the relentless sun, so we find a shaded garden to stroll through. I notice there aren't many parks or even patches of grass throughout the city. It's a cobblestone jungle.

My entire world is heightened—the saturation and brightness turned up to its highest point. The sun blinds me enough that most of my memories from the day are blanketed in light. I hear every static from the radios inside the shops and gelaterias we frequent. I notice every half-smoked cigarette nestled between the centuries-old cobblestones. Maia and I want to coddle and care for every stray cat we come across and we're grateful we don't come across stray dogs. There isn't an expense we wouldn't cut to save it.

Panhandlers dot the most crowded areas, even using their children to beg for money. As I take in the surroundings, I look for a place in their society I could fit into. What can I offer them? Maldanians love their history and culture; their maroon and white flags hang everywhere.

And as much as I hate to consider it, I'd be stupid not to: racism. I can't tell if the stares Maia and I get are because we're Black or being followed by two men. Locals mistake me for Maldanian, which isn't only the utmost compliment as a tourist, but it also tells me something about their culture and expectations. The island's proximity to North Africa is a clear reason for much of the population—the city population, at least—having generally deeper undertones. I close my eyes. This isn't school anymore. *Stop overanalyzing.*

Maia tugs on our interlocked arms. "What are you thinking about?"

Black and rusty lampposts line the curvy stone paths, leading us by outdoor cafes lining a town square. We walk around a fountain together, a few mopeds circling the roundabout. "I'm just thinking about what we could offer as royals. You hate performative charity as much as I do."

She sighs with an exhausted look as though she's been ruminating on the topic just as hard. "I was thinking we could change that—be *different* kinds of royals, but isn't that what politicians say? They'll be different, but once they get into the system, they wind up being the same because change is too hard."

"And then we can't forget it'll be even harder because we're Black."

"That, too. But Maldana's culture isn't like other European countries."

I glance behind me, my curls tickling my exposed back. I take advantage of wearing sunglasses by tracing my gaze down my bodyguard's figure. He's so... *climbable*. The regality of his posture only adds to his allure.

"Why don't we ask actual Maldanians?" I suggest before beckoning them.

"Is Beck even from here? He has an American accent."

"He was born here; his mom is American." I don't sugarcoat the question by the time they reach us. "Are Maldanians racist?"

Mason recoils in surprise; Beck doesn't react. The two of them exchange glances.

"There are certainly some of us who are," Mason admits.

"Well, of course," Maia agrees, "but as a whole?"

"Compared to other EU countries, no," Beck says. "But

both of us are white. We cannot speak for Black Maldanians."

I don't give him too much credit for what *should* be a basic point of view, but I'll be damned if I don't find him hotter for it. Common sense is attractive, and that can be hard to come by in men.

CHAPTER THIRTEEN

NINA

Giddiness runs up my core as we pull through the palace's iron gates for lunch. It sits huge among pristine and colorful landscaping. *My family lived here. My* mom.

Maia and I are so caught up in a conversation about the charity we could do as princesses that I forget to change into the heels I brought.

"Damn. Go on without me while I change my shoes."

"I'll go use the bathroom and then come back for you," Maia says, sliding out of the town car and leaving with Mason in tow.

Beck opens my door and waits as I put on my cream-colored heels and scoot to the edge. Before I can place a foot outside, his open hand waits in front of me. I pause at the sight, then sneak a quick glance at him. His entire effect is aloof, so I match it. I place my hand in his and hate the way his fingers clamp around mine automatically.

He's a gentleman helping me out of the car, and I can only imagine what it would feel like to have his hand else-where on my body. I inwardly groan and push the thought back as far as possible. No way in hell will I make a move on my bodyguard. The rejection would make my life painfully awkward.

I step out of the car into a private, circular driveway on a different side of the palace. This is much different than the public section. I meet Maia at the garden entrance, and when we reach a fork in the path, I notice Beck walking the other way.

"Where are you going?"

"I don't need to remain with you on palace grounds, madam."

"Fine... Hey—Beck." I wait until he looks back. "Don't call me *madam*."

He gives a curt nod, which I find oddly amusing. I have yet to see a handsome man as stoic as him. Every beautiful man I've come across *knows* they're hot and uses it as an excuse to be a dick one way or another.

I follow Maia down the path until it reveals a yard of flowers, a daybed, a pool, and a table under the shade of a huge tree. Security guards dot the area, and I spot the multiple cameras in trees and even on a few statues. The walkway leads to the table, saving me from walking on grass with heels.

"Girls! I'm so pleased you could join us," Aunt Beverly exclaims, extending her hands for us to grab. Maia takes one and I take the other.

"Of course," my sister says.

Even though I feel slightly out of place, I feign gratitude and joy. "Thank you for inviting us."

My aunt beckons us forward. "Come, meet your cousins, plus Roman."

Three people step up like little soldiers, but one moves closer. He's shorter than me with dirty blond hair that ought to be combed. "I'm still a *plus*? Mrs. Elias, you know you love me like a son."

She smiles. "Roman is my son's best friend, but for all intents and purposes, he's part of the family."

"I'm Vanessa," a girl says. She has tanned, freckled skin. Her light brown hair is bobbed, and she blinks pieces of her bangs away from her eyes.

"Jason—Jace for short," the remaining boy says.

She and Jace would be inseparable.

That was in Mom's letter to Aunt Beverly. She wanted Jace and me to be friends. Another mournful pang echoes through my stomach at what could have been. My cousin is tall with pale skin and brown hair.

I offer a polite smile. "Hi, I'm Nina, this is—"

"Maia," Roman interrupts, taking my sister's hand and shaking it even though she hadn't offered. "The goddess of love." I don't like the way he's looking at her. He acts like those beautiful men who know they're beautiful, but he's missing the most important part.

Maia has enough manners to pleasantly return the greeting, but I notice her wiping her palm on her skirt. I already know who Vanessa and Jace are from my extensive Google search. Ever since my mother's death, the royals have mostly stayed out of the public eye. The monarch has remained dormant, not improving, not declining. People have been calling for the end of the Maldanian monarchy while others want the tradition to live on. Vanessa and Jace offer enough publicity to remain relevant enough to collect taxpayer money, but they're largely boring to the public. To me, that's a good thing.

But Roman wants to change that. We spend an hour chatting about their lives as royals and how they can improve. Roman makes it clear he thinks Maldana can get richer if the royals become a consistent part of the media. While I remain guarded, Maia is more candid. She talks about what she would want to raise awareness for—specifically causes that pertain to the environment. In turn, Roman brags about the countries he's traveled to.

After another slice of tora di pomke, I excuse myself to stretch my legs before the main course is served. I wander through the garden, regretting it more with each heeled step on the grass. City noises erupt in the distance, but the area is serene. My fingers brush over hydrangeas and marigolds, and I perk at the sight of lilies. Without hesitation, I stick my nose in them and inhale the aroma. Serenity, indeed.

"Your mother designed this garden," Aunt Beverly says softly, appearing to my right.

I back up from the shrub. "She did?"

"She loved helping people as queen, but this—this was her happy place." She looks at the vine-covered arch above her. "Gardens."

I bite the inside of my cheek. "Maia loves plants."

"I know."

Silence topples over us. What am I supposed to say to her? All I can think about are the missed years—missed birthdays, Christmases, family vacations. I may not remember much of anything about Mom, but I know this would sadden her.

Despite being at least six inches taller than Aunt Beverly in heels, I shrink when I notice her staring. "What?"

"Sorry—that was rude of me." She blinks herself back to reality, running manicured fingers along her hairline. "It's only—you're all grown up."

And you missed it.

She notices my discomfort. "You're mistrustful of me,

rightfully so. But please understand—I was given no warning when Ophie left, she—"

"Over twenty years ago," I interject. "If you didn't want to be in your nieces' lives after her death, then you couldn't have loved her all that much." Or *me*, for that matter. I fail to keep my voice from cracking.

There's nothing Maia could do that would drive me away. If I was Aunt Beverly, I would make the Atlantic Ocean look like a puddle with how much I'd travel. Better yet, I'd relocate.

"It's not that simple."

"It is. You'll excuse me for being so forward, but I recently discovered my family *chose* to stay out of my life." The words are harsher than I want them to be, but I didn't realize my level of hurt until she started talking. I curve around her to head back to everyone else. She let Maia and me down when we needed her. Dad never recovered from Mom's death.

"I'm sorry," Aunt Beverly exclaims, and I halt. "I did not think—I did not consider you or your sister... I've made a horrible mistake. I know that now. I don't deserve it, but I'd like the chance to fix it." She takes a few tentative steps toward me. "You are *wanted* here, Nina. Say the word, and we'll let the adventures begin so we can show you that."

"Adventures?"

"The kids want to show you girls around the country a little bit, and the Higher Court is dying to meet you and Maia. It won't be a commitment," she rushes to add at my hesitation. "They can answer any questions you have about the institution. It is just an introduction."

I exhale. It doesn't sound appealing. I don't want to learn about the institution. I want to learn about Mom.

"I'll think about it. But, um... would it—would it be

okay if I spent some time with the letter Mom sent you? The original one—in Maldanian. And the... the scrapbooks you made."

"Oh," she says, her blue eyes wide in surprise. "Of course. I'll have them safely delivered to your room."

I rejoin the lunch with less animosity toward Aunt Beverly. It may not be wise to dwell on the past, but it's hard when that past is my childhood.

By the time the meal is over, I'm overwhelmed with the amount of social interaction and want to avoid conversation for at least two hours.

What I love most about Maia is that she understands my need to be alone sometimes. I've been the calm, responsible one in the family for years, and I need my own space to keep doing that. She doesn't argue when I tell her I'll meet her for dinner later this evening.

For the next few hours, it'll just be me and the streets of Kosita.

And Beck, of course.

CHAPTER FOURTEEN

WESLEY

During Nina's lunch, Mason and I meet at Jack's office. There's an array of food when I arrive, and my stomach growls loudly.

"Have a seat," Jack says. "Help yourself to any of it."

And I do just that. The large, round conference table holds a monitor showing CCTV footage. Mason and I get to supervise our clients while eating. Nina sits quietly among the group while Maia seems to chat endlessly.

"Princess Beverly wants to get a feel of how they're liking the country," Jack explains as he gathers his plate of food. "Anything you two want to add?"

"She and her sister are talking about the charitable things they can do as princesses," Mason says.

"They also asked Mason and me about what the racism is like here," I add.

Jack raises a brow. "And what did you say?"

"Better than others in the EU, but Black Maldanians are really the ones to ask," I reply with a shrug. When Jack purses his lips and nods in approval, I add, "Would it be all right if I directed them to you for those questions if they bring it up again?"

"Sure, I don't see why not."

Silence falls over us as I resume eating with frequent glances toward the monitor. I spot a table filled with tea, coffee, dessert, and seasoned bread with olive oil—a Maldanian tradition. I stare a little too hard at Nina's ass as she walks and later bends over to sit. Did she have to wear that dress today?

Thwack.

I nearly choke on my sandwich as my head gets smacked forward. I chew furiously with incredulous eyes on Jack, and he narrows his gaze and points to the screen. "If there is anyone who's off limits, it's her."

Mason laughs.

Have I had less-than-holy thoughts about her? Absolutely. But I would never act on them. This job is too important to mess up. I shove down a final bite and clear my throat. "Sir, I would never—"

He holds up a hand to cut me off. "Do not forget why you're here—*how* you're here. To a lot of people, you're nothing but a criminal who flipped for a deal."

"That's—"

"*I* know the truth. Not everyone does. You'd be in prison right now if not for your conscience and bravery."

Brave is the last word I would use to describe myself. There's nothing brave about the things I've done. I started because of the money. I finished because I was too scared of dying before doing some good in the world.

I don't tell Jack I would be *dead* rather than in prison. Santiago wouldn't have been caught if not for me. He was too smart to be on the police's radar for years. I made the right choice by turning on him; he lied to me. He promised he wasn't trafficking people, and the memory of those chained-up girls still haunts me.

I was a straight-and-narrow soldier before Santiago found me. I might've been an army ranger, but I was the quiet one. Most of my underground jobs were quick, in and out on a private plane overnight or less. The few times a year I would see Santiago or his associates, none except him would look me in the eye despite being depraved criminals themselves. That should've been my first hint to quit.

"You got me this job," I remind Jack. "I wouldn't disrespect you—or her—by crossing that line."

He leans back in his chair. His expression is either unamused or disbelieving; I can't tell which. He sighs and tosses his napkin over his empty plate. "Princess Beverly intends to introduce the girls to the Higher Court."

"Is the plan still to keep their identities concealed?" Mason asks.

"Within the Court? No."

I take a bite of a cold french fry, and it reminds me of Nina's grimace when she ate the fries from Moritzi's. She hated them but was considerate enough to keep that to herself. "Then what are the plans to ensure they won't sell the information to the highest bidder?"

"NDA contracts in addition to all members giving up their phone upon entry and being searched for wires or other devices."

We continue the discussion even as Nina gets up and wanders the garden. Jack switches the footage on one of the monitors for me. After a few minutes, Princess Beverly joins her.

Even with no set date for the introductory dinner, the three of us review the security plans.

"We'll finish this later," I say before we start reviewing

the guest list. With a glance at the monitor, I spot the group rising and exchanging farewell hugs. When Mason and I reach them, I notice that Maia has made a good bond with Princess Vanessa. Nina doesn't share their enthusiasm.

The sisters have a short conversation before Nina tells me to drive her to the heart of the city and park—the same thing we've been doing so she can explore on foot. Her sister doesn't join her this time, and it's just me trailing behind.

I analyze the vantage points from the windows of each road we walk through. The buildings are made up mostly of family homes, yet plenty of my assignments were in residential areas.

I close the distance between us the more crowded it gets. She doesn't notice the number of men ogling her as she strolls through an outdoor market. One man, though, stares a bit too hard at her. He's pale, Caucasian, five-foot-ten, with dirty blond hair and a long nose. He wears a white T-shirt and cargo pants with *many* pockets. He looks Nina up and down. If I didn't know better, I would've thought he was watching her ass. When he steps beside her and fakes interest in the stall merchandise, he swipes her phone from her bag.

I reprimand Nina in the back of my mind. She made it too easy. In a blink, I hold the man's wrist at an unnatural angle. He cries out and lowers his body, leaning into my hold. I pluck the phone from his hand, shake it in front of his face, and say in Maldanian, "Go find someone else to victimize."

Nina gasps and snatches her phone. "How did he—?"

The thief doesn't have time to get angry with me. I release his wrist and shove him back. He stumbles to the ground, fleeing as soon as possible. I hear the *zip* of Nina's bag.

I take her purse and shift it on her body. "Keep it in front of you at all times."

She stiffens as if suddenly mistrustful of all the people around her. I follow her out of the market and onto the road. Another twenty minutes pass. I watch her shop and buy a souvenir—an espresso cup. She buys a cup of vanilla gelato and I buy a bottle of water. She buys another souvenir. This time, it's a necklace. She slides it right over her head, so I know it's not a gift. She stops at almost every street performer and tosses in a coin or two.

While this day is mundane to me, I notice her discomfort break apart at the small activities. Nina stops to get french fries from a vendor, and she gasps after taking the first bite.

"Oh my god." She inhales another one. "These are delicious. You want to try some?"

"No, thank you."

"Are you *sure*?" she sings. "They're the best I've had in the country so far."

The corner of my lips quirks at her enthusiasm. "No, it's your—"

She plunges a crispy fry into my mouth, far enough to stop any protest. "You're not really living until you've tried one of these."

I chew the rest of it, savoring the salty and seasoned flavor. Pretty good, can't deny. She chuckles at my expression, angling the paper cone toward me.

"Told you. Want another?"

This might be crossing a boundary—sharing food. *But it's really good.* I shrug and accept one more.

"You have a lot of scars," Nina blurts, and I notice her staring at the mark on my forearm.

I stiffen. "It happens."

She points to the inch-long scar. "What's this one from?"

I inhale a long breath, debating how honest I ought to be. "Knife fight in Lisbon."

She points to another on my bicep, right under the sun and moon tattoo on my shoulder. "This one?"

"Fell from a rooftop in Amsterdam. No—Berlin." The pipe I fell on had been less than a foot away from impaling me through the ribs. The three-inch scar doesn't show justice for the physical pain I felt that day.

"And the one on your hand?"

I don't tell her it's the most recent one. If she has any knowledge of wounds, she might figure it out herself. I clench and unclench my fist, studying the pink flesh. "I, uh —fire. It was in a fire."

"Sheesh," she huffs. "No wonder you're always grumpy."

"I'm..." I want to protest, but I can only imagine how rigid I appear to the world. "I'm selectively pleasant."

Nina laughs, her eyes widening when a snort escapes. She claps a hand over her mouth, but a smile threatens my lips. Does she not remember she laugh-snorted this morning, too? It's almost endearing—a humbling sound from such a graceful woman.

"Okay, let's go before I do anything else embarrassing." After tossing her trash in the bin, she nervously glances around, but suddenly gasps and snatches my arm. "I want to ride a moped."

I follow her gaze toward the motorbike rental place up

ahead. Dammit. I shouldn't be surprised she'd want to do that.

"Do you have a license?"

"Of course," she scoffs.

"An *international* license?"

"Oh." Nina slumps her shoulders and laces her fingers in front of her. She purses her lips in thought. "No... but *you* do," she says quietly, flicking her big eyes up at me in a pout.

My stomach tightens and I shake my head. "No—"

"Oh, come on!" she wails. "Please?"

"Absolutely not. This isn't part of my job description."

"You don't have to ride it! Just sign the paperwork and I'll be off." A hopeful smile spreads across her face. While I won't say yes to that, I'd rather not be the one to steal her hope.

"I go where you go," I remind her. "And even so, what if you crash?"

Nina shrugs. "It can't be that hard to drive."

"That makes me feel so much better."

"Please? It'll be so much fun! I'll just—take a joy ride around the block and that's it."

"No."

She grabs my elbow. "Then *you* can drive! I'll sit on the back."

Shit. If I don't think of something quick, I'll be stuck driving her around the city on a moped I'm too big for. It's annoying enough doing so in a car. "You're wearing a dress," I point out. My hesitation only fuels her. She thinks she's breaking me—and she is.

"I can sit to the side."

"I—that's dangerous."

Nina crosses her arms with an amused expression. She

sees right through my excuses. "I'll hold onto you *super* tight. Pinky promise."

"No."

"Please?"

"No," I insist.

She grips my arm and tilts her chin up toward me. "Pretty please?"

"No."

From this close, I notice a single, faded freckle under her left eye. She continues pouting her lips and I keep pushing myself to be annoyed. Shooting things down is easy when an arrogant soldier gets ahead of himself, but I've never had to turn down someone with doe eyes before. And fuck, I'd rather go back to boot camp.

My head starts spinning when she does little bounces and says, *"Please please please please please please please—"*

"Nina—"

"Please please please please please please—"

"All right, fine, fine. Just—stop."

Anything is better than Nina bouncing like this in front of me. She doesn't hesitate to push me toward the rental place. "Yay! Come on."

I spend the next ten minutes filling out paperwork and tampering down panic because Nina is waiting around the corner; the clerk will watch me drive off and won't allow her to sit sideways. She should be supervised at all times. I only allow it to slide if she sends me fifteen-second updates. The rental clerk looks at me with skepticism at my consistently buzzing phone, but I couldn't give two shits. Rather than count fifteen seconds between each text— because according to her, *"it's annoyingly specific"*—she sends a slew of random shit.

NINA

Still alive.

I haven't died.

Yet.

I want gelato again.

Get the pink moped.

Wait no, the red one.

Or the blue?

What about a classic black?

No, the cream-colored one.

Fancy and won't absorb heat.

A lady just let me pet her dog. It was really
cute.

I'm hungry.

Can we find a bookstore?

Wait it would probably close soon, right?

It's not even five thirty, but everything
closes early here.

Still alive.

A woman walked by dressed as an
absolute icon and I want to be like her
when I'm 70.

I want to drive up to Moritzi's so I can
watch the sunset again.

I'm sorry, but I can't eat their fries again.

Are you done yet?

"Follow me," the clerk says.

I pick out the beige moped as Nina wished and opt for one with a sissy bar for added protection. After disinfecting the rental helmet twice, I zip off around the corner. If I wasn't so pissed at myself for caving into this stupid moped, I would have chuckled at her squealing when I roll to a stop in front of her.

"It's perfect!"

It's the most excited I've seen her since she arrived in Maldana.

I take off the helmet and hand it over. "Get on, then."

"You expect me to put that thing on my head?"

I sigh. After watching her constantly put on hand sanitizer and carry a cloth in her bag specifically to keep her bare legs from touching public chairs, it wasn't a far-fetched guess she wouldn't want to wear the helmet. I hold it closer to her.

"I made sure to clean it myself," I say, and when she hesitates, I add, *"Twice."*

Only then does Nina accept the helmet and climb on. I manage to remain neutral with my tone and demeanor; it takes more effort than usual. Regardless of her sitting behind me, of her arms snug around my waist, *I'm working.* She's my client who manipulated me into getting what she wants. I'll stop so she can get fries she likes and I'll drive up to Moritzi's so she can watch the sunset again. The light will outline her and the word *angel* will haunt me. If doing all of this will keep her content and quiet, then so be it. I can deal with intrusive thoughts and ignore deep desires.

But if she begs me for something—anything—again, I'll be undone and won't trust my decision-making.

CHAPTER FIFTEEN
NINA

I want my own moped.

Even riding on the back of one is *way* better than I imagined—as long as I avoid overthinking the cleanliness of this helmet.

The road Beck drives us through has a perfect view of the sea, the sparkly waters blinding. I unwrap a hand from his waist and let it curve with the wind, but the moped suddenly slows and he snaps at me to hold onto him with both arms. I groan but comply and enjoy the rest of the ride to Moritzi's while pushing aside the thought of how comfortable I am with my chest pressed against my bodyguard's back.

There's way too much on my plate to even consider his attractiveness. I may have spent the last few hours doing anything I wanted, but the reality is that I'm here to accept a title. At least, that's what my aunt and cousins want. During lunch, they gushed about life as a Maldanian royal —about all the *good* we could do.

Since I arrived in Maldana, different emotions have been hitting me left and right: excitement, confusion, grief, anger, and fear. Today, I feel tricked. I was tricked into this vacation, lured into a falsehood of relaxation when I truly have to determine the future of myself and a whole country.

The job sounds enticing. I would never have to worry about rent or dinner. I could travel without issue. But at what cost—the taxes of the woman running the fruit stand Beck drives us past? What gives me the right, and what would I do for her in return? Oh, right. I would attend charity auctions and gatherings while wearing a ten-thousand-dollar dress.

"Pull over," I tell Beck.

He hesitates. "We're two minutes out."

"Pull over!"

Panic seizes me. If I decline the crown, I won't just disappoint my family; I'll disappoint an entire culture that loves tradition. But accepting it means defying my values.

Beck stops on an emergency shoulder. I rip off the helmet and drop it before walking paces ahead toward the sun. He asks me what's wrong, but I don't answer.

New emotion unlocked on this trip: *powerless.*

No matter what I choose, someone will be hurt. I can't stop that. I place my hands on my knees to catch my breath. The wind pushes a curl in my face, so I begin twirling my hair into a low bun. I can control having a face clear of loose hair. *It's not enough.* I glance over my shoulder at Beck. He studies me through his sunglasses.

I reach for the keys. "I'm driving."

"No, you're not," he says, lifting them from my reach.

"I can drive a stupid moped."

"I know you can, but I'm not giving you the keys until you take a minute to calm down."

I flex my fingers and take a deep breath. The easy thing

to do is threaten to scream if he doesn't give me the keys, but that's not the kind of person I want to be. He hands them over after a few calming moments.

Controlling this vehicle is the most I can do. It's best to get out of my head and root myself in the present, but the present includes sitting between Beck's legs and it's *really* hard to ignore what I feel pressed against my ass. Rather than hold my waist, he reaches under my arms to grasp the inner part of the handles. I turn my head to secure the helmet clasp until I feel a hand on the back of my head.

"Watch where you're swinging that thing."

"Ugh," I huff, taking it off. "You put it on."

He leans back. "Absolutely not. *You're* wearing it."

"No, I'm not. If you insist on reaching forward to hold the handles, I'm not wearing the helmet because I'll knock you out by accident. And as appealing as that sounds..."

His expression doesn't falter. "Put the helmet back on."

I push it in his chest. "No."

"You won't knock me out."

"Wanna bet?" I challenge, shifting closer. I quirk my brow. "Pick one, *Wesley*. Will you hold onto the handles—or me?"

His jaw ticks at my use of his first name. I admit, I like the way his name sounds on my tongue. His eyes bore into mine for another few daring moments before he grumbles, "Put the helmet back on."

I smirk in triumph before sliding it over my head. The moped sputters as I get the hang of it. When he tries to reach forward and help me steer, I smack his hand away.

"I got it, I got it."

The moment I turn us back onto the road, the tension inside of me begins slipping away. The wind against my body is like a massage wiping off my worries if only for the time being. Most of all, it's the safety and comfort building up that calms me. And it's not from the element of control but from the begrudging bodyguard enclosed around me like a cocoon. His hold on my waist is firm but respectful, making it as hot as if he was full-on grabbing my tits. I selfishly pull a U-turn at Moritzi's and head back down the hill because I don't want to move. Beck doesn't say anything as I drive us toward the city.

Our interaction replays in my mind. I may have only wondered what he looks like naked once or twice, but now the possible image burns in my mind at *everything* I feel pressed against my ass. I can't detect the precise size, yet I can tell he's not lacking anything.

I drive us through an eclectic neighborhood, the homes on the skinny road bursting with color. Yellow, pink, and blue flank us. If only he wasn't a buzzkill, I would have the helmet off and the wind blowing through my curls. The breeze would bring unruly frizz, but it'd be worth it. Cracks and vines crawl up centuries-old buildings, their iron balconies exploding with colorful flowers and greenery.

After checking the rearview mirror, I jerk the moped to the right to stop in front of a gelato stand.

"*Karitó*," Beck curses—*shit* in Maldanian—while the moped skids to a halt. My stomach lurches as his grip around my waist tightens, the momentum shoving him into me. I would've flown from the seat if not for his hold. Shivers run down my spine at the feel of his chest against my back.

"A new gelato place!" I exclaim, peeking at him through the sun visor.

He glares, then shows me his watch. "Ten minutes and then we have to return the bike."

Days later, I hear Maia's muffled voice as she approaches my room. I unravel my nightly braids and eavesdrop on her talking to Beck.

"Good morning, Beck!" she exclaims.

"Madam."

"I have a question."

"What is it?"

I roll my eyes at his monotone, almost curt, answers. It sounds... fake—and I realize he speaks that way to everyone but me. When we're alone, at least.

"Are you like a cop?" Maia blurts.

"No, I'm not."

"So... if you see us committing a crime, would you arrest us? Turn us in?"

"Depends on the crime I suppose."

The absurdity of her questions has me opening the door. "Maia, why are you talking about committing crimes before I've had coffee?"

My sister grins ear-to-ear and holds up a bag of green clumps—*weed*. "Because I got the good-good."

Excitement fills me. After the stressful week I've had, that's exactly what I need. "Oh, *hell* yeah."

I pull her inside and notice something different about Beck. I lift my brows. "You shaved."

He shaved his scruff to stubble, and while I still wouldn't mind sitting on his face, his scruff was my favorite part.

"I did," he says simply, and I hum with a pout before slinking back into my room. My grogginess got the best of me, and my manners slipped; what he does to his own face is none of my business.

Ten minutes later, a joint is rolled and Maia and I are on my balcony passing it back and forth. Since we're the only hotel guests, I'm not worried about the smell disturbing anyone. She told me the marijuana is a complement from our cousins Vanessa and Jace.

I take a puff. "Is it even legal here?"

Maia lazily tilts her head toward me, the morning sun illuminating her brown skin. Her cheeks sparkle with beads of sweat. "Not in this quantity. She told me we have princess privilege here."

"Is that really a thing?"

She giggles. "No."

My and my sister's legs are draped across each other's laps, our hands entwined.

"I needed this," I mutter with a sigh. The sun blinds me, so I close my eyes and revel in the heat against my face.

"You did," she agrees. "I did, too."

I call for Beck to let the room service in, and the hotel employee rolls the cart right onto the balcony. Once I hand over the tip, I wait until we're completely alone to talk about our new family. It's eight in the morning and my parents are at the spa.

"Do you think she's full of shit? Aunt Bev."

We haven't spoken much about the lunch. Ruby took us to get mani-pedis the next day before a little shopping and wandering.

Maia sighs and squeezes my hand. "I don't know. It feels fake. All this formality makes it feel less authentic. It's tough to make a connection."

I chuckle. "Roman's trying *real* hard for your attention, though."

She snorts. "I know. I liked his boldness at first but he quickly turned into a pathetic waste of a trust fund."

I bark out a laugh as my sister takes a puff and passes it back to me. With the joint between my lips, I sit up straight and flip my curls from one side to the other. "She sent over those scrapbooks and the letter Mom sent her."

"You asked her to?"

I shrug. "I just really want to know more about Mom."

Maia presses a button on the wall that pushes an awning over the balcony. The sweltering sun no longer beats down on us. "Me, too. Does that mean you want to accept the crown?"

"Do *you* want to?"

She hesitates. "I think... we can make history."

"We shouldn't accept it just for that."

"Of course, but... I don't know—I'm torn about it. It would be so much easier if it wasn't sprung on us. We're not the only ones who want change, but we *are* the only daughters of Queen Ophelia. That has to count."

"We resent people who believe they're important because of their parents."

"Then we show the world that we're not like that."

I laugh. "Coming from the girl who *never* gives a single fuck what others think of her."

"Just... before we give an answer, I think we should consider what this could do for *us*. How will this improve *our* lives—and how can we navigate it without compromising our morals?"

I stare at my sister for a long moment. Her long curls spill down her chest and her once round and soft face has a bit more edge and maturity. Pride swells inside me. She's no longer an impulsive teen, but a thoughtful twenty-one-year-old. "You've grown so much, Maia. I'm proud of you."

She looks away shyly. "I learned from the best."

Maia and I chat for the remainder of the morning, and she mentions a club that Vanessa told her about. My sister loves a good party, and I'm ridden with guilt every time I turn down her offer. This is no different. She tells me constantly that I need to live it up in a foreign country, gain experiences, be wild, but I don't imagine a nightclub as part of it. The more she presses, the more I deny it, and the more I feel shitty for letting her down.

Ruby and Dad stop by after the spa, but it's nothing more than a surface conversation and telling us that they're taking a trip to southern Maldana for a few days. I hate hurting him with every curt reply, but I could've had years to think this princess thing over. Instead, I have three months.

He's not the only one with grief; I grieved the part of my dad that didn't show up every day.

As the time inches closer to noon, we change into bathing suits to head to the beach. The thought of Beck being there makes me regret bringing a one-piece, even if it rides high over my hip bones and has a low V-neck.

I stop in front of the mirror, my gaze dipping down to my ass as I pinch the extra skin. A lot of people expect tall girls to be stick-thin the way my sister is, but having hips and height means I take up more space than I want to. I've spent years making myself smaller, stopping only out of exhaustion, not desire. Low-waist bikinis make the bone structure of my hips look wider than I want them to, and high-waist bikinis or one-pieces are the only swimsuits I feel comfortable in.

I huff, sliding on my cover-up. This is as good as it gets.

CHAPTER SIXTEEN

NINA

We spend the next few hours at a picturesque beach only a few minutes outside of Kosita.

From here, the city looks etched into the side of a hill, its architecture marking just how old it could be. I read a chapter or two of my book before texting Raven; she watches too many kidnapping movies and is terrified I'll be a victim. I don't tell her a brooding tree of a man is guarding me, but I assure that I'm fine. I send a couple of pictures from my days, and she gushes over the aesthetic of it all.

RAVEN

OMG! Please please find a Maldanian man
to have a fling with so I can live vicariously.

I chuckle, glance at Beck standing dutifully behind me, and type a reply.

I don't think Zafir would like that or that it's
gonna happen, girl. Sorry. I'll be sure to
take pictures of parliament, though!

My soon-to-be-diplomat of a friend is as nerdy in her

field as I am in mine. It's why we're still so close. She doesn't ask for details about Mom and it's nice to text back and forth about normal travel things.

> I think I could live here forever.

Uh oh. That has more weight since your mom's from there.

When are you coming home?

> My return flight's been canceled.

????

What is going on? Am I never seeing you again?

> Of course you will!!

> I still have a lot to sort out here.

She's skeptical, but lets me know she has my back. With a full heart, I pull up Instagram to make a few posts to my stories. So far, the day is good. Clear skies. Calm waters.

So why do I pull up James's Instagram page?

The most recent post is a group picture with the friends I always hated. A pit gathers in my stomach when his arm is around a woman. She's beautiful, but judging from her severely ripped jeans and crop top, she's not his type.

Why do I care?

I lock and shove my phone into my bag with more force than necessary. Drinks. I need a piña colada. My high has worn off enough to warrant one. Maia's swimming in the clear blue water, flirting with a guy. After a quick scan, I notice Mason watching her. Good. The best part about having a bodyguard is that I don't have to worry about my little sister too much.

I sit peacefully at the beach bar until Beck lowers beside me ten minutes later. His sunglasses are removed and slung over the neckline of his white button-up. The sleeves, rolled to his elbow, hug his muscles and a fleeting thought of raking my nails over them crosses my mind.

I stir my piña colada. "I don't need protection here. It's a private beach."

"Three different men have been staring at you around the beach for an hour. Two of them moved to the bar since you sat here."

I glance around, but no men catch my eyes. None I'd fuck, anyway. I want to tease Beck, ask if he's jealous, ask how he'd know I wouldn't want the attention of the men who'd been staring. After all, it's not his job to fend off interested suitors. But it wouldn't feel right because I *want* him beside me. Having him around flows so easily that it unsettles me, so I order another drink.

The bartender says something in Maldanian to Beck, who offers a polite expression—not quite a smile—and responds in turn. They speak so fast that I don't get a chance to decipher much of the conversation.

"You're kinder when you speak Maldanian," I say, taking a sip of my second piña colada.

"How would you know?"

I scoff. Way to rub it in that I'm not fluent. "Language is more than just words. It's tone, body movements, and general attitude. It's called secondary linguistic personality. For example, I'm more laid-back when I speak Spanish."

The bartender sets a wet glass of ice water in front of him, its condensation instantly creating a puddle.

"Interesting. Second language per—"

"Secondary linguistic personality. So you're cold in English and a gentleman in Maldanian." I smirk and take a sip of my drink at his glare. "Let's only speak Maldanian. I need to learn it."

"I'm not your teacher."

I scowl. "Don't be a dick. It's unbecoming."

The corner of his mouth tilts in a smile. He leans back and crosses his arms. "You don't need me to help you. It won't be long until you're fluent."

"What makes you say that?"

"You already know both Spanish and Italian. Your knowledge of Greek will help, too." His matter-of-fact tone is rattling.

I set my drink down. "How do you know all of that?"

"It was in your file."

"I have a file?" A new wave of discomfort washes over me. "What else do you know about me?"

Beck shrugs. "Enough."

"That's not an answer."

"It is. You just don't like it."

"*What else is in that file?*"

Any relaxation I gathered in the last few minutes vanishes entirely. How many people researched me? I imagine someone taking photos of me while on campus, at a volleyball game, on a date with James. My Instagram account shows very little of my life and I keep my posts private. That made no difference. A whole team excavated information about me.

"Information. I know that your ex cheated and that your best friend just moved in with her NFL player boyfriend."

My stomach drops. "You... you know about James?"

Oh, god. I can only imagine what he thought the moment he learned I was cheated on. That someone didn't think I was important enough to stay loyal to. He shouldn't know about James and Raven and Zafir. They're not secrets, but they *are* pieces of my life that I haven't shared with him or anyone in Maldana.

What did those people think of my life? Did they think I should've done more? Were they judging me—thinking I'm nothing like Mom and can't fill her shoes?

"You had no right," I blurt.

"Excuse me?" He doesn't speak as if offended.

"You had no right to dig through my life like that!" I slip out of the chair, bag in hand, and start to walk away. Beck shouldn't know these things and I feel weirdly violated that he does.

He trails behind me. "*I* didn't do any digging. They handed me a file and I read it. It was a required step to protect my client adequately."

I whirl on him, not caring if I'm loud. "I'm a *person*! My life is not a—not a *step* you have to take for a job!" I move closer, angling to look up and challenge him and his bull-shit vague answers. "How would you feel, huh? If every detail of your life was displayed for people you *barely* know to analyze and make judgments? Don't act like I'm not justified. Would you want strangers reading about *your* worst mistakes, Wesley?"

He sighs. "If it makes you feel any better, very few people have access to your file."

"You didn't answer my question."

"You don't want me to."

"Yes, I do."

My bodyguard hesitates as he searches for the right words. "My worst mistakes would scare the reader more than me."

"Of *course*." I roll my eyes. Did I expect anything different? I turn on my heel and snap, *"Do not follow me."*

It won't matter; he still will. I slam into the empty restrooms as every reality crashes in on me within seconds. The crown. My father. My lack of privacy. *Wesley Troutbeck.*

I stare at myself in the mirror. Maybe I panicked because of James. He's across the ocean and I still let him rattle me. I like to be confident in all my decisions, and slipping onto his Instagram page reminds me of everything I'm unsure of.

What's the plan, huh? I don't fantasize; I calculate steps toward my goals. There is no point in thinking of Beck —*Wesley*—past his responsibilities. I'm not the type of person to act surprised when I suddenly find an interest in someone I've already known. I'm an observant over-thinker. I see a life story, a potential relationship, with every attractive man I meet.

Given, my interest often fizzles quickly, but it's the opposite with Wesley. I keep waiting for him to do some-thing to turn me off for good, yet every turn makes my cheeks flush and my heart race. It has to stop because I draw a blank when trying to thread a future with him, and a life without a plan is unacceptable.

A blinking light in the upper corner of the restroom catches my eye. It's a camera angled toward the door, and I wonder whether he's watching me from his phone. It's a gross invasion of privacy. It turns my stomach to be entirely monitored by a team. Wesley's job is to protect me, but it infuriates me that it feels as though he means it.

I need to snap out of it. After washing my hands, I splash my face with cold water and pat it dry with the shirt in my bag because European bathrooms rarely have paper towels. I reapply moisturizer and sunscreen and stare at my reflection. I'm pathetic. *Wondering if he actually* cares *about me?* Having a bodyguard just shows me how lonely I am. In a burst of motivation, I grab my phone and text Maia.

Let's go to that club tomorrow.

Seconds later, her reply chimes in. She must be out of the ocean.

FUCK YEAH.

After another moment, she attaches that popular GIF of Tina Fey and Amy Poehler dancing in sync.

How many times in my life can I go clubbing in a foreign country? I won't have to worry about being the inspiration for another *Taken* movie franchise—I have a whole team monitoring my safety.

I step out of the restroom and find Wesley waiting patiently, my piña colada in hand. With renewed energy and confidence, I accept the drink and take a sip.

"Feel better?" he asks, and I resist another roll of my eyes. *Arrogant ass.*

I shield my face from the glaring sun. "I'm calling you Wesley from now on."

"Weren't you already?"

I smile at his indirect approval, plucking the umbrella from my drink before sucking off the residue and sticking it behind his ear. "And Maia and I are going to a club tomorrow."

It's easy to miss, but there's a subtle fall in his expression.

On the drive back to the hotel, I spot an adorable café passing through the Milagro neighborhood. The tables and chairs are angled for people watching near the fountain in the center of a roundabout.

"We have to stop there! It's so cute and I'm starving."

Maia agrees, and Wesley and Mason sit at another table when we arrive. My sister groans, exasperated. "Enough of that! I'm tired of you guys sitting over there like stalkers. Just sit with us."

Mason sighs. Wesley looks at me for confirmation, but I shrug and say, "I agree. It's weird."

The moment they settle on either side of us and I open the menu, I realize something. "Wait—I haven't seen either of you eat today."

"I'm fine," Wesley says, shaking his head.

Mason nods. "As am I, Your Highness."

I huff and stick menus in front of them. "Oh, my goodness. Eat! What do I look like, the queen?" At their knowing stares, I hold up a hand. "Don't answer that."

"Yes, Your Highness," Wesley says, his demeanor steady and obedient. Maia busts out laughing, and I watch him in disbelief before giggling.

"Well, well, well. Someone *selected* to be pleasant this afternoon," I taunt, hiding my smile by surveying the menu between us. It's unlikely he'll ever make a move—he's far too reserved—but at least we can be friendly.

CHAPTER SEVENTEEN
NINA

At seven o'clock on the dot the next evening, Maia and a slew of people enter my room.

"Whoa, what's happening?" I ask as the random people roll in a clothing rack and at least half a dozen glittery cases. "Who are they?"

Maia grins. A woman who seems to be in charge looks me up and down. She has a thick accent. "We're your beauty team, courtesy of Princess Vanessa. We work on your clothes, hair, makeup, and jewelry together."

I choke out a laugh. "Oh, no. That's ridiculous. I don't need a whole team for that. And I don't like other people touching my hair."

"They're professionals," Maia says.

"Yes, but I'm capable of doing my own hair."

She releases a breath and takes my hand. "My fifth and eighth grade dance, all four of my homecomings, and my junior and senior prom. You did my hair and makeup for *each and every one* of them, including some of my friends. And then *all* of your own, too. Let yourself be pampered. Please. For me."

I huff. Truth be told, I was dreading figuring out what to wear. I didn't bring any clothes to wear to a club. What clothes would I even *wear*? I've never been to one. "Only 'cause you said please."

I let this group of six women turn my room into a beauty parlor. My phone buzzes with a text.

MAIA

No princess talk. They don't know who we really are.

I respond with a thumbs-up emoji. One woman takes my measurements silently before she starts tapping on her phone. The leader, whose name is Greta, gives me a list of options about what to do with my hair. Maia says hers will be in an updo, and I don't want to worry about whether this group of white women know how to do Black hair.

"Just—straighten it."

My sister notices and frowns. "Are you sure? They know how to do our hair."

"I want this to be simple. And you know I never straighten my own hair the right way."

The team of women pamper me with products I can only dream of affording. Maia connects her phone to a speaker and plays some soft R&B. The club is supposedly extremely upscale with acrobats dancing in the sky and good music. We're arriving separate from Vanessa in case paparazzi show up, and it jars me that I would have to deal with that if I accepted the crown.

What if Maldana hates me?

The world hated Princess Diana, and now she's beloved. The world loved Meghan Markle, but soon turned against her—the hatred only inflamed because of her race.

Given, the British population is different from a Mediterranean country, but racism is everywhere.

"Hey—no thinking," Maia interjects, looking at me from her spot on the divan. "Tonight, we don't think. We party."

"You're right, you're right," I mumble.

The stylists straighten my hair before adding waves with a perfect amount of swoop. It curls away from my face to frame it and I would *never* have gotten this result on my own. I ask them in Maldanian if they could do my makeup light instead of heavy. The results are sleek, and it feels like I should be going to an event that's way more important than a club. They show me an array of dresses that fit my measurements. I'm hesitant to pick the black-and-silver glittery one because it's short. The neckline is a cowlick and no matter the angles in which I bend to test it, no boobs pop out. The material doesn't slide up my thighs, so I won't be constantly tugging it down.

It fits *perfectly*.

Maia gasps. "You *have* to wear that!"

I smile, holding back a giddy squeal. "I've never worn something that fits me so well."

It shows me that I've *always* struggled with clothes that were too big or too small, wearing only on certain occasions or with certain shoes. Confidence surges through me at wearing clothes that fit like a glove.

My sister's multi-colored, shimmery dress has a lace butterfly covering her back where the tips of the wings turn into straps. The style matches her personality.

The two of us are already tall—she's five-eleven and I'm five-ten—but we tower over the entire beauty team once we step into heels that match our dresses. We have an iPhone photoshoot on the sofa and divan. Unlike before, I feel comfortable enough to be in front of the camera, and it helps that my sister is my biggest cheerleader.

Not long after arriving at the club, Maia insists we go to the lounge so she can order some food. Her excitement triples when she learns they serve vegetarian burgers. Leave it to my sister to order food the second we arrive.

"Shit!" Vanessa curses, scrubbing at the bread dip that fell onto her dress.

I lean over, then wave a hand. "Oh, that'll come right out. I have a stain stick in my purse. Come on, let's go to the bathroom."

"A *stain* stick?" Vanessa echoes, scooting out of the booth.

Maia laughs as her food arrives. "She's not kidding."

"You coming?" I ask.

She pouts. "My burger just got here, though."

"Okay, watch the drinks, then." I pluck a couple of fries from her plate. She tries to smack my hand away.

"Hey!"

"Older sister tax," I tell her while sliding out of the booth and holding the fries up in salute. "Thank you!"

Vanessa spends more time marveling over my stain stick than I do using it on her dress. "It's so useful! And quick!"

"It's definitely a lifesaver."

The bathroom has more places to sit than pee. A large mirror and empty counter line one wall while a couch and chairs line the other. The sconces look more expensive than my college degrees.

"This isn't your thing, is it?" Vanessa suddenly asks.

I perk, noticing my bored demeanor in the reflection. I smooth my hair. "Getting dressed up, yes. Going out, no."

"It's fun a little bit, no?" Her accent grows thicker the more nervous she is.

I square my shoulders and shake it off. I'm better than letting people feel uncomfortable in my presence. "Oh, yes, of course. I get to spend some time with you."

She and Maia have already created a bond, and I suppose we haven't because I don't try. But that's how it's always been. My sister goes out to have fun while I consider the heavier, practical stuff.

I clear my throat in the silence. "What was it like... growing up here?" *Being a princess. Being Aunt Beverly's daughter. Being part of the Elias family.*

"A little lonely, if I'm being honest," Vanessa says, wringing her hands together. "Jace didn't really want anything to do with me until I turned twenty. You know, the younger sisters are never cool enough." She chuckles shakily. "I felt—frozen. Everything was. I kept asking my mother why she wouldn't just become queen. The palace and the Higher Court were holding their breath, yeah? Waiting for something... For you. Everyone is much happier since you and Maia arrived. It's like they have hope."

"Hope for what?"

"For people to look at Maldana and see beauty. Strength. Family."

Being the face and representation of such an amazing country is not the worst fate that someone can have. But the pressure to be a picture-perfect daughter makes me want to reject it. It's unwise to let these decisions sway me because my past is done—I'm a grown woman and I can do as I please. If anything, my childhood can help me navigate the road ahead and avoid falling into those same patterns. Yet my stubborn side doesn't want to do any of it. The alternative is starting this new job that I hate.

Was it ever really a choice?

Is my answer going to be yes?

"It's..." I exhale. "It's so much to take in. All I wanted was to learn about my real mom... and I get all of this."

She tsks and sarcastically says, "Life is so unfair."

The two of us break out laughing. I might not have grown up in a palace, but I'm among the richest in the world. Not by money, by having a loving family, an education, and food security.

I can help others have that, too.

Vanessa takes my hand. "I understand it's overwhelming. But the Higher Court is filled with good people, and so is *our* family."

CHAPTER EIGHTEEN
WESLEY

This woman is going to be the death of me.

She's charming and sexy. That, I already knew, but the moment she stepped out of her room, all feeling rushed to my groin. The dress stretches across her ass and the back dips low, revealing skin I ache to learn if it's as soft as it looks. From the mouth I want to consume to the mile-long legs I want wrapped around my waist, Nina Laffley is the woman I wholeheartedly crave.

The club is everything I'd expect a royal to frequent. Its modern elegance says no one with less than a few million dollars in their checking account is here. Medium crowd, predominantly men. Dim, cool lighting. Acrobats twist in the air.

The building is square with exits only on the east and west walls. Nina enters a lounge with her sister and cousin. I stand across from the roped-off section, my back against the north wall to keep both exit points within view.

I watch as my client does her best to have a good time. Her hesitant smile and minimal words tell me her discomfort. She's more open and relaxed when wandering down a quaint street, conversing with locals in her slow, choppy Maldanian, and when she spots a bookstore with an English section. She prefers cultural experiences more than any of this.

Dread suddenly slices into me. I'm not one to pay this close attention to a person's life unless they're my target. I study their habits, strengths, weaknesses, looking for areas to exploit.

Nina is not my target.

Why do I have to remind myself of that? I have less control of my own mind than I thought. The muscles in my arms twitch, aching to move. The push-ups I did last night weren't enough. I need to do *more*. Do something to make me feel alive.

I don't exist to kill.

"If you're not killing men for me, then what are you good for?"

I roll my neck, reveling in the crack. Santiago is dead. I'm alive. There's goodness in the world—I'm looking at her now. My chest weighs with fear. How can I live up to everything she is?

Bloody memories claw the edges of my vision. No one here bore witness to what I've done. Nina's curious and starting to ask more questions. Her pleads usually overpower me, but I won't let her win this one. She can never know. My final hope of being a better man would vanish if she discovered the type of person I truly am. She looks at me like she trusts me. As if I'm someone worth trusting.

I'll do whatever it takes for her to look at me like that forever.

I blink myself back into reality when she and her family switch to the dance floor. I shift my spot for a better view before eating a protein bar from my shirt pocket. My shift is going on fourteen hours. It's not my longest, but I need to do little tasks to keep going. It's best when the girls are in the same room at the hotel; Mason and I alternate so we can take breaks. I spot my coworker from the other side of the room and offer a nod.

Every now and again, a woman will saunter up to me and suggest I buy her a drink or take her dancing. I brush them off as politely and quickly as I can. I lose my manners with the more stubborn women; the only stubborn woman I want tonight doesn't spare me a single glance. Not as she dances with her sister and not as a man approaches her. The hairs on the back of my neck rise in warning.

It's a club, Wesley. People flirt and dance at a club.

Still, I glare at the six-foot Caucasian man with blond hair as he slides behind Nina. My chest doubles in weight when she tosses him a considering look before backing into him. His hands find her waist—the waist I'd caressed just days ago—and dip lower to her hips. My ears burn. My jaw aches from how hard I clench my teeth. Images of snapping the man's wrists flash across my mind, followed with breaking his neck as he lowers to kiss hers.

I shut my eyes from the crushing realization that tonight, I won't be sliding up that glittery dress and tasting every drop of her. I won't be feeling her twitch and hearing her moan while her thighs tighten around my head as a climax overtakes her. I take a few deep breaths, my hands clasped in front of me to hide my hard-on. They dance together for the next few minutes, and I watch in agony.

A good man wouldn't imagine all the ways he'd kill a person simply for touching his client. He wouldn't dream of putting a bullet through said person's throat.

Luckily, I can't call myself a good man just yet.

A woman appears at my side, her breasts grazing my

arm. I step away. She persists by shifting in front of me. I glance down into blue eyes, and before she speaks, I demand, "Leave."

"I'm sorry?" she says, recoiling.

When I don't reply, she mutters a slew of curse words as she walks off. I resettle my attention on Nina only to see that a second man joined them. Roughly the same build as the first, but with brown hair.

Between them, Nina stiffens. She offers a polite smile as she tries to peel the second guy's hands off her. The first man presses her closer to his body. I take a step ahead, my hands itching to hurt *someone*. Again, she tries to move from between them, but they're persistent and lost in the music. She lifts her head, gaze searching the area until she finds me. I raise a questioning brow, and at her frantic nod, I spring into action.

I cut through the crowd without caring who I bump into. The goal isn't to kill despite my growing wish to. I slip my arm around Nina's waist, shouldering between the man in front of her. She swiftly escapes from them, her hand wrapped around my elbow.

"Are you okay?" I ask.

She nods. "I'm fine. He wouldn't let go."

I fight every instinct to confront them, but my job is to protect Nina and avoid all conflict. Which is why I nearly smile when the unwanted guest claps a hand on my shoulder.

"Wait your turn," he says in Maldanian.

The bass thumps in my chest. I look at him, studying his pointy features. "Please remove your hand from my shoulder."

He laughs, tossing a look at his friend. Nina shifts closer to me, her arm still around my elbow. Her presence is a reminder—deescalate and leave. But the man's hold tightens, and I think of this exact hand touching her without permission.

In a fluid motion, I contort his hand until I feel his wrist snap. He yelps, almost dropping to his knees as he cradles his broken bones. His friend rears back with a fist, but I send the knuckle of my index finger to the pressure point between his brows. His head reels back from my phoenix eye fist, so disconcerted that he collapses. Nina gasps and the crowd backs away.

Maia appears, asking what happened. When Vanessa pops up, I pull Nina aside and tell her we need to leave.

"What? Why?"

"The bouncer will more than likely kick both of us out. That will bring attention, especially with Princess Vanessa around."

Nina doesn't hesitate. When she grabs her things and heads to the restroom, Maia walks up to me with Mason not far behind. In heels, Maia is at least an inch taller than me.

"Are you taking her home?"

"If that's what she wants," I say.

"Well, are you going to take care of her? She's drunk."

A minute ago, I broke someone's wrist and wounded another because they put their hands on Nina. And Maia is still ensuring that I'll take care of her sister.

"I give you my word that she'll return safely."

She points a threatening finger at me. "She fucking better."

The corner of my mouth quirks. After slipping out the private entrance, Nina latches onto my arm as we head toward the main road.

"I can't believe you did that!"

With the amount of entitlement those two men had, they would have gone to great lengths to inconvenience my life. It isn't a notable event to me, but she's thrilled by it.

"You won't get in trouble?" she asks, stumbling over the cobblestone.

I reach out to steady her. "No. He came at me first."

She laughs. "That was so cool! You know, I punched someone before."

"Did you, now?"

She doesn't notice my sarcasm. Her hold on my arm tightens as she staggers over the bumpy street. I've seen my share of drunk women; being around *any* drunk person gets old fast. Not Nina. She doesn't do this often—the fact that she can't hold her liquor tells me so.

The road is mostly empty, considering all the shops are closed. The neighborhood is wealthy, making street crime less likely.

"I was a freshman in high school," she begins. "Me and my friends were hanging out in a parking lot and I had Maia with me because I picked her up from school. She was only in sixth or seventh grade and this boy called her a bitch! So I punched him in the nose and it got blood *every-where*. Maia was *totally* being a bitch but I wasn't about to let anyone else call her that."

I scratch the back of my neck as she presses her body weight into me with each step. For six years, I worked for one of the strongest crime bosses and arms dealers. I've been shot, stabbed, and done things that warrant a death penalty—and Nina's bragging about giving a boy a bloody nose a decade ago.

Yet when she leans her head on my shoulder, a hint of contentment punctures my chest.

CHAPTER NINETEEN
NINA

I don't know why I let Maia talk me into those two vodka shots or why I thought a strong margarita afterward was wise. I haven't had alcohol like this in months—I can't hold it for shit.

I made it a mere street over from the club before lowering onto the stoop of a small apartment building. I can't walk in these heels on cobblestones while drunk. The worst part? It's not even midnight.

"I don't wanna go back," I whine. "But I can't walk in these."

Wesley huffs, sliding his hands into his pockets. He's rather calm for someone who just broke another man's wrist. "Then what do you want to do?"

I look up at him through my lashes, fighting to keep my gaze steady. "Wander. Go to the square over there." I point toward the bustling area that erupts with street performers.

He contemplates for a moment. "Stand up."

"But I can't—"

"Stand. Up," he says, firmer this time.

I roll my eyes but accept his outstretched hand. Before I

can steady myself, he scoops me up bridal-style. "What are you doing!" I screech as he starts walking down the road.

"You can't walk in those shoes?"

"No."

"Then be quiet."

I smack the back of his head. "Don't talk to me like that."

He groans in annoyance. My heels weigh my feet down like anchors, and I can feel my panties exposed down below.

"Wesley—my dress." With one arm wrapped around his neck, I reach under me with the other. There isn't enough fabric to pull down.

"I'll blind anyone who looks," he deadpans, and my stomach flips. After what happened at the club, I believe he would. It silences me for the rest of the walk.

My head slumps against his shoulder and I squeeze my eyes shut to curb the dizziness. The world spins, and I hold on tighter to Wesley in an attempt to ground myself. I expected panic to kick in, considering I'm drunk and in public in a foreign country late at night. Yet I don't feel a hint of it. From jet lag to my unfamiliar drunken state to my life on the verge of flipping upside down, a sense of peace and safety washes over me for the first time in months.

When we reach the car, he sets me down and opens the passenger door.

"But I wanted to—"

"*I know,*" he says in an exasperated tone, and I want to smack his head again because of it. He instructs me to sit down, and I do so with my legs still outside the car. He kneels before me and unbuckles the clasp around my ankles.

"What are you doing?" I ask.

"You ask too many questions."

I don't argue that. Wesley reaches toward the car floor and grabs—slippers? He tosses my heels inside and slides the UGG slippers onto my feet.

"Where did you get these?" I wail. They're padded on the bottom, suited for the outdoors. I click my feet together, reveling in the plushness and warmth. I look at him, bewildered yet joyful. "They're so soft!"

"Now you can wander," he says, rising and gesturing ahead. "After you."

I squeal like a child and jump to my feet.

The city square is vibrant with life in spite of the time. Most shops and stalls are closed or preparing to, but people continue to pour out of bars and sit on stone ledges that lead to more of the city down below. If I look up and to the right, I can spot the restaurant from my first night in Maldana.

A street performer plays EDM music from a speaker and dances with glow sticks taped to his arms. Women offer roses in attempts to earn a euro. They back off when noticing Wesley behind me.

A few people stare as we pass through quieter streets. I hop up on the edge of the sidewalk, his hand capturing mine to steady me. I regain balance and tiptoe like it's a tightrope. Placing one slippered foot in front of the other, I hold my arms wide and squint to focus.

"Watch where you're going," Wesley says from behind me. There's nothing in front of me, so I flap my wrist to shush him.

Suddenly, I feel his hand on my forehead, the pressure making me stumble back into his waiting palm on my waist. I look up at the stop sign that would have whacked me in the head.

"Ohhhhh," I drawl, pointing down, then up. "I thought you meant watch out down here but you meant watch out up here."

He sighs.

"First the club and now this. You're such a good body-guard." I pat his cheek, then reach up to smack the sign, my rings clanking on the steel. "You can't hit me! As Avril Lavigne once said, *I'm the motherfucking princess.*"

"All right, come on," Wesley says, guiding me away.

I stroll down a road not ten feet wide. This one is nearly silent, save for the man sitting on a short stool playing the saxophone. Water from this afternoon's rainfall drips from the roofs around us. Wesley is far behind me, half of his body cloaked by shadow. I ignore him and sway to the music, its smooth melodies wrapping around me. A young woman passes by, and she gives Wesley a wary look before continuing.

"People are going to think you're stalking me if you stay that far away," I say to him, and he shrugs. I huff, head still spinning and body still loose from alcohol. "Dance with me."

I'm suddenly thankful for the streetlights being behind me, as the backlight will hide my surprise. Why the hell would I ask that? Alcohol takes away what little filters I already have.

Wesley barely reacts. "No."

The ease of rejection stings—and I fight it the best I can. I convinced him to ride a moped with me. This is much less dangerous. I walk closer. "People have been staring at you for following and not talking to me. It's creepy."

"I'm not concerned about them."

I suppress another roll of my eyes. "Please?"

It would be easy to miss, but I've spent enough time

with him to notice the little sag in his shoulders. It only fuels my stubbornness. His Adam's apple bobs and a smirk tugs at my lips. I take his hand and lower my chin to look up at him with doe eyes.

"One dance. Please?"

Wesley glares at me, knowing the trick I discovered. Yet to beat me at my own game, he presses his palm against the small of my back and pulls me against him. My chest slams into his hard enough to knock the air from my lungs and fan the hair around my face.

"*One* dance," he says in a stern voice.

If only he knew I'd give him hell just to hear him talk to me like that again. It takes all my will not to melt entirely onto him, which means there's none left over to curb the desire clenching my gut.

I curl my arms around his shoulders and imagine if there weren't layers of clothes between us. We sway to the saxophone music, my head tucked where his neck meets his shoulder. I close my eyes, but I can't feel or sense if he has an increased heartbeat like I do. Is he not as stirred as I am? Is his chest not enflamed like mine? Or am I just drunk?

It has to be the alcohol and the fact that I haven't had sex in over a month. All I want to do right now is snake my hands through Wesley's hair and feel his lips on mine. I ache to know what he tastes like. The night is warm, but shivers cover me from head to toe. I bet he fucks like a god. He's a man of few words; I doubt he holds back in bed.

My hand clenches his shirt when his fingers graze up my spine. I release the fabric and subtly smooth it.

Shit. Fuck. Damn.

He definitely noticed. I don't expect his grip on my waist to strengthen and our swaying to the classic music to increase. He's teasing me. If I wasn't enjoying it so much,

I'd be surprised he has it in him. I didn't think he would care to do anything. As he caresses my bare back—only fueling my wish for him to slam me against the wall and kiss me—I slide my fingers through the hair at the base of his neck. His shoulder twitches ever so slightly and I suppress a smirk.

We dance through teasing one another until my body is so tight with lust I can't think straight. When a lone pedestrian walks by, Wesley pulls away and I stumble.

"How do you feel?" he asks, steadying me. "You had a lot to drink."

I lower my head, my hair a curtain around me as I pinch the bridge of my nose. Of course. Have I lost my mind? I'm drunk. He's my bodyguard. I need to snap out of it because there's no way that wasn't in my head.

"I'm fine." I square my shoulders and lift my gaze for any type of distraction. With a quick scan around, I notice an alleyway to the left. Stairs lead upward with a statue in the center of it. I narrow my gaze on it. A woman. "What is that?"

The musician still plays his saxophone. While I usually tip street performers, I walk up the uneven steps toward the woman, my stomach stirring in unease. The plaque reads Queen Ophelia. Rusty lamps reflect an orange glow on my mother's stone face. A blank expression—frozen in time.

I wish the sculptor had given her more emotion. This is the closest I've been to her since she died. Real life. 3D. I take her hand in mine, brushing my fingers over the cold stone. What did it really feel like? Soft or callous? Did she always have a fresh manicure, or did she habitually bite her nails the way I used to?

Both fresh and decaying roses scatter around the statue and there isn't a spec of dirt in sight. A few pedestrians trot down the steps that curve around her. They have no idea I'm her daughter. I constantly ask myself if the public would hate me, and the pressure is almost enough for me to decline the crown entirely.

Mom was supposed to be here. She was meant to guide me through this decision.

"Maldanina," Wesley blurts.

I jump, so lost in my own world that I forget he's here. "What?"

"Before we gained independence from the Greeks, we were called Maldanina."

"Why was it changed?"

He shrugs. "Wanted to create our own name I guess."

Maldanina—*Nina*.

A wave of grief and love slams into me. I grip my mother's stone hand tighter. Everywhere I look in this country, I discover more pieces of myself, of who I want to be. I have to try. I have to see if I can do it—and I can start by going to the introductory dinner.

In the morning, I'm woken by Maia jumping on top of me.

"*Buenimara!*" she sings.

I groan and cover my head with the pillow. My temples throb in pain as all memories of last night still burn my mind. Every agonizing moment of thinking Wesley was teasing me. If only I drank enough to forget.

"How are you not hungover?" I muffle into the pillow.

"I didn't even drink that much. And *you're* the light-weight, not me. What do you wanna do today?"

I pull the pillow away and stare at the golden-toned ceiling. "I saw a statue of Mom last night."

She perks. "Really?"

"It was like... she was real." I exhale. "I got to hold her hand." I sound like I saw her ghost. It's almost as if I had.

"Are you okay?" Maia asks, her voice suddenly soft.

I turn toward her. "She was supposed to be here. She would've—" I cut myself off. There are dozens of ways to finish that sentence. "Everything would be different... but I think we should go to that dinner Aunt Beverly told us about."

"Really?" she repeats, lifting her brows. "The one to meet the Court? What makes you say that?"

"This was a big part of Mom's world whether we like it or not. I think we owe it to her memory to try."

She pulls her lips aside in consideration, but agrees, which makes Aunt Beverly ecstatic when we tell her. The dinner can't be scheduled until next Friday because Helen, head of the human resources department, is recovering from an operation.

I stay in limbo with Dad over the week. It teeters on normal every so often—as normal as we can be while ignoring the elephant in the room.

I FaceTime Raven for hours one night and while I trust her wholeheartedly, I keep the princess news to myself. *I hardly have a grasp on it*—perhaps it's best to tell her after the introductory dinner. Once I meet the Higher Court, I feel like I'll have my answer.

I opt for minimal details about my family and highlight the culture here. Raven, like me, loves to learn about the different traditions around the world. The only difference is that her parents are rich and she's actually *seen* the world, whereas I've just read about it.

I tell her that a lot of people know at least a little English, but largely act like they don't. I suppose it's from their love of tradition and culture. They want tourists to absorb as much of their culture as possible. According to Raven, plenty of Europeans want to practice their English with Americans, but it appears Maldanians don't. They are strong, stubborn people with open hearts.

I like the thought of never leaving Maldana, yet I couldn't ignore the ache from leaving my home. I don't hate America; its founding principles of diversity and freedom are revolutionary. Except those haven't been upheld, and I haven't felt proud of my country in a long time. Maybe it's a sign to share my pride.

I avoid everyone during these relatively empty days and create a self-care routine of morning yoga, journaling, and reading. I'll then walk to the farmer's market, inhaling the damp morning air and avoiding the already-roasting sun, and order a crepe or croissant.

Every so often, I'll go with a slice of tora di pomke. Some street vendors sell rings they craft themselves, and one morning, I turn to the forever-silent Wesley behind me and ask for the credit card. He always hands it over without a word.

Given, the palace is paying for everything, but still.

My memories often drift back to that night—of his fingers trailing down my spine, leaving shivers in their wake. I'm more than fresh out of a relationship; I hadn't been touched or held in that way even months before I broke up with James.

My body ignites every time Wesley touches me, and I don't know if it's because I've been so deprived.

When Friday afternoon arrives, the same team that prepared me for the club rolls in with their equipment. This time, the dresses they have for me are formal. I quickly settle on a maroon mid-calf dress. The front folds over my chest, exposing my collarbone and shoulders. My throat clogs with nerves. The Higher Court will be studying me for signs of Mom. How can I become her if I don't know her?

I stare at my reflection as the team straightens and curls my hair again, twisting it into a low bun. I search my wide brown eyes for a hint of her. She had blue eyes. Perhaps we have the same sharp cheeks.

I shiver when the loose curls around my face tickle my neck. Greta sets a chunky ruby necklace against my chest, and frankly, I'm scared to ask what it's worth. I struggle to steady my breathing the entire drive to the palace, but my thumping chest tells me this dinner will change everything.

CHAPTER TWENTY
WESLEY

I wake up covered in sweat.

The wound on my left hand throbs. This nightmare wasn't about the boy I saved from gunfire; I relived each kill like a movie with Nina, Cora, and Mom as my audience. My chest caves at the sight of their horrified faces. Nina flinched from me. Mom couldn't meet my eyes. My mind and body betray the efforts to improve, as if life in the underground is a muscle memory, utterly ingrained in my heart.

Maybe it's who I'm meant to be.

El Revalté.

I've stared at the ceiling so often that I memorized each cobweb and spec of dirt. I heave a sigh, waiting for the urge to throw in the towel and call Trakas to offer my services. It would be so easy. Before I can push myself to do it, Mom, Cora, and Nina appear in my mind—asking me why.

Why would I become an assassin? I tell myself it's because I wanted to be part of something bigger. I wanted to put my mark on the world. But after my third or fourth target with Santiago as my boss, I realized it was the soli-tude. It was good that I wasn't in society. The less I spoke to people, the better. I just so happened to be skilled with long guns and staying in the shadows. As much as I hated Santiago naming me The Ghost, it fit—and I liked that no one knew my real name. Almost like it wasn't really me committing these acts.

I sit up and swing my feet over the edge, head in hands. How did I end up here? All those years suddenly become clouded, poisonous memories. My military career could have been promising if I hadn't spent half of it searching for targets underground. Even as a ranger, I did things my family wouldn't be proud of.

More than anything, I want to disappear. Not leave, not move to another city or country. I want the half of me that feels like a ghost to overtake me. The few moments I feel grounded are when Nina's near. She was ecstatic to see a damn cat napping on the back of a Great Dane. She shoved a french fry into my mouth because I wasn't *"fully living"* until I tasted it. She doesn't have to search for joy, it lives in her, and she uses it wherever she can.

Nina reminds me of a reality without darkness. A world with light.

I spend the next two hours trying to get my head on straight. I make the bed, sweep, clean the kitchen, eat breakfast, clean the kitchen again, shower, and shave my beard. I almost trim it further until remembering Nina's reaction the last time I had. I could tell she hadn't meant to react, but my stomach lurched at her pout.

Even though I'm off duty while she dines with the Higher Court tonight, my chest caves as she walks in the opposite direction, her dress swaying around her legs. I don't know if I'm addled with constant thoughts of her or if the prickling along the back of my neck is a warning. My instincts are reliable, but I hate that they blend with Nina.

Yes, I constantly wonder what sound she makes when having an orgasm and what her nails feel like digging into my back.

Yes, it's been a while since I had sex.

I haven't slept with anyone since Daria, and these intrusive thoughts of Nina make me consider calling her. But Daria wouldn't hesitate to pull me back into underground work. Anything involving my ex-girlfriend has a hefty transaction, and she's not worth the risk. Regardless, the thought of taking any woman who's not Nina to bed makes me nauseous. She's the only woman I crave. I fall hopelessly into every opening she gives me. All she has to do is give me those doe eyes—and I'm done. I release a long breath.

"What are you doing here?" Jack asks as I stride into the security room. Monitors cover every inch of a wall, displaying camera footage of the dinner location in the Maia wing.

"To offer extra hands."

He hands me an earpiece. "Then you can go check the blind spots on the upper external floor."

"Yes, sir."

For the next fifteen minutes, I help identify and cover the blind spots and bite back a retort about how this should've been done long before the dinner started. I do an extra lap of the patios with alcoves overlooking the garden. Parallel to the nooks, French doors lead to an interior balcony around the perimeter of the circular room.

Down below, the Higher Court starts gathering

amongst a seating area to the side. Only a few members arrived, and they're chatting with the sisters. Nina glances up and spots me walking along the balcony. Her brow knits, but she visibly relaxes before turning back to the Court. She laughs at something her sister says, a smile brightening her brown skin. I shift focus before I start picturing myself kissing her bare shoulders and collarbones.

Jack redirects me to double-check a blind spot outside. Once finished, I turn and find Nina twenty feet away with a curious expression.

"What are you doing here?" she asks.

I fight every instinct to rake my eyes down her body. "Working."

"Obviously," she scoffs. "Why? We're in the palace. You don't work when I'm in the palace." She studies me. "Are you okay?"

"Uh—yes, I'm fine."

"You seem... stressed."

I inhale and subtly lift my posture. "No. I'm okay." If I'm in her presence any longer, I won't be able to stop the compulsive images of touching her curves beneath the dress. I fix the cuffs of my white dress shirt as I walk by. "Just enjoy your night, angel."

It's not until I'm way past her that she blurts, "Angel?"

I halt. *Fuck.* Did I say that out loud? I hesitantly lift my gaze. "What?"

"You called me angel."

"Must be mistaken," I brush off. There isn't a chance in hell I'd admit it.

"I'm not," she says, a cocky hint in her voice. The flirty smile on her lips makes my blood rush south. "But I like it."

Nina leaves without another word, her heels a *clack* on

the marble. I force myself to continue right away. There are cameras everywhere—and I'll be lucky if no one overheard that interaction. When I return to the security office, Jack's lingering stare digs into me, but I do the same thing I've been doing about my growing feelings for Nina: I ignore it.

CHAPTER TWENTY-ONE

NINA

I'm surprised at the relief washing over me when Aunt Beverly arrives. Perhaps it's the familiar face at a stressful dinner.

Tonight, I genuinely consider my future.

Ever since discovering my lineage, I haven't considered the history of the crown or its function. I need to learn about the government and understand its fine-tuning. My aunt explains that Maldana has a constitutional monarchy—they're the face of the country and show strength, courage, and excellence. I don't know what it means to be a princess, let alone a queen.

But my stomach sinks at the idea of taking this administrative job in September. It's not what I want. My goal has always been to bridge the gap as a translator, possibly for an organization as big as the United Nations. I love to help people, and my knack for language science is the way I can best help them.

But what if I can do more?

As we wait for the remainder of the guests to arrive, I sit in a lounge area with Maia, Aunt Beverly, and two other early arrivals—George and Nico. George is from the Higher Court's communications office. He has *plenty* in mind for what my sister and I can do and is convinced the public will adore us. I'm not eager to find out. Nico, the head of the Lord Chamberlain's office, explains how he and his people arrange our trips and functions.

"Functions for what?" Maia asks.

Nico gives a hearty laugh. He leans back on the loveseat and sips his liquor. "Everything. The list goes on. Dinners, ceremonies, luncheons. We're your calendar come to life."

Maia and I exchange glances. The thought of being busy enough that we need an entire office to manage it is a little more than intimidating. It's frightening.

Within the next twenty minutes, the heads of the human resources and treasury offices arrive, and so do the staff belonging to them. I ask about Helen's recovery when she arrives, and she's pleasantly surprised by the question. By far, she's the kindest member of the Higher Court by trying to learn more about Maia and me as individuals, while the rest like to dive into business, contrary to what Aunt Beverly had told me. At least twenty-five people fill the room, and I stopped memorizing names after the tenth person.

Despite Wesley being largely out of sight tonight, it's a comfort knowing that he's here somewhere. He handles everything with ease and relaxation, and even his distant presence inspires me to emanate that.

When all the guests arrive, we settle at the table in the center of the circular room. Aunt Beverly had taken care to inform the kitchens of my and Maia's vegetarian diet, and although I'm reluctant to taste the eggplant parmesan, it's delicious.

The Court becomes more welcoming as the evening

goes on, and it's noticeable that they love Maldanians. Even though they praise the people, I'm skeptical of anyone who holds power like theirs. Should I ask them candid questions about where taxpayer money is spent? Where the funding comes from?

The attention of the gathering is so focused on Maia and me that it's difficult not to close into myself. My sister, on the other hand, thrives in it considering she typically loves being the center of attention.

Once dessert is served, conversations disperse among the many seating areas around the room. I slip free from my discussion with Helen to head upstairs to the balconies. I've been socializing for over two hours and my body is starting to send me warning signs.

I let the fresh air calm my rapid heartbeat. For the first time tonight, I slouch my shoulders and roll out my neck. Tension slowly leaves my body as I spot an alcove overlooking the barely lit garden. I flinch at the sound of shuffling feet behind me.

I huff. "Can you—not now. I need a minute alone."

"I won't speak." Wesley knots his hands in front of him, and although the sight would be a pleasant distraction, I want privacy.

"No," I insist, waving a hand and gesturing for him to leave. "Go away. Vanish. I need space. You said yourself the palace is heavily guarded—so *shoo*."

Shooing him away reminds me of Maia. Before I fall into a state of worry about how my sister would adapt to being princess, I push everything from my mind and take a sip of my drink.

For a single moment, I don't want to think about anything. Not my crippling relationship with Dad. Not the check-in texts Raven sends me. And definitely not how invigorated Wesley makes me feel from a simple touch, yet at the same time, his steady presence calms me beyond expectation. I press a hand against my cheek and close my eyes.

Breathe in, breathe out.

"You should see it in the autumn."

I try not to get angry at the gentle voice. A brunette man around my age saunters up to me, his dreamy gaze on the dark landscape. In heels, I have a solid four inches on him.

"Yeah," I breathe out, my hand tightening around the champagne glass. I don't even like champagne. "I bet it looks breathtaking."

I don't remember his name or know how to politely tell him to leave me alone. "What do you think of the country so far?" he asks, his Maldanian accent strong.

I have yet to come up with a blanket reply to people asking me this question. He's seeking a hint about what my decision will be. "It's absolutely beautiful here. I love it."

"Do you feel at home?"

I tense. What a weird question. "Well—with my mother from here, I certainly feel a connection."

From the corner of my eye, I spot him nod. He speaks in a soft voice. "Nice... That is nice."

Awkward silence fills the space. It's odd that he doesn't get the hint I don't want to engage in conversation. My answers are brief, reserved. I need this time alone before I go back to the crowd.

Speak up, Nina. Demand your space.

"Um, if you wouldn't mind—"

I barely have time to gasp as his hands around my throat dig into my windpipe. My chest immediately explodes with pain, begging for more air. The man's kind eyes turn dark as he leans into me, and my entire body is aflame with nerves when I feel the breeze against my bare arms.

He's choking me.

He's *killing* me.

Panic washes over me and I don't know what to do first. Grab onto the ledge so he can't throw me over. *Hit him with the champagne glass!* But my hands are empty. When did I drop it? I don't remember hearing the glass shatter.

"We don't want you here," the man whispers, his hold around my neck tightening as his breath fans my cheeks. "Death to the monarch. Vi ponte lo revínastí."

Is this going to be the last face I see?

My ears burn. My vision blurs. No amount of clawing at his face and hands stops the breath draining from me. I have no more energy to panic; all of it rushes to my core and tries to fight for air. Black dots hover in front of me. My legs weaken, and he starts to lower with me until two big hands cover his face from behind and rips him away like it's nothing.

I collapse as air rushes back into my lungs. *Alive. Breathe.* Tears well in my eyes, a few escaping despite the effort. Through my foggy vision, I can see who tore him off me.

Wesley.

CHAPTER TWENTY-TWO
WESLEY

At first, I assume the red I see is from my anger.

And then I notice the blood on my hands.

"All right, *he's down!*" Jack yells, pulling me off the attacker after my fourth punch. I stumble back, swiping my mouth with my wrist. My knuckles throb, but I forget about any discomfort when I see Nina collapsed on the floor with a hand on her necklace as she struggles to catch her breath.

"Get back," I snap when a security guard reaches out to help her.

Nina looks at me, her face red and eyes glassy, and I pour my focus into getting her out of here before I finish the man who tried to kill her. I take her trembling hand in my bloody one as I reach my other arm around her waist. My stomach caves at the sound of her ragged breathing.

"Take her to a safe location," Jack demands as I'm already leading her away.

Everyone bustles around in a panic. Up ahead, Maia rushes to meet us. Mason is but a foot away from her, and I assume she refused to leave without Nina.

"Nina!" Maia exclaims, a look of horror and fear on her

face. "Oh my god. What happened? Your neck..." She extends a hand, stopping midway.

Nina shuts her eyes, overwhelmed. She curls her hands against her chest. Even if I wanted to step back, I couldn't. She leans into me.

"Someone attacked her," I say. "He's in custody, but we need to get her to the hospital."

Her voice comes out in a single, rasped sound. "No."

"You need to be examined."

"No hospital," she insists. Amidst the chaos around us, she stares at me, defiant.

"There's an on-call doctor for tonight," Mason suggests. "What if we bring him here?"

Nina lowers her gaze from me and nods. Mason and I stand on either side of the sisters as we lead them to the designated safe room in the palace's Jolie wing. Palace employees bustle around, and I soon find Jack trailing behind us.

"Have the on-call doctor meet us," I tell him.

"What? She needs to go to the hospital."

I lift my shoulders. "She refuses."

My boss sighs before taking out his phone. When we reach the room, Nina sits on the leather couch with Maia. Her hands haven't stopped trembling. I step to the mini bar and pour a bottle of water into a glass. Mason appears at my side with a bowl of ice, and I drop a couple into the water.

"It's for your hand," he says, and I walk away without a reply. I can't begin to think of myself until Nina calms down.

I hold out the glass to her. As she accepts it, her gaze lingers on my shredded knuckles. The doctor arrives only a short time after. She flinches away every time he tries to examine her, and remains adamant that he only looks at her neck. I notice that Maia and I are the only ones she allows to touch her.

"You will be okay," the doctor says, his Maldanian accent so thick he's difficult to understand. "You have the, uh"—he gestures around his neck—"the bruise, but it heal soon. You should get scan of head to be safe."

Nina attempts a smile, whispering, "Okay. Gracea," as he packs his things and leaves.

Jack steps toward her with a solemn face. His voice has an unusual gentleness to it. "I can show you to a room you can stay tonight." At her confused look, he adds, "Here, on palace grounds."

She shakes her head. "No. I want—I want to go back to the hotel."

My chest constricts. We don't know who attacked her and how he got access. Chances are, he has a group of people who, at the very least, know he was planning this. He could have a back-up plan.

"Your Highness, it is safest if you stay here," Jack says.

"No." Like before, she speaks definitively. My boss gives me a look. Part of me almost demands that she stays here, but I can imagine what she's going through. She's feeling destabilized. I clench my jaw and nod to Jack.

"Okay, then. Our security is still securing the perimeter of the grounds. Once it is secure, you may go." He gestures for Mason and me to gather in a corner of the room. We speak in Maldanian. "Do you think Maia will agree to stay here?"

"Absolutely not," Mason says in a grave tone. "The only reason I did not take her to a secure location right away is because she screamed at the top of her lungs when I grabbed her arm."

It's a scene I can picture.

Jack sputters. "Oh—okay, then. Have Gregory and Silas sweep the hotel before you arrive. I'll send back-up in a few hours so you can have a break and call me the *moment* they're settled so we can debrief."

As the minutes tick on, I realize how *slow* time has moved since the incident. A few crazed, violent seconds changed the whole trajectory of the night when I've moved on quicker from even bloodier fights before. It reminds me that civilians aren't used to this, but I'm strangely shaken tonight.

I flex my bruised, swollen hand that's still stained with blood. Every safe room has a medical kit, so I hastily clean and scrub my wounds.

"Can someone turn off the radio?" Nina asks in the silence. She holds her hands on either side of her head.

Maia touches her shoulder. "I... There's no radio."

She must hear a ringing or buzzing sound—common after strangulation. I suppress the urge to insist she goes to the hospital for a scan. The more I would encourage, the more she would resist.

The ride to the hotel is quiet. Halfway there, I get two messages. Gregory and Silas find no red flags at the hotel, and Jack sends me a single name.

Anton Robert.

Her attacker. It's a name I don't recognize. I stop myself from mulling over it and focus on getting Nina to bed. In the hallway, Maia says to her, "I'm going to shower and change. Will you be good for a little bit?"

Nina nods and sinks into her sister's hug. I notice Maia's tears. She wasn't the one attacked, but her love runs so deep that she takes some of the pain, too. It makes me think of Cora—how I haven't been around to look after her all these years.

Nina jumps when she sees two people from the beauty team in her room. The lead woman, Greta, speaks to me, likely because of the apparent agitation on my face.

"We are here to retrieve the dress and jewelry from Miss Laffley."

"Not now," I say. "You'll—"

I feel a hand on my arm. "It's okay."

Greta has no criminal affiliation and neither does her assistant, Chloe. Still, I watch as Nina steps out of her heels and hands them over to the women who look at her with unease and pity. The redness in her face has calmed, but her neck has splotches and discoloration. I turn from them when she steps out of the dress and wraps in a silk robe. Other than the few shed tears right after the attack, I realize that she hasn't cried.

Until now.

"*No—!*" I warn when Greta stupidly reaches to remove the necklace from Nina, who lashes out and shoves the woman with full force to the ground.

Nina gasps, a horrified expression on her face as she covers her mouth. "I'm sorry. I-I-I didn't mean—"

"It is all right. I am fine," Greta says as Chloe helps her up.

Second by second, Nina breaks down. Tears spill over as she brushes her fingers over her neck. "No, I... I didn't—I'm—"

All the emotions she suppressed over the last two hours free themselves with a vengeance. I stop her from collapsing with an arm around her waist. I glare at the two women. "Go. Now."

"The necklace. It's worth—"

"Get the fuck out," I sneer. They flinch at my tone and scramble to gather what they can. Nina falls against me, her sobs uncontrollable as I lower us to the ground. Her anguish carves into me, and I feel sudden resentment toward Jack for not letting me kill Anton Robert.

"It's all my fault," she rasps, her head against my shoulder as she fights to catch her breath. "I-I-I just stood there and let him choke me. I froze. I did nothing."

"Nina," I say, my voice grating with unexpected emotion. "Nina, look at me." I shift until she faces me and meets my eyes. With one arm still around her, I hold her cheek with my free hand. She doesn't flinch away from my touch; she watches me with vulnerability I haven't seen before. "It doesn't matter. You can freeze again and again because no one will *ever* get another chance to lay a finger on you, okay?"

She doesn't say anything as she nods, her eyes falling shut. My heart doubles in weight when she curls against my chest. I slide my fingers through her hair, forcing away my violent plans for Robert. My voice doesn't raise above a whisper.

"I promise."

CHAPTER TWENTY-THREE
WESLEY

The plan was to turn on the bathtub and leave her alone.

But after seeing her struggle to take off the necklace and pull the pins from her hair, I find myself standing behind Nina and doing both of those things for her. My groin stiffens when I notice her slipping robe in the mirror. I turn my attention to these hairpins as she fixes it, but her nipples poking through the thin material don't help.

She steps to the claw-foot tub and moves to undress. *Is she trying to kill me?* My subtle attempt to leave results in my shoe scuffing the ground as I stumble. "I, uh—I'll—I'll give you some privacy."

"What?" Nina tightens the robe as she whirls toward me, panic filling her eyes. The look is clear enough: *don't leave me alone.* I bite the inside of my cheek and chide myself for getting hard right now. I gesture to the tub before turning my back to her.

Get it together.

The water trickles as she dips inside. I wait another few

seconds to turn back. She curls her knees to her chest, the puffy bubbles blocking the side of her breast. I sit on the bench beside the tub, examining my bruised hand as a distraction. Anxiety pumps through my body.

I shouldn't be this turned on right now, but the thought of scooping her from the bathtub and kissing every inch of her body intensifies with each second. She briefly dips under the surface and pulls her wet hair aside, revealing the slope of her neck. I nearly fall to my knees and press my lips to every drop of water on her honey skin. My eyes land on the growing bruise around her throat and my chest wrenches painfully.

Nina lathers shampoo through her hair, her soft cries filling the otherwise silent room. I don't know why I do it, but I shift closer on the bench and offer to take over. There's no time for embarrassment; she leans on the edge of the tub, her head angled toward me as if she wanted me to offer. I roll my sleeves to my elbows and dip my hands in the warm water behind her before squeezing more shampoo out of the tiny bottle.

"I don't mean to be difficult," she says in a small voice.

I'm not good at comfort. Being open and gentle has never come easy to me, but all I'm sure of is that I don't want Nina to feel like she's a burden.

"You're not being difficult," I reply as gently as I can, my fingers rubbing the soap into her scalp. The tension in her shoulders starts breaking apart. Her breaths become longer, body becomes stiller, and I slip further into the kind of man who would do anything she asks.

"He spoke to me," she suddenly whispers. She inhales a strained breath. "He said '*we don't want you here. Death to the monarch.*' And then something in Maldanian."

I keep my tone steady. "Do you remember it?"

"No." Her voice breaks. "And I'm trying really hard to. But I just—"

"Don't worry," I say, still massaging the shampoo through her hair. "It's all right."

For a few delicate moments, the only sounds are the light trickling of water with each of her movements and the suds on my hands.

"Neen?" Maia calls, and I don't have the chance to panic before she appears behind me. If she's surprised to walk in on this, she doesn't show it. Nina doesn't react to her sister's arrival. I rinse my hands quickly in the bathwater as Maia nods toward me. "I'll take over. Thank you."

"You're not leaving, right?" Nina asks when I reach the door.

"I'm not going anywhere."

While Nina is with Maia, I use the time to debrief with Jack over the phone.

The name Anton Robert echoes in my mind. I list various ways I can make him suffer. Scream. Beg for death. Breaking each of his fingers would be the start. His eyes would be the final parts I torture before killing him; I want to be the last thing he sees.

"They were able to repair his eye socket. He'll have brain damage, but he'll survive," Jack says.

"A shame."

I should've smashed his head into the marble floor. The feeling of his skull cracking would satisfy me.

The meeting lasts an hour. From a quick glance, Anton

is average with no red flags. Born and raised in Kosita to a middle-class family. He worked in the treasury office for three years. I tell Jack that Anton spoke to Nina, and neither of us knows the phrase *death to the monarch* to be tied to a group.

Jack doesn't protest my decision to work through the night. Once we're finished, he sends me the security footage of the incident. At first, Anton's demeanor is normal, perhaps a little tense, but that's expected when talking to Maldana's princess. The two of them briefly talk; Nina is oblivious to him inching closer. My grip around my phone tightens when he lunges at her, hands latching to her neck. With one arm around the balcony edge, she tries to fend him off. The attack lasts exactly fifteen seconds before I run up and clamp my hands over his eyes, digging my elbows into his back and yanking him to the ground.

I lock the phone and shove it in my pocket. Closing my eyes, I lean my head against the wall. My heartbeat is steady. Exhaustion can be easily controlled, but my mind has never been more at war. Fifteen seconds. She had no protection for fifteen fucking seconds.

How could I have let this happen?

Nina's safety is my responsibility. Apprehension had nagged me beforehand, but I fought my instincts in order for her to have a moment of privacy. Beck would have ignored her protests; Wesley is trying to be better, and good men respect boundaries. I continue blurring the line of expectations as her bodyguard. If I push her boundaries, she'll distance herself. If she does that, she might end up out of my reach altogether—especially when I need to be closer.

I shouldn't dedicate this much of my emotional

capacity to my client. At the same time, I don't have a choice. From the day I met Nina, all I wanted and all I can be is because of her. It may be unhealthy, but she's the first light I found on the other side of who I was.

In the following hours, Mason and I don't take breaks except to use the restroom. Christopher Doukas, the hotel busboy, rolls up a cart of food for us.

"From the chef," he says in Maldanian, which I'm sure is Jack's doing and the chef isn't working at two in the morning. We thank him anyway and devour the huge plates of chicken alfredo. Maia leaves the room not long after, and I resist the urge to check on Nina or ask how she is. But after another forty-five minutes, Nina's bedroom door opens and she leans on the threshold, peering up at me with red-rimmed eyes.

"What's wrong?" I ask.

"I can't sleep," she says with a shrug. She feigns indifference. "Do you want to play UNO?"

I blink, unsure if I heard correctly. *Boundaries.* This would break so many boundaries. I can say no, that it's not appropriate, but it may be too late for that considering I washed her hair while she was naked in the bathtub.

"All right."

I leave the door ajar as I follow Nina inside. Her hair is in two braids. I assume Maia did them since she could hardly take the pins out of her hair earlier. She wears an oversized Wilton University T-shirt and short shorts. My hands ache to replace my gaze caressing her slender legs. I tamper my disappointment when she tucks them beneath her as she lowers onto the sofa. I sit on the other end while she deals the cards. It's been over a decade since I played, but the rules are simple enough.

The game is quiet, save for the few huffs and whines

when I set down a plus-four or a color she wasn't hoping for. I win the first round. I'd let her win if UNO was a game more of strategy than chance. But I'm dealt with another plus-four that I have no choice but to use since I'm out of reds and twos. She glares at me, slapping a hand on the cushion.

"Seriously?"

I shrug and say nothing despite the crack in her voice. I want to make sure she has enough water, to ask if she needs painkillers or if the buzzing sound stopped. But I continue the game and listen to the cicadas and crickets singing outside.

Nina squeals when I toss in a blue seven. She starts slapping down cards like money. "Skip, skip, skip, reverse, three, eight, and plus-flour. *UNO!*" She holds up her final card with a grin.

"Wait—"

"You've hit me with *two* plus-fours! How's it feel?"

Damn. I forgot how much I hate losing. I stutter as I study my new cards. "Not—not great."

She picks the color yellow. I set down a yellow three and, as expected, she tosses in her last card and quips, "I win!"

I huff, a smile tugging at my lips.

I gather the deck to shuffle, and Nina suddenly asks, "Where is he?"

"Who?" I look up, only to realize she's staring at my damaged knuckles.

"The man. The one who—"

"The hospital," I interject, dreading what the end of that sentence would be. She watches me, waiting for more detail. I clear my throat as I start dealing the cards. "I broke his eye socket. He'll have brain damage, but he'll live."

She hesitates. "Do you feel guilty?"

The question surprises me. "No," I say, staring at her bruised neck while I finish dealing. "I don't feel guilty."

I feel homicidal.

But she doesn't need to know that.

CHAPTER TWENTY-FOUR

NINA

My head is heavy in the morning. The dryness in my throat is so painful that I throw myself toward the nightstand, knocking off my phone and nearly tipping the lamp over to reach my water bottle. I chug the water despite the dizziness and throbbing ache.

I collapse back onto the pillow with instant regret. My neck twinges in pain, the soreness echoing through my body. Tears spring to my eyes.

Powerless.

I stood there doing nothing. I let him choke me.

We don't want you here.

A painful sob chokes out of me. I clench the comforter and fight to inhale a single breath. But the raw, paralyzing feeling of last night rips at my throat and blocks my airway. I wish I hadn't woken up. I wish I could stay asleep until this trauma passed like a bad cold. I dig my face into the pillow until I'm composed enough to breathe.

My first instinct is to call out for Wesley. He let me cry on him last night, took care of me; he's done more than enough and I don't want to bother him. Besides, what would he do? *Crawl into bed with me?*

Perhaps it's not too far-fetched of an idea considering he washed my hair. It was intimate in a way I hadn't experienced before. I might have been naked, but nothing about it was sexual. I felt him weaving into my soul, thread by thread. It's not because he stopped my attack. If I told anyone about my growing feelings for him, they'd say I'm projecting my trauma. He washed my *hair*. A normal bodyguard wouldn't do that, right? Or was it out of pity?

For thirty minutes, I toss and turn until the need to pee is too intense to ignore. Afterward, I look at my reflection for the first time. I pointedly ignored it last night, too afraid to face how much of a wreck I am. Red spots scatter through my right eyeball. A purple handprint marks my throat. It's noticeable but will fade quickly. I've never been one to bruise easily.

I shove my feet into slippers and check the time. 7:13. My eyes are still heavy from exhaustion. I poke my head outside my room, expecting to listen for any sign of life downstairs, but I jump at the strange man in Wesley's spot. He has sandy hair, thick brows, and a lean build.

"Who are you?"

"My name is Silas."

"Where's Wesley?"

"He is sleeping in that room, Your Highness," Silas replies in a strong accent, nodding to the room across the hall where the door lies cracked open. Of course. Did I expect him to stay awake forever? He needs rest.

"How long has he been asleep?" I ask, my voice suddenly quieter.

"I take over his spot for three hours."

"Okay. Don't wake him up."

"He instructed me to wake him when you do."

"Well, don't. Let him sleep."

Silas hesitates. He opens his mouth to speak, searching for the right words. "I'm sorry, Your Highness, but I must do as he says."

If I was him, I'd be frightened to disobey Wesley, too. He was fiercely protective last night. But not everything is up to him, and Silas should be more concerned about *my* wrath if he doesn't let Wesley sleep.

I lean closer. "Silas, do not wake him up unless you want me to make your life a living hell."

Do I know *how* I would do that? No, but where there's a will, there's a way. He stiffens, considers for a moment, then nods. "Understood, madam."

Downstairs, I ask Dora in Maldanian if she could bring me a cup of coffee. She doesn't stare at my neck like the other hotel employees. Dora brings me coffee with a slice of warm tora di pomke once I settle on a lounge chair under the shade.

"For you," she says.

"Oh—gracea mucho, Dora."

"Parafóré."

I've been receiving special treatment ever since I arrived here, but Dora brought me this pastry out of pity. There are worse things than pity cake, I suppose. I spend the next ten minutes in the silence of the garden until Maia joins me. She doesn't ask how I feel, thankfully.

"Where's Beck?"

I sip my coffee. "Sleeping. I told the other guy not to wake him."

"Dad and Ruby are on their way back. They didn't find out what happened until they woke up this morning."

I hadn't even considered my parents over the last

twelve hours. It's a good thing Dad wasn't here; he would've been overbearing and worsened my anxiety.

Dora walks outside, her shoulders tense and face struck. "Uh—Prince Jason and Princess Vanessa are here to see you."

Her shock is endearing; I can only imagine her reaction when she learns out I'm royal, too. My cousins walk outside.

"Gracea, Dora."

I sit up on the lounge chair as Vanessa lowers onto the edge. Jace pulls up another seat.

"How do you feel?" Vanessa asks, almost hesitant.

I clear my throat, trying to hide the aching wince. "Like someone tried to choke the life out of me."

She falls quiet and glances at Jace, who leans his elbows on his knees.

"I, uh... When I was eleven," he begins, "I was away on holiday—in a camp. A man with a gun showed up looking for me... I had to hide in a small cabin for three hours as the police searched for him."

Maia perks. "Did they ever find him?"

He nods. "He had a—rifle." He stares at me, unwavering. "And grenades."

"They told you that?" I ask. I have a hard time believing they would've revealed that information to an eleven-year-old.

"I heard my mother talking when she thought I was asleep."

"That must have been scary," Maia says.

"It was. He didn't touch me, but I understand the fear. People don't think of us as humans sometimes."

I don't say anything. Is this a regular occurrence? Will a lot more people try to hurt me in the future? I believe

Wesley when he promises no one would ever touch me again, but he won't be at my side forever. The reminder twists my stomach painfully.

"We want to take you out of the city," Vanessa says in the quiet, placing a hand over mine. "We can go on a boat ride along the coast toward Antina. It is a very beautiful and peaceful town. A lot quieter than Kosita."

"For how long?"

"As long as you want. A night, a week."

"Where will we stay?"

"We will drive to the boat and take it down the coast to a small neighborhood where we have a house. No one knows about it. Very private."

"I promise you'll like it," Jace affirms.

I look at Maia, who only says, "It's up to you. I go where you go."

Part of me hates the pressure. I hate to disappoint her if she wants to go, but a change would be good, and I want to see more of the country.

"I would love to."

When my cousins leave to arrange the plans and transportation, I don't get a chance to slip upstairs with Maia to pack because my parents arrive.

"We came as soon as we heard," Dad says, dropping his bag. "Beverly didn't call until this morning."

I'm enveloped in a hug in the middle of the lobby. My body tenses when his arms wrap around my shoulders, far too close to my neck for comfort. I fight every instinct to shove him off as my heart thunders in my chest. I squirm out of the hug when I feel his hand on the back of my head. He only means well, but I battle the returning emotions from last night. I don't want anyone touching me above my shoulders.

"This happened last night?" Ruby asks, surveying the damage to my neck. "Why the *hell* didn't Beverly tell us right away?" I've never seen her this angry until now.

"I'm fine. I'm okay."

"Like hell you are," Dad snaps, his hands shaking with either worry or anger.

"Dad—please."

"Where's the man who did this to you?"

"In custody."

"Did he say why?"

"Pierce," Ruby warns, noting my demeanor. She squeezes my arm and brushes a curl from my face. "Let's calm down. It's been a long night for her. She needs rest."

"You're right." He sighs, and I notice the redness under his eyes. Ruby's, too. They were crying. I shouldn't be shocked—they're my parents.

"Vanessa and Jace invited Maia and me to travel down the coast to Antina. We're gonna go."

"Are you sure—" Dad cuts himself off after a glare from my stepmother. "Okay. What about—your security will be with you, right?"

"Yes, Wes—Beck will be there. He'll probably be more overbearing than you."

"Good." He hesitates as if searching for the right words. "I know we don't see eye to eye right now, but I love you, Nina. So much."

"I know. I love you, too."

He pulls me into another hug, his arms low this time. I let my head fall into the crook of his neck.

"My baby girl," he mutters, pressing a kiss to my temple. I'm still so upset with him. I expected more from Dad—more of everything. And I realize now that it's not simply because he's my father, but because I love and want him to be a better person.

It's ten o'clock by the time I'm done packing, which means Wesley had almost six hours of sleep. I tiptoe into the room to see him fast asleep on his back, his face soft and unguarded. Typically, his expression is irritatingly neutral. Nothing fazes him. I could stare at this peaceful version of him forever, but I don't have the time nor patience. I nudge his shoulder with my palm.

"Wesl—"

He snatches my wrist before I can finish, his iron grip softening as soon as he sees me. It happens so fast that I don't have the chance to be frightened. So much for being in a deep slumber.

"Nina," he whispers with a huff, almost relieved as his thumb brushes the inside of my wrist. "Are you all right?"

My stomach flips from the way he whispers my name in a husky morning voice. It rattles me enough that I forget to answer at first. "Oh—I-I'm fine."

Wesley blinks himself awake and I regret not waiting another hour for him to rest. I rake my gaze over his messy hair and hunched shoulders and my belly churns from the thought of shoving him back against the bed and crawling on top of him. He runs his hands over his face.

"What time is it? Where's Silas? He was supposed to take over."

"It's ten o'clock—"

"*Ten?*"

"I told him to let you sleep."

He shakes his head, snatching his watch from the nightstand. "He shouldn't hav—"

"I threatened him," I blurt.

He recoils as he fastens the watch. "You... threatened him."

I interlace my fingers in front of me. "I sort of told him I would make his life a living hell if he woke you up."

"Sort of?"

I whack his shoulder. "Stop repeating everything I'm saying and pack a bag." I can't help but smile in excitement. "We're going to Antina."

CHAPTER TWENTY-FIVE
NINA

It takes a lot longer for us to prepare for the trip because of protocols.

Vanessa sends my sister and me a group text explaining the preparations that need to be made to ensure our safety and that we won't be picked up for another *two hours*. Yay for being princess.

In the meantime, I get dressed and put makeup on. As I apply eyeliner, I spot Maia through the mirror as she plops onto the divan. She opens the same photo album we've gone through a dozen times since Aunt Beverly gave it to us.

"All this security stuff is annoying," she whines. "With Mason, it's like having a dad around all the time." I chuckle at the memory of her bodyguard chasing off that boy on our first day. *"Don't do this, that's dangerous, don't swim too far,"* she mocks, lazily flipping through pages. "At least yours doesn't talk and is boring as hell."

I stop my eyeliner mid-brush as a knot of agitation flies up my core. "Wesley isn't boring!" I shut an eyeshadow palette and toss it into my bag with a *clank*. My sister's jab at him shows me the impact he has on my day. "He's just... *calm*." I re-dip my eyeliner brush. With a sigh, I add, "The only calm part of this trip."

I have no idea what the future would look like if I accepted the crown. But if I don't, I wouldn't see Wesley anymore. And the thought of that slices my chest with dread. I shouldn't become queen just to see him more, although it's certainly a perk.

When I finish my eye makeup, I spot precisely what Maia's wearing through the mirror. "Why are you wearing my shirt?"

She glances at her chest. "I'm not."

"You are. I got it at the mall with Raven."

"But it's not your shirt."

"Yes it is!" I insist, walking out of the bathroom and putting my makeup bag into my duffle. I remember picking the red shirt instead of the lavender and how I would only wear it when I was feeling particularly saucy because it was the one revealing shirt I have. And Maia's B-cups don't fill it the way my D-cups do.

"I've literally had this for months so it's not like you were missing it."

"So you admit that it's mine."

"What does it matter? You don't wear it!"

"It matters 'cause it's mine."

"Oh, my god. It's not a big deal!" she wails, getting to her feet. The shirt looks good on her, can't deny, but I'd rather die than tell her that.

"How about you don't take my shit?"

"How about you get over it?"

"How about you grow the fuck up?"

"I don't have to—you act old enough for the both of us."

"Because nothing would ever get done!" I screech, wanting to throttle her for the childish way she said *I don't have to.*

"No one told you to act like my mom!"

"You're so—" I clench my fists with an annoyed groan. The number of times her crying ass came to me with her homework or over another boy she liked! I push out a sigh. There's one focus here, so I hold out my hand. "Give me my shirt back."

"No," she quips. "It looks cuter on me."

Fuck this. I'm not her mom. Which means I can hit her.

I lunge to wrap my arm around her neck, slapping aside her raised hands. As I haul her to the ground, I shout, *"You don't even have the boobs to fill it out!"*

"What the—" Maia stammers, struggling to get off her back. She might be an inch taller than me, but she's also a twig. "You're psychotic!"

"I want my shirt back!"

She tries to shove her knees between us and I push them away and reach for the shirt zipper on her back. She squirms away. "Too bad!"

When she slices me with her unreasonably sharp nails, drawing blood, I slap her in the face. *"Don't scratch me, you little bitch!"*

"Get the fuck off—" She groans in frustration. *"Nina!"*

"All right, enough!" Wesley snaps, hooking an arm around my waist and lifting me off my little sister.

Mason intercepts Maia from hopping up and lunging at me. As her bodyguard pulls her away, I notice she's slipped off her sandal and raised her arm to either throw or hit.

"Drop it," Mason demands, loosely holding her wrist. At her silence, he adds, *"Maia."*

The sandal drops to the floor with a thud.

"Good girl," I taunt. "Now *speak*."

Mason stops her from lunging again. As he ushers her into the hallway, Maia points at me and says, "Don't act like I won't bite you."

I crinkle my nose at her.

She held back. We've been in enough brawls for me to know her dirtiest moves; she could've landed a punch or another skin-splitting scratch. She may have been comfortable enough arguing with me, but she went easy physically.

Wesley sighs. "Why are you fighting her? She's your sister."

"Oh, please." I level a judgmental stare at him. He has no idea what sisters are like. I hold up my bloody forearm. "This is nothing."

He sighs and examines the wound. "Easy fix. Come on."

Without waiting, he walks into my bathroom and takes out a first aid kit. Instead of asking why he knew where that was, I say, "I can do it myself."

"I know."

I rinse my arm in the sink and dry the wound. Wesley tries to use the antiseptic wipe on me, but I smack his hand away and do it myself.

"I don't need a babysitter to clean a scratch."

He grits his teeth and fishes out a Band-Aid, holding it up between his two fingers. I take it without looking at him.

"Your Highness," Mason says as he urges my sister ahead. "Princess Maia has something to say to you."

"No I don't."

Mason glares. It's the most expressive I've seen him.

"I'm sorry I stole your shirt," Maia drawls, "and that I said it looks cuter on me. Even if it does."

I chuckle. My anger dissipated the moment Wesley

pulled me off her. I mostly want to thank my sister for not walking on eggshells around me.

"I'm sorry I said you don't have the boobs to fill it out. Even if you don't."

She pulls me into a hug. We break out into laughter when Mason says, "I'm so grateful I was an only child."

CHAPTER TWENTY-SIX
NINA

Maia, Vanessa, and Jace probably can't see that Wesley is more attentive than ever.

At the start of summer, his indifference was infuriating. He's more present and talkative when it's just the two of us, but he's largely withdrawn. Now he's more brazen—asking if I want french fries delivered to the boat, pointing out cute dogs we pass. I would love it if it wasn't coming the day after my attack. I question the authenticity of it, and that alone leaves a pit weighing my stomach down.

Four bodyguards trail behind us as we head down the dock. Suddenly, Roman pops up on the upper deck of the boat, his arms spread wide. I shield the sun and my disappointment with my hand.

"Your Majesties have finally arrived!"

"Oh, Roman is joining," Maia says, trying and failing to sound upbeat.

"I know he was a bit over-the-top when you first met him, but he will be on his best behavior," Jace assures. "I promise he's a lot of fun when you get to know him."

A man around sixty years old steps off the boat. He

opens his arms for a hug from Vanessa. "Vanessa! Jason! It's good to see you again."

"Captain Thomas!" she exclaims.

He pecks her on each cheek and I wince at the kissing sound. He's around my height with skin wrinkled from years of sun exposure. Greasy hair snakes out from beneath his sailor's hat.

"This is Nina and Maia. They'll be joining us," Jace explains and gestures to the two of us.

Captain Thomas gently shakes Maia's hand. When he turns his attention to me, his interest visibly piques. "Look at how beautiful," he says. Instead of shaking my hand, he caresses and traps it with the other. He looks at me as he adds, "It is a pleasure to meet you both. I look forward to exploring the waters with you."

I stiffen as he starts to bring my hand to his lips. Wesley steps closer behind me and I don't have to pull away from Captain Thomas; the look my bodyguard gives him is enough.

"I, uh—follow me," Captain Thomas says awkwardly to the group. He walks toward the boat without waiting. I wipe my hand on my dress. Wesley's intimidation was subtle, but Maia and my cousins noticed. Vanessa's smothered chuckle comes out in a comical snort, making my sister laugh, too.

My cheeks warm at the thought of them reading into Wesley's defense, so I hurry onto the boat. Maia gets attention from Roman, and I get attention from a greasy sixty-year-old. I don't want either, but one would make me less disgusted than the other. I hold back mortified tears. Vanessa and Jace put this trip together to help me feel better. It will be best for everyone if I packed away these childish insecurities.

The boat is the size of the house I grew up in. An array of fruits, vegetables, and other snacks lay in wait for us near the lounge area under the shade. The bodyguards disappear up into the room where the captain works, which I notice has its own lounge, too.

"Let's get this party started," Roman says, and I wish I had enough time to take a picture of Maia's reaction when he turns on techno music. My sister immediately protests this music taste, surprising him and my cousins.

"You don't like this?" Vanessa asks as she clips her short brown hair behind her. She tugs down a few pieces to frame the bangs across her forehead. "It's popular here."

"*Techno?*"

"EDM!"

"ED-no." She outstretches her hand for whatever phone is playing the music. "I'll show you some better stuff."

Roman laughs and hands her his phone. "Play what you like. I want to hear your music taste."

The slick attempt to include his interest in her makes my sister roll her eyes. She types and scrolls until *Iced Tea* by Joyce Wrice thumps through the speakers. The R&B helps calm me as the boat steers farther from the dock and sails through the crystal blue waters.

I marvel at the sight of Kosita. Half of the city looks etched into a mountain, some of its buildings blending in from the ancient structures. It's the epitome of a preserved world.

As Maia and the rest chat and joke, I wander to the bench along the perimeter, folding my arms over the edge to watch the horizon. The breeze whips through my curls. It'll soon be so frizzy that I have to twist it into a bun, but I focus on the sway of the boat on the waves. The sea before me is wild and the sky above is endless. Puffy clouds dot the atmosphere, far beyond my reach. It's more jarring to remember how infinite the world is beyond the clouds.

Suddenly, my attack feels less powerful, less hurtful, in comparison with the world's vastness.

It won't last, but the taste of relief—no matter how fleeting—offers hope I hadn't possessed before. I slip back into the shade the moment I feel a drop of sweat; I spent far too long covering the bruise around my neck to sweat it off.

We float past dozens of mansions perched along the coast, flanked by pillars of cypress trees. None of the houses has a dock because of the hundred-feet-tall rocks between the surface and sea. Vanessa eventually puts traditional Maldanian music on, the guitar and accordion melodies drifting throughout the boat.

In spite of Roman consistently invading Maia's personal space, she maintains an upbeat personality, and I know that it's for my sake. Roman is the type to keep his advances subtle—a brush of his hand or shoulder against hers, asking her every opinion. It would make her look dramatic if she were to ask him to stop.

As we sit around the table playing a game of UNO, a longing pang for Wesley hits me. I don't like it when he's not at my side. Vanessa starts to deal out another round, and Roman steals a card to gather the white powder he dumps on the surface. He sets up two lines and snorts up one while Jace snorts up the other. *Coke?* I glance around to see if anyone is as uncomfortable as I am.

"Is that—?" I ask.

Roman holds up another little baggie of white powder. "You want some?"

"No, I, uh—I need to use the bathroom," I stutter, jumping from my seat and heading around the corner. I disappear from the main deck, grateful for the temporary moments to gather myself.

"Neen?"

I whirl toward Maia. "They're snorting *coke*?"

She sighs. "I know, I know, but that's their choice. We don't have to. I'll ask them not to do it anymore." She turns me toward the view of Maldana's mountainous landscape across the stretch of blue sea in front of us. "We're here to relax. Look at where we are! It's insanely beautiful here. Why don't you go ask Mason and Beck to come relax with us?"

I look at her over my shoulder, eyes wide in question.

"Roman's getting a little too close," she admits. "This is the one time I want him to run interference."

I choke out a laugh and head upstairs to search for the two bodyguards in question. In truth, it will calm me with Wesley in sight. Part of me panics at the chance that Maia knows this, which is why she suggested they join.

"Wes!" I perk at the familiar figure walking down the exterior hallway. I hold onto the railing to my right. We might be in water, but this is still too high for comfort. "Maia and I want to invite you and Mason to come relax with us," I explain when Wesley faces me. "Like we did at the café in Milagro."

He hesitates. "No, we're fine up here."

"Really? I know the others are all about business, but you and Mason are different."

"I understand. I don't—like to be around people much."

He's antisocial. This much I know. But it still stings. I want to show Maia and Vanessa the side of him that I love being around. How he's smart and thoughtful. How he gives me subtle reassurances and knows what I need before

I know myself. Maybe I'll keep the second part close to the vest.

"Are you sure?"

"I'm sure."

Disappointment fills me, and I try to keep it out of my voice. "Okay," I quip. "Um—well… Maia wanted to invite Mason because Roman keeps getting too close to her. Can you let him know?"

Wesley nods and continues down the hallway. When I return to the main deck, the group falls silent. I suppress a huff. They could at least attempt to be normal.

"Let's go swimming!" Vanessa exclaims, getting up and pulling three donut floats from a closet. Jace and Roman rip off their shirts before launching themselves over the edge without warning. I can't help but laugh at the funny sounds they make while sailing through the air.

I shed my cover-up, still stuck with my one-piece that I regret bringing more and more. I put on my jumbo black sunglasses and climb onto the air-filled donut. Maia flips the music back to R&B and I let my anxieties melt away with the boiling sun as I brush my fingers through the surface of the crystal-clear sea. Every few minutes, I splash some water onto my chest and legs for temporary relief from the heat. If this float had a headrest, the gentle waves would have rocked me to sleep a long time ago. I'm already looking forward to my nap later.

From a quick glance up at the boat, I spot Wesley and Mason outside, both leaning their forearms on the railing as they chat. All the way over here, I study the curve of Wesley's biceps and the width of his shoulders. I would have been more surprised if he *had* accepted the offer to spend time with everyone; it doesn't mean I don't feel slightly rejected. And I hate that feeling and I hate how much I crave him.

Letting myself fall for Wesley will only complicate things. I'm his job—one he takes seriously. Sleeping with me wouldn't look good on his resume; he would get in trouble with Jack; the Higher Court would never look at me the same. With Queen Ophelia as my mother, they expect me to have some natural streak of regality.

I live for the ease of my family. I missed school dances because Dad was drunk and throwing up and Maia was lost on the proper way to take care of him. Until I was fourteen, Dad would try to drive, leave, or wander when drunk. Maia went out. I stayed. I never resented her for it—it was my job.

Do I want to risk the way my family and the Higher Court view me over some lustful thoughts about my bodyguard?

I blink myself out of my reverie, glancing around to spot the mountainous lands hundreds of miles across the sea. *Yes.* A distraction. I point toward them. "Are those part of Maldana?"

"Yup!" Vanessa exclaims, flailing her arms to twist the float toward me.

"Do people live there?"

"No, they aren't livable. Something about the environment."

The island view takes my breath away, but it's not the one I crave. The real view is sitting on the second floor of the yacht in front of me.

CHAPTER TWENTY-SEVEN
NINA

After docking in Antina, Jace and Roman leave for the house while we three girls search for french fries at a nearby restaurant.

"Wait—where's our luggage?" I ask, mid-chew of a fry.

Vanessa chuckles. "It will be waiting at the house for us." She plops on a sunhat and guides us into the village where the paths are like a fairytale. Although the walls and buildings are dirty white, the roofs and shutters are either sky blue or shades of pink. Cats trot along the ledges, hopping from one side to the other. I thought the stone roads in Kosita were hell, but Antina is worse. My eyes glue to the ground with each step. Mason even catches Maia's stumble once or twice. Shops flank either side of the narrow walkways. Trellises provide shade in some sections, the greenery and pink flowers making a pleasant umbrella.

"Neen! I found a black cat!" Maia squeals.

Vanessa blanches. "You don't think they are bad luck?"

My sister gives the cat little scratches. "Look at this face! How can anyone look at this precious creature and think he's bad luck?"

Just then, the feline stretches its long body and rolls to expose its belly. Maia damn near cries. She presses a hand to her heart.

"Nina. I want him. This is my baby now."

I touch her shoulder. "This is his home. You don't want to take him away from it."

As expected, she pouts. I gather my sister in my arms and steer her away from the cat. We get little relief from the heat, and I drink in every breeze as it whooshes the skirt of my long dress around me. After following the path down-hill, the roads get wide enough for cars and we almost get mowed down by a motorbike.

"Ay, prosíttento," Wesley snaps, gripping my arm to push me out of the way as it zips by.

Be careful.

The same thing happened my first night in Maldana. In a subtle moment, I realize he's been in my life the entire time I've been in this country. As if he's weaved into my attitude and assumptions toward Maldanians.

I love this country.

Would that mean—

No.

While I might be turned on every time he speaks Maldanian, those thoughts will lead me nowhere. I scold myself for forgetting so quickly.

"They drive so damn fast here," Maia says, tugging me deeper into the sidewalk.

Each time I meet the eyes of a stranger, I wonder what they'd do if they discovered I'm the princess and possible future queen. Would they attempt to hurt me like that man did? It guts me to realize that I'd be hated for existing.

We don't want you here.

Maia's gasp rips me from my spiraling thoughts. "Ice cream!"

"*Yes,*" I insist. "I'm dying out here."

My bodyguard curves around me to open the door for us. It's nothing new, but he pointedly doesn't look at me. I roll my eyes while passing him.

What I thought was an ice cream shop turns out to be a bakery that sells gelato. Maia squeals at the macaroons and their reasonable prices. I can feel us planning to buy a bunch of desserts just because we can.

The woman baking behind the counter stops mid-whisk to greet us.

"Ne tora di pomke?" I ask. She replies in Maldanian, telling me the next one will be done soon if I want to wait. I nod. "Sì, parafóré."

We order gelato in the meantime. Before I pay, I glance behind me to check if any of the three bodyguards want something, and Mason actually takes me up on it. We settle amongst two tables with Vanessa and Maia in the chairs against the wall. Wesley disappears to the bathroom, and I take the chair in front of my cousin.

I slowly eat the gelato, savoring its cool taste in my sore throat. Did I apply enough foundation? I should have double-checked before stepping off the boat.

I flinch when Vanessa leans forward to lazily wrap her arms around me. She plants her chin on my shoulder. "Your bodyguard is flirting," she says.

"What?" At first, I don't think it's me she's talking to. Wesley doesn't flirt. He's far too serious.

And sure enough, he's standing at the glass display counter with an elbow propped up. The perky blonde on the other side—the same one who greeted us—is so invested in the conversation that she wouldn't notice if an earthquake struck. They speak in Maldanian, but they're too far for me to translate. I lean my head against Vanessa's and ask, "Can you tell what they're saying?"

My cousin hums, straining an ear. The baker lifts her arms on the case, closer to Wesley's, as she swings her ponytail over her shoulder. Shouldn't that bitch be wearing a hairnet?

"She's talking about the beach and how she loves to go there. He's saying that he likes it there, too."

"How riveting," Maia mumbles.

It's a conversation. I shouldn't be jealous, but betrayal coils around me in a searing grip. He told me just a few hours ago that he dislikes being around people. What makes it so easy to talk to her and not me? Does that mean what happened in the bathroom last night was truly out of pity?

Maia looks at her bodyguard. "You should start flirting, too, Mason." She gestures to his face. "Ladies love that silver fox look."

"I'm married," Mason replies, and I raise my brows, but Maia squawks in response.

"*What—since when?* You don't wear a ring!"

He clears his throat. "She died."

"*Awwww.*" She leans across the table and grabs his hand. "We'll talk about getting you back on the horse later."

"No, we won't."

"We'll see."

"We won't."

"*Sure,*" Maia sings.

While Vanessa turns her focus elsewhere and my sister finds a way to debate with everyone possible, I untangle from my cousin's arms and head to Wesley with squared shoulders. I slip into the space between his chest and the display counter.

I peek into the paper bag on the surface. "Is this ours?"

"O-oh—yes," the baker stutters.

"Gracea mucho!" I say, turning to Wesley and holding up the bag. "Carry this for me?"

He looks at me, confused, but accepts it, nonetheless.

So much for getting over him.

After walking through a few narrow and bumpy streets, we arrive at our destination—a white house tucked between other pristine courtyards. The walls are just high enough that I can't see over them.

The path to the other side of the house reveals an infinity pool, a few lounge chairs, and a broad, unobstructed view of the sea. It's eight o'clock at night and the sun is just beginning to set on the horizon.

"I can die happy," Maia says.

I nod, marveling at the vibrant shades of orange. "This is where I live now."

Remembering that I'm here because my birth mother was a queen makes it even more surreal. Vanessa takes us on a quick tour of the three-hundred-year-old house, pointing out its modern upgrades made for longevity. I head straight to the shower when I'm brought to my room. Though I typically lock the door when I shower, I leave it open for the possibility that I fall asleep under the water.

CHAPTER TWENTY-EIGHT

WESLEY

The best part of this job is Nina.

But I forgot how peaceful Maldana's views are. The scenery along the boat ride and in Antina reminded me why I didn't return to America with Mom and Cora. It's a paradise for many reasons and can be summed up to the comfort my home gives me.

Remembering this feeling has a hint of familiarity—and I realize it's shared with the woman currently giving me the cold shoulder. Does she regret what happened in the bathroom last night? Maybe it was too vulnerable.

By the time I finish sweeping the perimeter of the property, Maia is waiting at the front door with a concerned look on her face. She's a softer version of Nina, with rounder cheeks and eyes.

"What's wrong?" I ask.

She folds her arms and leans against the threshold. "I'm worried about Nina."

"Did something happen?"

Last I checked, she's in the shower. But Maia shakes her

head. "No, just with... the whole attack. I tried, but—she won't talk about it. Not even to me."

If this were any other client, I'd stay out of it. I protect Nina; her emotional healing should not be my concern or responsibility. But that's not the case with her—and I'm loath that Maia notices. I can't imagine the secrets these two sisters share.

"Are you trying to ask me something?" I scrounge up my kindest tone, and I still come across as bothered and irritated.

Maia smothers a frustrated scoff and turns around. "Never mind."

I bite my tongue. I thought I was getting better at a sympathetic demeanor. It doesn't seem so. "Tell me what you need," I call after her, not in the inviting way she might want, but we're both worried about Nina—even if I won't say it out loud.

"To just—look out for her."

"That's my job."

She groans. Not in the adorable way Nina does—as if she's determined to make us see eye to eye. Maia groans as if my incompetence is a burden. Which I can respect.

"Then be a human," she says. "Ask her if she's okay. Tell me if she's getting more depressed."

"What—like a friend or colleague?"

She rolls her eyes and throws her hands in the air. "Whatever you want to call it." She pushes off the door-frame and mutters, "I have no idea why she likes you much."

My stomach flips, and I resist asking her to confirm that before she walks off.

Nina sleeps for the rest of the evening, and I check in with Jack about the security footage around the property. The house is in a cramped neighborhood, but all windows are one-way.

Vanessa's and Jace's bodyguards will reside two houses down for the duration of the trip. Mason and I would have been there as well if not for the sisters wanting us closer. Nina and Maia have been thoughtful since day one; asking if we're hungry or thirsty, noting that it's been eight hours since either of us used the restroom. In spite of Nina being largely silent and Maia being endlessly witty, they're quick to build relationships with others, making whoever they meet feel important.

It didn't take long for the Laffley sisters to charm Mason and me; it just so happens that I'm falling completely in love with one of them. It's difficult to comprehend that Nina might have feelings for me, too. She's friendly toward everyone, but the growing possibility sends apprehension through my body because I know I won't resist her. I don't resent myself enough to deny her on the basis that she deserves better. She does—and I'll be that person because she makes me believe I can be.

Jack would be furious, but even the thought of being with Nina in every way I imagined is worth it.

CHAPTER TWENTY-NINE

NINA

Yesterday morning, I woke up wanting Wesley near me.

Today, I avoid him.

I'm surprised at how frustrated and almost agitated I am with him. I have no right to be upset that he flirted with a baker yesterday, but the lingering sense of betrayal still scratches me raw. Perhaps it was the stinging realization that he's just my bodyguard, not my friend and definitely not my boyfriend. He keeps me safe and fends off overstepping men. Why would he socialize with me or my family? It makes more sense that he would chat up a cute baker.

Maia and I want to spend the day at the house, and Vanessa happily agrees. It's relaxing whenever Roman isn't trying to blast music or doing cannonballs into the pool. Around noon, someone walks through the back gate with a package for Vanessa. She passes it right to me.

"What's this?"

She blushes and gestures to her midriff. "I, um, it gets hot in that swimsuit, no?"

I glance down at my black one-piece. "Yeah, but it's the only one I brought."

"I asked Greta to pick out a few. She used your measurements, so they should fit. They are for you to keep."

Maia pouts in awe. "That's so stinkin' cute and thoughtful."

I lean across the lounge chair to hug Vanessa, holding back tears at the idea of being considered and cared for. Anyone going out of their way for me never fails to make me emotional.

"Gracea mucho," I whisper. "This means a lot."

I slip upstairs to change. In the elegantly wrapped box are three triangle bikinis, one pink with flowers, one solid blue, and one crocheted red. I select the pink one and tie on the top piece, instantly feeling more confident from the way it accentuates my boobs. But when I slide on the bottoms, I have to resist putting my one-piece back on. It's low on my hips, making my bone structure look wider. If only they were high-waisted. Tall girls are supposed to be dainty; I could knock someone out with my hips.

I blink back tears again. Stop. This was a gift, and I'll look like an asshole if I don't wear it. But as soon as I return to the backyard, Maia whistles.

"*Goddamn, Neen!*" she screeches. "Titties and ass, hello!"

I clamp my arms over my chest. "Ugh, please stop."

Vanessa laughs. "It looks good!"

"Ugh, I'm so jealous of your ass," Maia says.

I scoff as I lower onto my lounge chair. "No, you're not."

"*I* am," Vanessa pipes. "I have *no* curves."

"And I'm scrawny," my sister adds. "No one takes scrawny women seriously."

As much as I hate to hear them talk so poorly about

themselves, I'm comforted in knowing I'm not the only one with insecurities. When I recline and check my phone, I open a text from Dad.

DAD
How are you feeling?

Fine. Just tired.

His reply is instant.

What are you girls doing today?

Relaxing by the pool. Yesterday wiped us out.

That sounds nice.

I lock my phone, unable to take any more of this dry conversation. The chef brings us fresh hummus, pita, and spanakopita, and I thank him profusely. I can live off these three foods for the rest of my life with no issue. With my sheer cover-up tied around my hips, I head into the kitchen for more water.

My stomach clenches at the sight of Wesley at the kitchen island, hunched over a laptop. I focus on getting a bottle of water from the refrigerator, reminding me that I would want to help make the faucet water cleaner if I become princess.

"That's a new bathing suit," Wesley says.

Butterflies tickle my stomach; I force them down and dryly respond, "Vanessa got it for me."

Awkward silence passes between us for the first time. When I start to leave the kitchen, he asks, "What's with the attitude?"

I stop in the doorway, rolling my eyes before facing him. "I don't have an attitude."

"You're pissed about something."

"Nope."

"Just—cut the bullshit and tell me."

"I'm not pissed!" I snap. He really knows how to charm a lady.

"Then what are you?"

I slump my shoulders and toss my head back. *Pick one.*

Sexually frustrated.

Angry.

Afraid.

Confused.

Completely falling for you.

"Nothing," I say. "I'm—nothing, Wes."

Part of me feels stupid for considering anything more with him. Maia would roll her eyes. Dad would probably ignore me. Raven would more than likely be intimidated by Wesley.

It's unprofessional. The Higher Court expects grace from me, similar to my mother.

And I'm lusting after my bodyguard.

That night, I toss and turn. The mattress puffs around me like a cloud, but not even the world's most comfortable bed puts me to sleep. I was exhausted enough yesterday that I didn't have a chance to overthink myself awake.

I cycle through the stressors of Dad, the crown, the attack, and Wesley. The ache in my throat has almost healed and the redness in my eyes has faded. The crowds in town stressed me out yesterday; having Wesley around helped, even if I'm a little agitated with him for no good reason.

Every time I start to fall asleep, I startle at the vulnerability of letting my guard down. I keep seeing the hatred in his eyes and hearing the venom in his words.

"*We don't want you here. Death to the monarch. Vi ponte lo revínasti.*"

The words hit me like bullets.

Vi ponte lo revínasti.

I sit up in bed, my heart racing. The moonlight streams through the white curtains shielding the French doors. Why am I just remembering this? How?

Vi is live. *Ponte* is long. *Revínasti* is revolution.

Long live the revolution.

"*We don't want you here. Death to the* monarch. Long live the revolution."

I snatch my phone from the nightstand and search the terms in Google, adding Maldana monarchy to the end. Then I come across the group name *Lo Revínasti*, The Revolution. How original. Some of their methods are near anarchy, but their intent is clear.

There's a housing crisis in Maldana and inflation is harming the economy and citizens. Tourism is booming and helps the country, but not actual Maldanians. The group notes that Maldana's royalty is a decrepit system that doesn't contribute to society. I fail to see the correlation between the monarch and the crises until I look at the balcony in my room, the statue on my nightstand, and consider the boat we took to come here. The monarch may not have started these issues, but it could be doing more. The group doesn't believe the monarch needs to exist at all.

Would it be selfish if I became a princess despite this?

Some news articles compare Lo Revínasti to the French

Revolution, which didn't end well for Marie Antionette and many other royals. Dread plunges straight into my stomach. I drop my phone, hands shaking, and jump out of bed. After what I read, there's no way I can get any sleep. I slide on blue jeans and a long-sleeved dress shirt.

The past two days have been lovely. Vanessa put a lot of effort into making me feel better and more comfortable, but I still notice the eggshells scattered around me. No one knows who I am in Antina. They don't know what happened and won't treat me differently. It's not quite my goal to meet other people tonight; I want to *witness* what they're like in the dead of night, when the darkness shelters possibilities both good and bad.

My phone is at thirty percent, but I don't plan to be out for long or scrolling through apps. I take note of wherever I pass, even placing a large rock in the middle of the path as a marker. I revel in the tranquility of the night and occasional purring of a cat.

The houses have a lot of charm but also cracks and sagging roofs. As the princess, I can redirect funds into rectifying this. How hard would that be? Does the Higher Court plan on turning me into a puppet for show-and-tell? Other than the conversations about the monarch's functions during the hors d'oeuvres at the introductory dinner, the night was about their plans *for* me, not *with* me.

I check the map on my phone to head toward the downtown area, only to notice my battery at ten percent.

"What the fuck?" I harshly whisper. Stupid foreign data eating at my phone battery. If I remembered that pesky fact, I wouldn't have ventured so far from the house. When I plug in the address on the GPS, the screen goes black, and the torturous loading wheel spins before shutting down completely.

Oh, shit.

Fear begins to stack inside me, but I knock it down and scan the area. Don't panic. No one here knows I'm a princess. I retrace my steps, halting at the sight of a demolished house. I definitely did *not* pass that before.

Phone, dead.

Sense of direction, gone.

I look up at the stars and moon, suddenly resenting myself for quitting girl scouts. My next option is to find help. It's a good thing Wesley made me memorize his number—all I need is a phone. The neighborhood is asleep for the most part, but I follow the sounds of laughter and light music, going down a path I know is farther from the house.

Slight relief ignites in my chest at the lively street. A bar is still open, and there's a café half-open. The small family who appears to own the place is sitting in their outdoor dining area. I'm surprised to see two elderly people awake at this hour, but the man softly plays the accordion and the woman funnels treats to the bulldog at her feet. A middle-aged man is hunched over a notebook and a stack of receipts.

"Ciao," I say, pulling out my best smile and tucking a curl behind my ear. "Siporí caporer a tu parné?"

The woman grins and gestures to the dog. "Sì, tofalimente, tofalimente!"

"Gracea mucho." I lower to pet the eager bulldog. "Ciao, panímorísi."

I glance up to find the man's eyes on me. *Please don't be creepy. Please don't be creepy.* He nods politely and asks, "Cómi stara?"

"Stari sto bueni. Ke tu?"

"Bueni. You are American?"

I chuckle. "Is it obvious?"

"We do not get many tourists in this part of town."

"I came to the right place, then. My name is Nina."

He holds a hand to his chest. "I am Sebastian, this is my niassa Eleni, and our neighbor Philip. He does not speak any English."

I reply in Maldanian. "It's lovely to meet you."

"Please, sit," Eleni, Sebastian's grandmother, says, pointing to one of the chairs, which I graciously accept. The bulldog curls up by my ankles and I reach down to scratch behind his ear.

"Is it your first time Maldana?" Sebastian asks in English, his accent heavy. I quickly rake my eyes over his lanky frame and his thin, long face.

"Uh, yes, it is," I stammer, and the four of us carry small talk for a bit. I keep my replies in as much Maldanian as I know for Philip. He smiles every time I speak. We chat about tourists and the way some of them behave. Sebastian talks about Antina's corrupt governor being why the streets are not being fixed.

"The government no help us." Eleni waves him off. "We help each other."

"Do you like living in Maldana?" I ask her.

She repeats my question with a laugh. She ponders for a moment. "It's all I know. Do I have a choice?" She notes my confused look and continues, using many hand gestures as she speaks. "I live here all my life. I work, I sleep, I raise family—uh, in Antina only." She pauses to find the English words. "I ask my husband—before he die—if he want to move to new city or country. He say we cannot afford it. I think he want to stay."

"He didn't want to leave?"

"No," she says fiercely. "He love Antina, but it get, uh. It get... Sebastian—" She then speaks quick Maldanian to her grandson, asking for the right word.

"Crowded," he offers.

"Yes, crowded."

"Antina is getting crowded?" I clarify.

She nods, but Sebastian answers. "All of Maldana is. We have a small population, but we are growing and don't have enough places to live. The prices go up and people who live here for many years, like my grandmother, cannot afford her own home anymore."

"That must be difficult. I'm sorry."

Eleni laughs again. "They can't take me from my home. I will have to die."

"*Niassa,*" he drawls, and I hold back a smile at her ardor.

"I have another question," I say. "The royal family, do you like them?"

She considers my words, then shrugs as she flicks her wrist as if to show her lack of care. "I don't care for them, they don't care for me."

Sebastian looks at me, capping his pen. "Why do you ask?"

The likelihood of him guessing my reasoning is almost nonexistent. I look nothing like my fully European family members. "I'm curious."

"They don't do much. Nothing to like or dislike."

"What about other Maldanians?"

"The same, I suppose. My little cousins used to love them. They are more liked by the children. Adults are too busy working to care."

Eleni nods in agreement.

"Now it is our turn to ask a question," Sebastian says, pressing an elbow onto the table. "You say you love it here; what is your favorite part?"

If not for his grandmother and neighbor as witnesses, I might be apprehensive about him, but he hasn't asked personal questions or called me any nicknames like baby or beautiful.

At first, I almost say the food is the best part, as it always tastes fresh and flavorful. Next, I want to say the views. The medieval architecture and ocean sights are otherworldly. But I could also say the people; everyone in Maldana is welcoming, and it's strong enough to over-power what my attacker said to me. The weight of comfort I find here hits me all at once.

I never want to leave.

"Everything," I admit. "Picking one thing is impossible."

Eleni rears back with a hearty laugh, clapping her hands together. The bulldog hops up at the commotion. "Lo tósché Maldasso."

I echo the words in question. Sebastian bows his head, hands pressed together as if in prayer. "It means The Maldanian Touch, and that we have done right by you."

I grin. "I haven't heard of that, but I believe it."

"Are you here with family?" Eleni asks in Maldanian, surveying the area as if someone might be searching for me. "It's not safe to be alone."

"I'm—I'm actually lost. My phone is dead." My face heats and I glance down, slightly embarrassed to admit it.

"You need to call someone?" Sebastian asks.

"Unless you have an iPhone charger?"

"Oh, no." He holds up his phone. "We have the Android. But if you need to call someone..."

I release a breath. "Thank you so much."

As I dial the number, it dawns on me that Wesley is *not* going to be happy.

CHAPTER THIRTY

WESLEY

Did I say those things today to get Nina riled up in that bikini? Partially.

All I could picture was pulling her onto my lap and feeling every dip and curve of her body with my mouth. The sight taunted me the entire day. I don't know how much more of this I can take. Our interactions break me apart inch by inch, and I'm not far from turning into a man who begs.

After a long shower, I sit on my bed and stare at my personal phone. I've been pushing myself to call Cora or Mom for the last ten minutes. Everything I say to them is wrong and comes out judgmental or awkward. I shouldn't have to struggle to be with my family.

I selfishly accept the affection they offer, but improvement means meeting their efforts. I can say that work takes up all my time. It does, but quick texts after my shift or the occasional call would go a long way. I know that. Doing it is another obstacle.

What if they don't want to talk to me? What if, with every conversation, they realize that they deserve better?

I hit *call*. My knee bounces the whole time it rings.

"Hello stranger," Cora sings, but I can hear the under-lying agitation.

"Hi."

"Isn't it late for you?"

I swallow my nerves. "A bit, yes."

"Are you okay?"

"Yes, I'm all right." I clear my throat. "I wanted to, uh—check in. How's the baby?"

"Your five-year-old nephew is fine."

Karító. Five? Last I heard, he was less than a year.

"And John?"

"Also fine."

"Mom?"

"Also fine."

I squeeze my eyes shut. "Cora..."

"What do you want me to say, Wes? We hadn't heard from you in *years* and a couple months ago you bounce back into our lives, but no, not completely, because you're still so secretive about whatever the hell—"

"If I could tell you, I would."

She groans. "What *can* you tell me?"

"That I'm sorry," I admit. "That I'm... I'm trying. I really am."

She sighs. "Look, I just don't want to get my hopes—"

My work phone buzzes with an incoming call from an unsaved number. This phone is protected from scammers and all unprogrammed numbers go through a scanning system before connecting. Which means this has to be related to work—to Nina.

"I-I'm getting an incoming call," I stutter to Cora. "It's work. I have to go."

"Are you kidding me?"

"I'm sorry," I say genuinely before hanging up on my sister to answer the other call. "Hello?"

The caller hesitates. Cold and wild panic washes over me when a timid, familiar voice says, "Wesley? It's Nina."

She's supposed to be sleeping down the hall.

"Where are you?"

"Did I wake you up?" she asks, and I shut my eyes to stop the frustration creeping in. She speaks as if it's a normal conversation.

I grip the phone tighter. "Nina... *where are you?*"

"Don't be mad, but um... I don't know."

CHAPTER THIRTY-ONE

NINA

"Nina."

I lift my head to see Wesley approaching.

Sebastian twirls me out of the dip, and Philip slowly stops playing music. When I mentioned I love the street music in Antina, Philip began playing his accordion and Sebastian offered his hand in dance. I was reluctant, until I remembered that he doesn't know who I am. He doesn't know the weight or trauma I carry, and he wasn't offering to dance because I'm the princess, but because I'm Nina.

"That was fast!" I exclaim, then look at Sebastian. "That's my friend."

I exchange grateful farewells with the three of them before following Wesley into the night. As we turn from them, I notice the disdain in Wesley's expression toward Sebastian. I quickly usher my bodyguard around.

"Don't kill him," I chide. "He was nice."

"I have a habit of breaking the wrists of men who put their hands on you," he says, his voice gruff.

I roll my eyes. He's referring to the men at the club and the one who tried to pickpocket me. It's no lie that the men who mistreated me walked out of the situation in a much worse state than I did.

Damn. I really needed a bodyguard after all.

"Well, he was respectful," I reply. "I promise."

He keeps quiet as we walk, but I can feel the tension. Ten minutes pass, and I start recognizing landmarks and come across the rock I set in the middle of the path. I kick it back to its place.

"Why didn't you wake me up if you wanted to go out?" Wesley asks.

To tell the truth, I hadn't even considered him. I jumped out of bed, got dressed, and left. With a shrug, I say, "Didn't think about it."

"Wake me up," he insists. "I don't care what time it is or what I'm doing. If you want to go somewhere, tell me so I can do my job."

I roll my eyes again in spite of the sinking stone in my gut. Why am I foolish enough to get disappointed with every reminder that this is his job? I shake my head free of the thoughts. "I just—I wanted to be away from all this royal stuff for a minute. I wanted to feel normal again."

This summer came at me fast. One day I was panicking about paying off my student loan. The next, I inherit a country. I wanted a break from the adjustments.

"Even then, you need to tell me."

By now, I recognize our street and don't need his help anymore. I shake my head. "You still don't understand."

"I understand perfectly, but I only care about keeping you safe. Leaving in the middle of the night without saying anything stops me from doing that. If anything happened—"

I whirl toward him. "It'd be my fault?"

He stops, leveling a glare at me. "You know that's not what I was going to say."

"Give me just a little credit," I groan. "Nothing happened. I'm *fine*. I'm not some fragile little—"

"*You got lost, Nina!*" Wesley shouts, and I flinch. "You've never been here before and you snuck out without even thinking about what—"

I shove his chest, anger simmering inside me as I lift my chin. "Don't fucking patronize me. I don't need to tell you shit. *I went because I wanted to.* I wanted a break from my fucking tornado of a life and I could forget how everyone feels sorry for me now. *Including you.*"

He closes his mouth, his brows creased and shoulders falling.

"See?" I press. "You can't even deny it."

My heart breaks as the silence continues. More than anything, I want him to say that he's not just my bodyguard. I want him to touch my waist the same way he did the night we danced together, to kiss me with such vigor I can't think straight.

I want him to want me this bad, too.

But he stands in front of me, mouth agape in a most uncharacteristic fashion as he struggles to find words. Yes, he's a quiet person, but not because he has nothing to say. His silence has always been by choice. Not tonight.

Finally, I break the moment and head up the hill toward the house. Exhaustion starts slipping into my bones, weighing my limbs down.

"I've thought of a hundred ways to kill Anton Robert— the man who attacked you," Wesley admits, and I halt just outside the reach of a streetlight. His voice cuts through the darkness, wrapping around my stomach as he walks closer with a solemn face. Out of the dozens of things he could've said, I hadn't thought *that* would make the cut. "I... I already can't forgive myself for letting him lay a finger on you." He looks down, tilting his head as if struggling to allow himself to say it. He sucks his teeth. "There are a lot of emotions I feel because of you, angel. Pity is not one of them."

Well, when you put it like that.

Wesley has never raised his voice at me before today. As grumpy as he can be, he's not an angry man. He's frustrated. I clear my throat. "I don't blame you for—"

"Doesn't matter," he says softly.

No one is around to see us. If we stand here in this quaint street with barely illuminated lampposts for hours, anything could happen. But the mere thought of being rejected by him is terrifying enough to silence me. I can't offer more of myself tonight if he doesn't, and he shows no sign of budging. The night's emotions rush through me, and unless I let it out in anger, I'll end up in tears within seconds. I inhale a breath, forcing back the sting in my eyes.

"Don't worry," I say while backing up to leave. "I'll still write you a letter of recommendation for the next job. Maybe ask your girlfriend at the bakery if they're hiring."

ROAMING HOLLOWS

CHAPTER THIRTY-TWO
WESLEY

I hunch over my coffee, bleary-eyed and yawning.

I was too stunned to sleep. It took me a few seconds to even understand what Nina meant last night.

I stare through the window across the room that overlooks the blinding ocean. The sky doesn't have a single cloud in sight, letting the sun beat relentlessly on the waters. Eight hours of thinking and I still don't know what to say to Nina. Guilt pierced me when Nina walked away from me on the yacht. She was disappointed, and I hate being the reason why. Crossed boundaries aside, I would've embarrassed her. My later conversation with Maia proved it, and my conversation with the woman in the bakery had been practice. Clearly, I need more.

Like the museum last month, I had tried to practice small talk and not make an ass of myself—specifically with people I don't care about. It so happens that the most talkative people are women. Maybe they were flirting; I wasn't. Nina hadn't liked it then, and I mistakenly believed that, after everything, she knew me better. Her attention is all I crave. No one else's.

For the last eight hours, I pictured everything I could have done differently last night. Some ended with her naked, but those scenarios were just for me.

Nina passes through the dining room. I sit up a little straighter when she slows at the sight of me.

I stir my coffee to distract my nerves. "Hey."

She acts indifferent. "Hi."

Before she can pass, I catch her wrist. "Are you angry with me?"

She doesn't reject my hold on her wrist, but her arm is limp. "Should I be?"

"No."

"Then there's your answer." She snatches her arm away and continues toward the kitchen.

"I wasn't flirting with her," I say. "I—we were talking."

Clarifying this means admitting she would care if I had indeed been flirting. I'm not sure either of us is ready to admit that—or she's as nervous as I am.

Nina stops in the doorway, head bowed. Her face tightens as if in pain. She shakes her head. "I went out because I remembered what he said to me," she mutters. "Vi ponte lo revínastí."

My mind blanks, ridding all thoughts of what I could and should have said last night. She doesn't wait for my reaction. I pull out my phone to text Jack the phrase immediately. *Death to the monarch* isn't a signature phrase, but *vi ponte lo revínastí* is.

Mason and I spend the rest of the morning researching the group and its known members. We agree to fly in Gregory and Silas as added security. Both of our clients would vehemently reject this, so they'll remain as distant safety measures. We change the designated safe houses and rendezvous points. If members of Lo Revínastí managed employment by the Higher Court, the circle of trusted individuals has to shrink.

Over the following days, Nina, Maia, and Vanessa visit museums after hours and dine on rooftops. Nina and I hardly speak, but I'm too focused on the information funneling through Jack about the militia that's Lo Revínastí. My boss has been talking with the head of the royal guard to reinstate the task force dedicated to hunting the militia. They've been dormant for years, but their knowing about the Laffley sisters is dangerous.

One morning, while Mason and I review the files of those enlisted for the task force, footsteps trample down the stairs. Curly hair flashes past the open door of the sitting room, the length telling me it's Maia.

"I call the pink one!" she yells.

Jace and Roman follow her out the front door. I stop in the threshold, Mason behind me, as Nina bounces down the steps with Vanessa in tow.

"Where are you going?"

She stops mid-run. Her bright smile lands on me with enough spirit to weaken my will. "We're gonna ride mopeds down to the farmer's market," she says, partially out of breath.

"Which one?"

"The one on Lordi Street," Vanessa answers.

Nina notices the hesitation on my face, but her eyes glisten with hope.

I wanted a break from my fucking tornado of a life.

When we return to Kosita, her security will be tripled. Fuck. I never stood a chance. With a sigh, I say, "I'll meet you down there."

I shut my eyes as she squeals with joy, bolting out the

door with her cousin, who mutters, "Does he have to be so serious all the time?"

Mason and I stand on the porch as Vanessa and Maia climb onto a pink moped. Roman gets on his alone and I'm grateful to see Nina head to Jace's. From the corner of my eye, I spot a black helmet.

"Wait—"

Nina turns to me, then slumps her shoulders. "Oh, come on. Seriously?"

I don't say anything as I slide it over her head. She sends me a withering glare through the open sun visor as I clasp the helmet.

"You've *got* to be joking," she deadpans.

I lower my head and lift her chin to focus on tightening the strap. "As serious as a heart attack," I mutter. Once I finish, I smirk at her and flick the visor shut to hide her glare. "Have fun."

I move to stand beside Mason, who doesn't speak until all three mopeds zip out of the courtyard and down the road. "You're sure this is a good idea?"

"Gregory and Silas shouldn't be far. They can track her phone and keep an eye out." I pull out my phone to call Gregory since Silas doesn't listen to my directions.

CHAPTER THIRTY-THREE
NINA

The five of us wander through the farmer's market, the branches of the trees to my right twisting above me to provide much-desired shade.

My fingers brush the overhang of leaves. The sea lies on the other side of the buildings and all the way from here, I can hear the waves lapping against the rocks.

I glance behind me to see Wesley fifty feet away. He nods once. I chuckle at his seriousness. We've barely spoken since the night I sneaked out. My face heats in embarrassment when I remember my pettiness toward him. I'm not entirely sure how to act around him anymore since I all but admitted how jealous I was. I hate that I get so territorial when it comes to him.

Over the past week, I became increasingly frustrated with myself for craving him in the first place and irritated when he doesn't make a move. I keep replaying what he told me, and butterflies tickle my stomach at the nickname "angel." That has to mean *something*. He first said it at the introductory dinner, and memories of that night flash in my mind—of his fury toward my attacker, of his softness toward me. He was off-kilter and as vulnerable as I was.

I approach a fruit stand, my touch drifting over the lemons in the wicker basket. Anxiety flutters in my stomach when the old woman who owns the stand smiles at me. I wipe my sweaty hands on my shorts. This is it—another chance to feel like a local. That is, if she doesn't spot me as a tourist from the get like Sebastian did.

"Ciao, buenimara," I try and say as naturally as possible.

"Buenimara," she says, her gaze lingering on me before she adds, "Sto panímorísi."

Very beautiful. My eyes widen. "Oh! Gracea mucho."

She outstretches her palm, and I gladly place my hand in hers. Maia holds up a pineapple to hide her chuckle and I spot Wesley in the corner of my eye.

"Tu milla, tu pielli. Tu stara sto panímorísi. Sto, sto, sto," the woman says. I'm no stranger to old people marveling over my skin and hair when they're feeling bold. It's almost objectifying, but affirmations from the elderly always boost my confidence. I thank her profusely before slipping off with my sister to avoid more prodding.

With our arms linked, I lean my head on her shoulder and inhale her flowery scent. Maia is the one part of the summer that hasn't wavered.

She senses my increased affection and tightens her arm around mine. "Love you."

With a full heart, I say, "I know. Love you, too."

It's been weeks since we last discussed taking the crown. Wesley is the only person who knows about what my attacker said to me in Maldanian, although I'm sure he's told Jack about it by now.

Once we return to the house, I fall behind so everyone

goes inside first. Wesley and Mason enter the courtyard next, and my bodyguard notices my lingering.

"Everything okay?"

"Yeah." I knot my hands behind my back, not trusting myself to refrain from touching him.

"Listen," he says, lifting his deep-set eyes to mine, and I lock my knees before they buckle. "I... I shouldn't have yelled at you the other night. I'm sorry."

I blink in surprise. "Oh—I was... I'm here to apologize to *you*."

"For what?"

"Everything. I—I know you were just trying to protect me."

He offers a small smile as if amused. "Good."

Wesley was violent the night of my attack and doesn't regret putting my attacker in the hospital with brain damage. I don't blame or hate him for anything that happened; he had been my only safe place, but violence doesn't suit him, and he said he's thought of at least a hundred ways to kill a man.

"I-I don't want you to think of any more ways to kill him," I insist, and it's Wesley's turn to blink in surprise. "Don't let him take your peace away."

The corner of his lips quirks. His shoulders ease. "Only if you don't let him take yours."

"That's impossible." I attempt a small, bashful smile. I untie my hands to poke his shoulder. "Mine is a six-two man of steel who pretends he doesn't have a heart made of gold."

"I'm six-three."

I roll my eyes. "Point still stands. You might know how to fight, but violence isn't your nature. That's not the man I

—" I cut myself off, heart pounding. "That's not the man I know."

I head into my room to find Maia and Vanessa sitting on my bed.

"Is there a reason for..." I gesture to them. At least they're not under the comforter in their outside clothes.

"We were waiting for you while you flirted with Beck."

My eyes widen. "I wasn't flirting."

My sister and cousin exchange looks, and Maia puts her hands behind her back and starts batting her eyelashes. Then she pokes Vanessa's shoulder.

"I hate you," I groan, my face heating as I flop between the two of them. I fall back on the bed, and they follow suit. "Why are you guys in here?"

"Your room had the better view for spying," my sister says.

I hum in response. The three of us stay quiet, and I revel in being able to do that with them. Since the attack, comfortable silence has been nonexistent. I could always feel someone scrounging up the courage to ask me something—*anything*. But I'm tired of thinking about the incident, tired of dealing with it, and tired of being tired. What happens next?

"I'm scared to become princess," I admit.

Vanessa puffs out a laugh. "You already are one. Both of you."

"What do you mean?" Maia asks.

"Even if you don't work for the institution, you'll still be princesses. It's a birthright."

My sister lifts her head. "Do I still get royal treatment?"

Vanessa laughs. "No, the treatment comes with the job."

"What's it like?" I ask. "The job."

We're a week away from August. The Sunday of summer. And I'm still conflicted about accepting the crown despite the amount of normalcy it already feels. I'm already making plans, but I'm terrified.

"It's different for me and Jace. I've lived as much of a normal life as I could as a princess. I grew up outside of the city, raised mostly by my dad, had normal teen problems. Pimples. Girls."

"Yeah, but, in a mansion, right?" my sister presses.

"Maia," I chide.

"I'm kidding."

"No, in a cottage," Vanessa says dreamily. "I have chickens there."

Maia sits up at that, a scandalous hand to her chest. "You have pet chickens and you never told me? I'm hurt."

I shake my head, refusing to get sidetracked. I stare at the ceiling. "I don't want to become another privileged socialite who worries about doing enough public charity work to save my reputation."

"Well, that's specific."

Vanessa nods. "I understand."

The more time I spend in this country, the more I feel like Ophelia's daughter. "I think Mom would want us to be here."

"*You're* the one who said we shouldn't inherit a country because of our mommy issues." She lies back down, propping on her elbow. "We're the type who talk about dismantling a system, not joining it."

I cover my face with my hands and groan. "If only we could just do *both*."

Maia chuckles and says, "If only."

But I hesitate.

What if we *can* do both?

"Wait," I whisper, sitting up in anticipation. "Let's do that."

"Do what?" Maia asks.

"Both!" I spin around to face them, sitting back on my heels. "Let's join the institution to take it apart!"

Vanessa matches my sister's position, propping onto her elbow.

"They wouldn't let us do that," Maia says.

"Think about it. The Court is fighting for us because they want to change the fact that over half the country wants to get rid of the monarch system. But Maldanians love their tradition and history, so what if the crown ends with us and we spend our careers making sure the institution is getting a proper close?"

My sister tilts her head, her big mandala earrings swishing forward before disappearing into her curls. "Nina, that's crazy."

"A lot of people would lose their jobs," Vanessa argues.

"Someone tried to *kill* me," I say, shutting them up. "He was part of a group called Lo Revínastí and even though they're violent criminals, they fight for what most Maldanians want. Who knows if it'll become the next French Revolution? If I accept the crown, they'll be a constant threat. To save jobs, we can—we'll have openings by turning different properties into museums. Even a hotel! Do you *know* how much tourist revenue that would make?"

After a long, considering moment, Vanessa says, "I... I think that's a great idea."

"And the housing!" I exclaim. "We could either redirect

funds or sell items to help build more homes and pay contractors to make the current ones safer."

Maia snatches my arm as an idea pops into her head. "We could use sustainable materials, too!"

"I—sure!" I don't know what sustainable building materials are, but she's excited about it, so it must be great. With each passing moment, we come up with more ideas about what we could do.

We did it. We found a solution.

Since learning that my attacker was with a militia, the security team wants to move Maia and me into the royal palace until further notice once we return to Kosita.

"*What a* bummer," Maia had said.

We stayed another few days in Antina before taking a three-hour car ride back to the city. I step into my room, ready to pack, and find Dad sitting on the couch twiddling his thumbs.

"Hi," he says.

I swallow the lump in my throat. "Hi."

"How was the trip?"

"Nice. Very pretty." I drop my duffle on the foot bench before taking my suitcase out of the closet.

"It's time we talk," Dad says. "This is getting a little ridiculous."

"Then talk." I should've known this was coming.

He rises, stuffing his hands into the pockets of his linen pants. "Are you really angry with me for not telling you about your lineage?"

"Mad doesn't come close." I plop the suitcase on the bed and zip it open. I hadn't expected to be riled up so quickly. "You did more than not tell me. You did *more* than hide my mother's title. You hid her entirely."

"I was doing what she wanted."

"Really? She wanted to be completely erased from her daughters' childhoods?"

He scoffs. "I was a new widow with two infants! I didn't know what I was doing."

"That much was clear," I retort, opening the drawers and throwing fistfuls of clothes into the suitcase.

"*Excuse me?*" Dad narrows his eyes, watching me carefully because we both know that, before this trip, our arguments were limited to his drinking.

"I have *always* had inconceivable expectations put on me. *You* wanted me to be the best, but I didn't know how to be myself. All I knew was how to be the girl you raised me to be."

He blanches. "And what's wrong with that girl?"

"*She's tired, Dad!* I am so conditioned to have everything done for everyone no matter how it might impact me."

He wags a finger. "We *all* had parts to play in keeping our household running."

I'm grateful that Ruby inspired and helped Dad clean up his act. It hurts that Maia and I weren't enough motivation, but my stepmom relieved the pressure for me. Ruby's presence created a rift, and since I was no longer the matriarch of the household, it was like Dad and I had nothing in common anymore.

It was like my skill as his caretaker determined my worth as a daughter, and I was no longer useful.

"No," I insist. "*Your* part was running away and emotionally abandoning your daughters and leaving *me* to pick up—"

"*Who the hell do you think you're talking to?*" he snaps,

voice echoing through my room. "Crown or not I am *still* your father and I will be treated with respect! Not everything is about you!"

"*YES IT IS*," I scream, and he flinches from my outburst because he expected me to cower. "I finally realized that *I* am the most important person in my life and *you* taught me how to take care of everyone but myself, and"—with a sigh, the tears break free at last—"now you expect me to take care of a country."

Dad stares at me, shaking his head. "You're using words you don't fully understand. I did not emotionally abandon you girls."

"You treated us like burdens," I seethe, my face heating. "We *never* did anything as a family until you met Ruby and even then—you didn't even care what we did!"

"Like when? Give me an example."

I throw my hands in the air. Every time we argue or have a confrontation, he wants multiple thorough examples to prove my point. Even then, he has excuses to debunk all of it.

"Fine. When I was sixteen, the four of us went to a water park and you told me and Maia to leave you and Ruby alone until we left." I start counting the incidents on my fingers. "You *never* came to our volleyball games. You never—made us school lunches, went to parent-teacher nights, picked us up from practice. I raised myself *and* Maia. Because of what? You were doing what Mom wanted? You were grieving? I didn't lose one parent from that car accident. I lost two."

He's at a loss for words, mouth agape. I only now realize that my door is still open and everyone and their mother probably heard the argument, including Wesley.

Dad's voice is gentle, quiet. "I... I'm sorry you think that."

I'm sorry you think that?

A new wave of fury takes me. "Get out."

"What?"

I grab one of the many pillows on my bed and throw it at him. "GET OUT!" I grab another and throw it. And another. And another. My eyes and face burn with tears. *"GET OUT GET OUT GET OUT GET OUT!"*

CHAPTER THIRTY-FOUR
NINA

After Maia and I spend the evening eating ice cream and bonding over our agitation with Dad, we team up with Vanessa for a few days to gather data for our meeting with the Court.

My cousin insists that Helen from human resources will back my idea instantly and that her department is loyal to her. On the understanding that rich people don't like their money being shrunk, we prepare statistics to emphasize the danger and legitimacy of Lo Revínastí and the probability of what the future of the institution looks like.

I haven't spoken to Dad since our fight, and I don't plan to. Not to mention that he thinks my childhood trauma is based on a misunderstanding. I hoped that argument was our moment of truth. With all emotions on the table, we'd have a chance to heal. But I've never felt so distant from him.

And because I'm living in the palace until determining the next step, Wesley is largely off-duty. I'm glad he has this time to himself, but it's been days since I saw him and I'd be lying if I said I didn't miss him. He might not be the life of the party, but he's my favorite part of each day.

One afternoon, Vanessa strides into my much-too-big bedroom with news. "My mom said the Higher Court wants to have the meeting in Corsos to be safe."

"Where is that?" Maia asks.

"A city at the very bottom of the country. About an hour and a half by plane."

Dread prickles my stomach. "How long driving?"

"Oh, uh... six hours, maybe."

I look at my sister. "Are you up for a road trip?"

"Hell no."

"What?" I squawk.

Maia reclines across my bed, propping on a single elbow. "That three-hour ride back from Antina knocked me out, so *I* will be flying and *you* can have a six-hour drive alone with the bodyguard you're pretending you don't want to take to pound town."

While Maia tends to be unrefined, she has a good point. She also gave me the idea to request a classic convertible for the road trip, which was granted, and now I'm sitting in the passenger seat as an unbelievably sexy man drives us through the winding roads of the countryside. Bless my sister and her ingenious mind.

Everything that happened in Antina was petty drama. It's not too awkward between Wesley and me, but there's a lingering curiosity each time we look at each other. Maybe that's in my head.

I watch as he focuses on the road, windows down and wind ruffling his hair, his stubble outlining his strong jaw.

I could look at him forever.

The words flash across my mind before I can truly register it. Not long ago, I told myself our future is blank—and now it's not. I could look at him forever. Fear spikes my heart at this sudden realization, but it soon turns into warmth.

"What?" he says, amused.

Shit. I was staring a bit. And I feel myself smiling.

The level of trust I have with him surpasses anyone in my life. I over-explain each thought for fear of being misunderstood. With him, I'm calm. The itch to elaborate on each thought is *gone*. I can sit with him in complete peace, knowing that I'm seen and understood. Even if he won't kiss me.

"Nothing," I quip.

Maybe he feels something for me, too, and is too afraid to act on it. Does it matter? The Higher Court might not take me seriously if they found out. Wesley could lose his job.

Maia has the paperwork for the meeting tomorrow and I regret giving it to her. We're nearly two hours into the trip and I could use this time to review the material. But I take a deep breath and watch the mountains slowly pass by, lighting up when I spot goats or horses. I almost ask Wesley to put the top down until I remember the amount of time I spent styling my hair. Despite my efforts to relax, I keep circling back to the knowledge that we're driving toward a life-changing meeting.

I turn to Wesley. "Do you think the Court will hate my plan?"

"What plan?"

"I didn't tell you?" I ask, sitting up straighter. With a sigh, I dive into all the details from memory. Saying it aloud helps me become more confident, and I genuinely want his input.

But when I'm done explaining the proposal, he hesitates, shrugs, and says, "I don't know."

I smack his arm, surprising him more than hurting him.

"*Ay*—what was that for?"

"After all that, you tell me *I don't know*?" I wail. "Do better."

"It is a strong plan." He lets his Maldanian accent shine when he sharpens the *t*. I'd be annoyed with that answer if he didn't sound so damn cute.

"But is it good enough?"

"I—" Wesley struggles to find the words. "I'm not part of politics. I've never contributed to the country in that way."

A cryptic answer, as always. I poke his arm. "Do *you* want a queen?"

"What I want doesn't matter."

"It does to me," I say firmly. "Answer the question: what would you think if I became the queen?"

The car slows as we approach the toll booth line. He shakes his head. "I can't answer that."

"You can."

"I can't."

"You can."

"I can't."

"You can." When he doesn't reply, I turn to my next method by leaning closer. "Please?"

He sees right through my attempt, his shoulders falling. "Don't—"

I tilt my head and bat my eyes. "Pretty please?"

"Don't do this to me." He looks at me, his expression almost desperate, which oddly arouses me.

"*Pleeeeeease* answer the question, Wesley."

He doesn't break eye contact as he shifts the gear between us. "You are killing me, woman."

The car pulls up to the booth and I smirk. "Isn't that what I'm for?"

After he pays the toll, I don't press the subject any further. There's still so little I truly know about him. He was in the army and alludes to supposedly frightening past mistakes. The drive continues in silence, and I keep wondering what his life was like before we met. I'm no doctor, but I can tell the burn scar on his hand isn't old. Most of his visible scars are on his wrists and hands. The one on his inner arm can be hidden easily with a sleeve.

Okay, maybe I look at him too much.

I flinch back to reality when Wesley speaks. "Were you truly upset... when I was speaking to that woman in the bakery?"

My cheeks warm. Damn. I thought we moved past this. I swallow the nerves lodging in my throat. "I... I asked you to join us—when we were on the boat and you said no. But you found some blonde baker more interesting." I squeeze my eyes shut, shaking my head at how pathetic I sound. "It's stupid, all right? Just ignore it. I did. It was right after the attack and I was... I don't know."

He doesn't answer at first, and I want to disappear more with each second he lets pass.

"I didn't want to embarrass you," he admits, and I stare at him, shocked. "I have made an ass of myself many times this summer because I don't remember the uh—how to socialize. And I can practice with strangers. Like *blonde bakers* I could not care less about."

Well, that makes me feel shitty. I can't imagine what he's gone through where he forgot how to *talk* to people.

"Why didn't you just tell me that?"

Wesley opens his mouth to speak, but no words come out. He focuses on the highway through a small mountain. I've known him long enough to decipher his body language. Right now, I can tell he's wrestling with himself. If he has trouble talking to others, it's probably a much harder obstacle to open up.

"You helped me through the worst night of my life," I remind him.

The furrow in his brow dissipates. "That was my job," he deadpans, and I notice the automatic nature of his reply. He's convincing himself, not me.

"It wasn't your job to hold me as I cried or wash my hair. It wasn't your job to play UNO with me at three o'clock in the morning. It's okay for—"

POP!

The car trembles from what feels like an explosion. I grapple for the door handle as my stomach lurches. "What is that? What happened?"

Wesley curses in Maldanian as he switches gears. "The tire probably blew out."

But the car keeps making weird noises while he hits the gas, aiming for the emergency shoulder up ahead. This is the one thing I hate about Europe: there aren't enough shoulders on the roads. If this happened three miles back, we would be screwed.

The car makes it just into safety before smoke starts to escape from under the hood of the car.

"I don't think the tire blew out," I say.

CHAPTER THIRTY-FIVE
NINA

Wesley has been on the phone for the last ten minutes.

I climb out of the car, unable to take the still heat any longer. The steep hill right over the edge of the railing has patches of green in the dirt. At least it's not a cliff.

"I don't fucking care if it's an old car! Did it even pass inspection?" Wesley snaps, then pauses as the other person talks. "The princess won't do that..." He sighs and drops his arm by his side, phone in hand. "Do you want a helicopter to come get us?" My wide eyes are enough of an answer; a helicopter is worse. He lifts the phone back to his ear. "The princess says no... We're still four hours away."

He looks at me for a long moment before turning his back and speaking quieter. Waiting a couple of hours for another car wouldn't be the hard part; the sun is nearly at its highest point.

After another ten minutes, Wesley walks toward the car with his phone back in his pocket. "Someone will pick us up and let us stay overnight. Jack will send someone with a new car for us sometime between now and morning."

I cross my arms. "Just like that?"

"Just like that." He ducks back into the car, and I follow suit.

"Who's picking us up?"

"You'll see."

That's a cryptic answer I'm *not* okay with. "You expect me to be okay with not knowing where I'll be sleeping tonight?"

He checks his watch. "You'll know in about forty-five minutes."

"What—"

"Nina," he warns, and I pause at the vulnerability in his eyes. "Trust me... please."

Forty-five minutes later, a pick-up truck approaches from the opposite direction and pulls a U-turn. By the time the driver gets out of the car, Wesley has our bags ready.

A man at least sixty years old dressed in linen pants and a shirt grins at my bodyguard. He's at least six inches shorter, forcing Wesley to bend as he hugs him.

Not quite the person I was expecting.

Nonetheless, Wesley speaks to him briefly before putting our bags in the bed of the truck.

When the man looks at me, I attempt a smile. "Ciao."

"Ciao, madam." He holds a hand to his heart. "Stari Dimitri."

"Stari Nina. Cómi stara?"

"Bueni," he says, giving a raspy little laugh as he opens the passenger door for me. Assuming I'd be sitting in the backseat, I glance at Wesley, who nods in confirmation.

Not long into the ride, Dimitri tosses a look to the back-seat before saying, "Tusé fimare? Te niassa comagri."

Are you hungry? Your grandmother is cooking.

Grandmother. *Wesley's grandmother?* I resist turning around and punching him in the arm for not telling me this right away. Why would he hide it?

The short drive leads us down a dirt path where a small house sits. Wind chimes dance and sing in the breeze; potted trees shield the seating area of the porch. Wesley told me he spent childhood summers and Christmases in Kosita and Palfu. Is this where he grew up? I check my location in the app on my phone. Palfu.

Branches spurting green leaves twist around the house, up toward the roof. The tanned face of an old woman pops up in the window framed by brown shutters and a pot of morning glory flowers. She gasps. "Ay! Íma cópente! Íma cópente! Mi Wesito stara eni!"

I may not be fluent, but I have enough of the basics down to understand that the woman rushing outside yelled, *"Oh! It's true! It's true! My* Wesito *is here!"* Wesito being Wesley. No—*Little Wesley.*

She's no taller than five-two, but it doesn't stop her from yanking Wesley down to her height and peppering his stubbled cheeks with kisses. Despite the pristine bun at the back of her head, I can tell her grey and dark brown hair is both long and thick. She claps her hands together when turning to me, tossing a knowing glance at Wesley.

"Ke sou stara estaf mianna panímorísi?"

And who is this beautiful woman?

My face flushes. "Ciao."

"Nina, this is my grandmother, Callie. Niassa, estaf ya Nina. Le veni di Amerikí ke le mila no Maldasso."

I elbow Wesley for telling her I don't speak Maldanian. "Ay, e pígo."

"Sto bueni," Callie says, then adds in a heavy accent, "Nice to meet you."

I grin as she takes my hand to guide me inside. His grandparents speak little-to-no English and Wesley speaks to them solely in Maldanian. My skills are tested and I wouldn't have it any other way. Callie gives me a quick tour of the one-level home with maroon tiles throughout.

When she speaks to Wesley and points to the stack of pillows and blankets, I can translate that he'll sleep on the couch later. The open living room has a step leading to the kitchen and dining area before turning into the hallway toward the two bedrooms, one of which I'll be sleeping in tonight. Sun-catchers and relics decorate the entirety as if it's a museum and not a home.

Callie gestures for me to sit at the round kitchen table, and I decipher what she asks Wesley.

"Did you feed the poor girl?"

He sighs, lowering onto a chair beside me. "Niassa... we just work together."

She shakes her head as she hands me a glass of water and a bowl of strawberries I hadn't requested, but accept graciously, nonetheless. "No excuse, Wesito. A gentleman does not ignore a struggling woman and you bring me *her*! She looks tired and starved!"

I press my fingers to my cheek. Tired and starved? "Oh —stari bueni."

He gestures to me as if I affirmed his argument. "Verá. Stara bueni. Parafóré, niassa. Niávo gi kest mianna kesmáris en e mondélo."

See. She's good. Please, Grandmother. I work with the most stubborn woman in the world.

There's something riveting about listening to a man speak in another language. Maybe it's a linguist thing, but I've never been more attracted to him.

My phone dings with a text from Maia.

MAIA

Are you okay? They told me your car broke down.

I notice my battery on ten percent once I send a response. I excuse myself to charge my phone in the bedroom, jumping when Wesley appears in the doorway.

"You scared me."

"Is this all right?" he asks, gesturing to the room. "I can tell them that you—"

I set my phone down. "No, it's fine," I insist, lowering my eyes. "I just wish you trusted me enough to tell me from the start."

"Hey," he says, stopping me mid-stride with a hand on my waist. "My trust in you is the only reason we're here. I haven't seen or spoken to my grandparents in years."

I blink in surprise. The people out there clearly love him. "How come?" At his hesitation, I add, "Is it... the socializing thing?"

He clears his throat. "Believe it or not, it's harder with family."

Wesley is naturally withdrawn, yet I can't recall him being anxious or awkward whenever we're together. "Were you... was it ever difficult to talk to *me*?"

He gives a bashful smile. "No. Never."

"Wesley!" Dimitri calls. "Va eni, verá, verá!"
Come here, look, look!
We find him holding up his iPhone, a broad smile

hidden by his distinct mustache. On the screen is a pretty brunette with clear blue eyes and a pleasant expression.

Wesley blanches. "Cora?"

"Yeah, it's me," she replies sarcastically in English. "The sister you never called back after hanging up on her in the middle of the night because you got a work call."

He sighs, failing to come up with an excuse as I figure out what *work call* she means. From his look, I realize it was the night in Antina.

I gasp, covering my mouth. "I think that was my fault." Dimitri hands me the phone. "I needed his help that night."

She lifts a brow. "At one o'clock in the morning?"

My face heats. The last thing I need is for Wesley's sister to think of me as *"the booty-call my brother hung up on me for."*

"I was lost," I hurriedly add. "I was out and—and my phone died so I had to borrow someone else's to call for help."

She smiles at my rambling attempt. "You work with Wesley?"

I nod. It's not how I'd describe our relationship, but the alternative is revealing that I'm the princess. Cora shrugs. "I know by now not to ask questions about the job. I'm Cora, by the way."

"I'm Nina. It's nice to meet you."

"Found 'em, found 'em!" a woman in the background cheers, running up the camera while sliding on a pair of glasses.

"This is our mom, Olive. Say hi, Mom."

Olive lifts her chin as she studies the screen, adjusting to her lenses. "Oh, she's beautiful."

Cora snorts. "She can hear you."

"Sì, panímorísi." Callie nods and smiles in understanding. "Beautiful."

"Oh!" Olive quips. "Hi! Sì, Callie. Sto."

Wesley takes the phone when Cora asks how we ended up here. Callie gestures for me to sit beside her as she peels some apples. Although strict with Wesley and Dimitri, she's kind and gentle with me. She's patient as I gather the confidence and stumble out my Maldanian words and tells me that my accent is good. We spend the first half of the evening peeling and chopping and she shows me how to make falafel balls.

My assumption about Wesley growing up here is true; he and Cora reminisce about childhood memories, including Cora streaking through the neighbor's orchard in the backyard on the night of her twentieth birthday. The conversations switch between the two languages as the phone gets passed from one to the other. There's laughter and sibling banter and I've never seen Wesley smile ear-to-ear before today.

Callie continues talking to Olive over FaceTime and gestures for me to follow. "You come, uh," she says in a thick accent, pointing to a basket by the back door. "We take the vegetables."

I slip my shoes on and step into the heat, which is only amplified by the patio's unshaded tile. The swirling tile designs make a path to the garden on the side of the house. All the while, she chats with Olive in Maldanian.

"Osé?" I ask, motioning to the array of growing vegetables that she might want. Callie has me pick the ones that she can't easily reach, and hands me the phone so she can do some of it herself.

I expected to see Olive, but Cora smiles back at me. The

expression in her bright blue eyes turns heartfelt. "Thank you, Nina."

"What for?"

"Bringing Wesley back to us."

Butterflies brush my stomach. "Oh, I don't think I can take credit for that. It's only luck that our car broke down."

"Physically, sure. But I got a real glimpse at the brother I hadn't seen in a really long time. I have a feeling that you're part of the reason."

"I, uh... we just—we just work together."

She waves off my response. "Whatever the situation, I'm thankful for it."

"Thankful for what?" Wesley says, coming up behind me and reaching for the phone.

"Seeing your ugly face."

He places a hand on his heart. "Ouch, and to think you cared."

So badly I want to shake Wesley and say *this is what I wanted*. The love he has for his family is genuine—and I got to see that even though I wish his broad smile was because of me.

CHAPTER THIRTY-SIX
WESLEY

We hang up the phone with Cora and Mom before eating dinner, and Niassa's cooking is as good as I remember.

This house is steeped in memories. I should've told Nina we were coming here; the alternative was to wait up to three hours in ninety-degree weather before continuing onto a four-hour drive.

Telling her right away would mean explaining what my grandparents are like and, eventually, why I haven't seen them in at least four years. I had to remind myself of those things first, which are consistently accompanied by the searing guilt and pain from what I let my life turn into. Daria had warned me to cut off my family a dozen times before I did. I could pretend for as long as I pleased, but physical scars are harder to hide.

Those were in the beginning of my life underground, when I was stubborn and craving action. I'd eliminate a target, fight my way out, escape wounded, and hunt the witnesses. It didn't take long before death's weight crushed my will. I cleaned myself up by the time Santiago became my sole employer.

Mom's petrified expression at the scars littering my body is burned into my mind. The ensuing arguments made me realize that if I loved them even a little, I had to go. I became someone they didn't recognize, didn't raise. I became The Ghost.

But tonight, I came home. My mother was smiling at me again. My grandfather didn't look scared of me.

"You like her, huh?" Niassa says, pulling me from my thoughts. Before I can answer, she adds, "Don't lie to me, Wesito. You were a lovestruck boy at dinner."

Nina is watching the sunset under the gigantic oak tree in the backyard. Every so often, I crane my neck from my seat at the kitchen table to check on her. "I'm not that obvious."

"You are to your grandmother. Tell her how you feel." Again, before I can answer, she adds, "And don't you dare tell me it's complicated." She wags a finger at me. Growing up, it was nearly impossible to get away with something. Her perception is unnatural.

As much as I want to tell Nina everything, I know it would be selfish. She's been through turmoil the last couple of months, and adding myself to the mix won't help. I can't do that to her. And not to mention my past; I couldn't keep it a secret forever.

"Niassa, I can't."

I'm grateful she doesn't push the subject. She hands me a glass of water filled with fresh fruit. "Then don't let her watch the sunset alone. Take this to her."

I pretend my grandmother isn't being a wingman as I head toward the woman sitting on a blanket under a tree. When Nina hears me approaching, she glances over her shoulder, the sunlight outlining her per usual. *Mi angeli.* My angel. She smiles.

"Hey."

"My grandmother made this for you. It's just water with a bunch of fruit. She drinks it almost every day in summer."

"Oh my, that's so sweet," she says, scooting over and patting the space beside her. I lower as she tastes the drink before setting it aside. Her eyes linger on my shoulder when I lean my elbows on my knees, the shirt sleeve riding up. "Can I see your tattoo?"

I tug the sleeve to reveal it. Her fingers hover over my skin, and her eyes watch me for permission. I nod, suppressing a shiver at her touch. I steady my heartbeat as she drifts over the ink.

"Are they letters?" she asks.

"C for Cora. O for Olive." The crescent moon is angled to look like a C while the sun, tucked in the C, looks like an O. Two years ago, an assignment in Istanbul led to a bullet grazing straight across my shoulder.

Nina must notice the flames around the edge, toward my back, because she asks, "Does this lead to a bigger one?"

"A phoenix across my back."

"Did it hurt?"

"Very much."

She refocuses on the sun and moon tattoo, her fingers tracing the scar that mars it. Despite the heat, I feel chilly when she pulls away. "Your family is really kind."

"Yeah, they're... they're something."

"Not at all what I expected," she adds. "It makes you seem... normal."

I release a low, sardonic huff. "Normal."

"Under all that... stony facade"—she motions toward all of me—"is just... a normal person with a loving family."

"That's not quite how I'd describe myself."

"It's how I would," she replies without a hint of false optimism. "Smart, too. Thoughtful... I've never seen you smile before today."

I recoil. "You've seen me smile before."

She shakes her head. "Not a real one. Those were polite smiles, but with your family, it was real. I could tell."

It was real because of you. It wasn't because of them. It should've been. With the military, I was Beck. With Santiago, I became El Revalté. With Nina, I get to be Wesley—for the first time in over a decade. And it pains me she doesn't know that.

"Don't give up on them, Wesley. They haven't given up on you."

Mom and Cora sent letters and emails for years, begging me to rejoin the family. And I return because of one woman. They deserve a better brother and son; I've long accepted that.

I shrug, my attention on the rows of orange trees in the distance. "They probably should."

Nina grabs my shirt sleeve and pushes it up to reveal the tattoo. "You didn't get *this* tattoo for people you don't love." She watches me defiantly, a curl drifting across her face with the breeze. "The people you love are worth fighting for."

There isn't a moment I forget about the sins I've committed. I can explain them away, but no one except for me will listen or care. I can find hope outside of Nina, but her very existence urges me to search for it. She enjoys the little things—people watching, petting a dog or cat whenever she can, testing french fries from different places, and watching the sunset and clouds at any available moment. She makes me want to search for little things *I* might enjoy. Like listening to her speak my native language, how dogs might be the best animal, how my city lights up at night.

Her hands haven't moved from my shoulder and I find myself studying every slope and curve of her angular face. From her long lashes to her full lips, I struggle to determine a good enough reason not to kiss her.

Nina notices my attention on her mouth. She bristles, subtly wetting her lips, but doesn't move away.

My head spins; she's worth any repercussions. I punch through the tension in my chest. "Fuck it," I whisper before catching her mouth with mine. Her breath hitches as she kisses me back, her soft lips sending shockwaves through me and my blood rushing south.

I just admitted that I can't tell her how I feel, but when she runs a hand across my chest and tangles her fingers in the hair at my nape, I resist pulling her onto my lap to explore every inch of her. She releases a little moan into my mouth when my tongue brushes hers, tasting strawberries. Fuck. It's not enough. I grab the back of her neck to deepen the kiss, and her hold on my hair tightens. Both of us become needier, sloppier, with her nipping my bottom lip and me gripping her waist to bring her closer.

My dick hardens when I fill one of my hands with her ass. She gasps at the pressure, arching into me.

My work phone vibrating in my front pocket is the one thing that helps us keep our clothes on.

"*Karító*," I curse, digging out my phone as Nina's hand lingers on my neck. "It's Jack—probably about our new car."

With only one bodyguard protecting the princess, I

can't ignore this call. I feel her nod, and I press a kiss to her knuckles before getting up to answer.

CHAPTER THIRTY-SEVEN

NINA

I feel dizzy for the rest of the night.

The last thing I expected was for Wesley to kiss me, and suddenly his lips were on mine and my body was on fire. Every glorious shift of his lips sent sparks straight down my center, and I replay the memory long into the night. While in bed, I keep putting my fingers to my lips.

I wanted that for months—and those blissful ten seconds were nowhere near enough. My stomach erupts in butterflies at the thought of doing more with him and my heart pounds at the increasing possibility of that happening. There are so many questions I want to ask him.

Why did it take you so long? Why now? Do you have feelings for me?

I shouldn't get ahead of myself, but it's impossible not to. Everything about it felt right. There was urgency in the kiss, yet I'd also never felt so peaceful. It was heaven.

The idea of sleeping tonight feels impossible, so at midnight, I slip out of bed for a glass of water. I pointedly keep my gaze away from the living room where Wesley is sleeping as I tiptoe into the kitchen. The glowing moonlight streams through the window above the sink, giving me enough light to quietly get what I need.

By the time I finish the glass, the toilet flushes, sending my heart into my throat. It's definitely not Callie or Dimitri. *Shit, shit, shit.* At least I haven't put my bonnet on or braided my hair yet. His footsteps shuffle behind me and suddenly stop.

"Are you okay?" Wesley asks.

I turn and lean on the sink. He stays just out of the moonlight, cloaked in shadows, but my stomach tingles at his black tank top.

"Yeah. I was thirsty. Are *you* okay?"

"Yeah."

"Good," I whisper, lingering in the moment. I can't move. I don't want to.

"I—" He pauses, scrounging up the words. "I'm sorry."

He steps closer, and my breath catches in my throat. His hair is tousled and his shirt hugs every muscle so perfectly that I know I'm seconds away from pouncing. I clear my throat. "For what?"

"For kissing you. I put you in an awkward situation—"

"Did I seem awkward to you?"

"Well, no, but... it wasn't appropriate. You're my client."

I release a breath and take a small step closer. "You might be sorry, but I'm not." I ball the fabric at his chest in my fist, yanking him down to me. His lips find mine like a magnet.

Sorry, my ass.

He falls into my kiss with a groan, his hands gripping either side of my face as we stagger backward. My lower back hits the counter and he doesn't hesitate to haul me onto the surface by my thighs.

This kiss is far more raw than earlier; we cling to each

other almost desperately. With his tongue in my mouth and hands traveling my thighs, hips, and waist, I arch into him with the hope he'll sate the wetness between my legs. His head falls to my jaw and leaves behind wet kisses down to my collarbone.

"Wesley," I beg, my hushed voice making me sound even more desperate. I need something—*anything*. His breath grazes my skin when he curses. I bring his lips to mine again, releasing an unintentional whimper at how savory he tastes. It's better than what I imagined.

Suddenly, a loud snore erupts from his grandparents' bedroom down the hall, making Wesley and I stop. It's a fifty-fifty chance it was Dimitri or Callie.

We catch our breath, heads bowed together. It's a relief to finally touch him without hesitation or apprehension, to feel him against me.

"M-maybe," I stutter, "maybe we shouldn't do this here."

"You're probably right," he whispers, voice strained.

I tighten my legs around him when he starts to lift me. *"Wait—"* I tug on his shirt. "Just... just a few more seconds."

I can't have more of him tonight, but I need it for a little longer. Wesley burrows his face in my neck, one hand flat against my lower back and the other caressing my thigh. He melts into me, reaching into every hidden corner of my soul.

I thread my fingers through his feather-soft hair, biting back a lustful sigh when I feel his lips graze the shell of my ear. He kisses me hard enough to send sparks between my thighs. And when he groans into my mouth, the sparks ignite.

Wesley suddenly lifts me off the counter and sets me

down. He forces himself away, catching his breath and planting one last kiss on my temple. "Good night, angel."

In the morning, after twenty minutes of saying goodbye, Wesley and I continue the drive.

I don't have time to ponder what happened yesterday; Maia calls me and we spend two hours reviewing the data and presentation, and I spend the other two hours sleeping.

I am trying to do something revolutionary. This can change the course of a country and will have more than a chapter in a history book—it'll need its own. I *should* be nervous. My heart *should* thunder in my chest because I hate being told no or feeling incompetent.

Neither my sister nor cousin warned me of Corsos's grandeur. Never before have I seen so many mansions. It's hard to marvel at the sights when I instantly think of the parents in Kosita who send their children to beg for money, of the city's homeless population. The fire in my chest intensifies, telling me this proposal is the right choice. I couldn't enjoy the luxuries of being a princess without doing *everything* possible to help the people I'd represent.

The car pulls through a private checkpoint and up to one of the mansions. Without enough time for a tour before the meeting, maids bring me right to my suite, which is unfathomably opulent. The plush bed has champagne and ivory pillows. Its fabric probably costs as much as my student debt. People live like this. *All the time.* My eyes snag on the box tied with a pink ribbon, and a thrill runs up my spine at the note attached.

Princess Nina,
We hope this care package comforts you during your stay.
The Higher Court

Princess Nina. Princess Nina. Princess Nina. It's not a joke, not a lie. It's *me. I'm Princess Nina.* I glance over my shoulder into the full-length mirror, at my curls, my brown skin, my tall frame. Princess.

It fits.

The passion hits me, quick and fierce. I want this. I truly, wholly want this.

CHAPTER THIRTY-EIGHT
WESLEY

When Nina went back to bed last night, I realized how far gone I am.

She is intoxicating. I'm at her mercy and I have been for months. It launches me into a dangerous game of balance; there's nothing I wouldn't do for her. She inspires me to become a better person, but I'd do unspeakable things if it meant keeping her happy and safe. In the underground, love is a liability and always will be.

During the four-hour drive from my grandparents' house to Corsos, I listed possible threats from my time underground. My work was thorough. While Santiago's death inconvenienced his employees and associates, the ones who knew me either hated him or feared me enough to stay away.

Even with heavy security at the mansion, I remain outside Nina's room. Employees are dotted around the property and we can't take the risk that one of them works with Lo Revínastí.

My phone rings with a call from my colleague and I answer, "Mason."

"Wrong," Maia says. "Nina's phone's off and I don't want to walk across the damn country in these heels. Where is she?"

"Inside her suite."

"Tell her that we're waiting," she instructs. "She needs to get down here. Now."

"Yes, madam," I reply, knocking on the door after Maia hangs up. Once Nina gives me permission to enter, I see her pacing. She wears a light pink pantsuit, her hair in a bun with curls framing her face, which I now realize is my favorite hairstyle of hers.

"The Higher Court is waiting for you."

"Okay," she exhales, shaking out her hands. "Just—I need a minute."

"Nina—"

She stops in the middle of the room and stares at me. "Please tell me if my plan is bad and I am *begging* you not to be impartial on this because you're the only one I trust to give me honest advice." She holds her hands against her stomach, entire body tense.

I hate seeing her like this, especially because of her brilliance. I've long known this, but listening to her talk to Maia on the way here showed me in a completely different way. She's compassionate, wise, and strong. People are drawn to her in ways she doesn't realize.

She's nearly my height in heels, so I don't dip my head to catch her gaze. I remove her hands from her stomach, folding them in mine.

"Nina Antonia Laffley, you are one of the smartest people I know," I begin. "Definitely the most stubborn. And charming. And out-of-this-fucking-world beautiful." She blushes. "This country is my home and the only place that felt right—until I met you. Which is how I know there's no one better to wear its crown."

Nina blinks away sudden tears, nodding. I almost panic that I said the wrong thing until she kisses me deeply. My head spins from her lips on mine. Since the day we met, I craved her taste. We've kissed three times in twenty-four hours and it's only the start of catching up.

But we're on a time limit.

I want her to succeed—and I may not be in the final picture. I'm not the person the Higher Court or her family would want by her side. Their input doesn't matter to me; Nina's does, and a good man wouldn't force her to pick between them and me.

CHAPTER THIRTY-NINE
NINA

I can't believe it worked.

Vanessa was right; Helen adored the idea from the start. The meeting lasted three hours, most of it locked into a somewhat respectful debate. Maia helped keep me level-headed for the simple reason that she became combative a few times. Her retorts were accurate, albeit abrasive, which helped my diplomacy shine. I couldn't have done it without her.

We discussed reallocating funds and increasing the institution's function by decreasing unnecessary profit. It helps that Vanessa and Jace are in favor since some of the secondary estates have been passed onto them. After reviewing the statistics and presenting the probable scenarios, the Court began to agree.

Maia and I take a long walk in the estate's humongous garden to decompress and debrief. The sun begins to set, the golden hour hues brightening the flowers. Mason and Wesley trail not far behind us.

"I could do a lot of experiments here," Maia says,

bravely poking a bee perched on a marigold like it's her friend.

"What do you mean?" I look down at my linen slippers, already stained with a little dirt. My pink toenails peek out from under the fabric.

"The garden. I'll have to find out who's in charge. Oh! There's a worker; maybe she'll know." She dashes off toward the gardener with Mason in tow.

"You did it," Wesley says, his beard curving with his smile. "I'm proud of you."

A grin spreads across my face as I hold my stomach to calm my nerves. "I feel like... I'm finally making the right choices."

It's more than the luxury of being called a princess or staying in palaces and mansions; it's that I can say I'm Ophelia's daughter and believe it. I can make a true difference in the world.

I step forward with the urge to throw my arms around Wesley, but my arms freeze as a voice calls, "Princess Nina!"

My face falls with disappointment, as does his.

"I'm not sure I'll get used to that," I whisper, turning to the maid walking toward me. "Yes?"

She knots her hands in front of her. "Dinner is ready for you and Princess Maia."

"Thank you. We'll be right in."

We stay at the mansion for another few days before taking the road trip back to Kosita. Each of those days, I had long meetings with George from the communications department about ways to introduce us to the public. We brainstormed speech ideas and locations for hours.

As soon as I climbed into the passenger seat of the black SUV, I fell asleep. I have a meeting with Aunt Beverly this afternoon about where Maia and I are going to live moving forward. As luxurious as the palace is, we don't want to live there forever.

Suddenly, I feel Wesley's hand on my hip, squeezing gently as he whispers, "Nina, wake up."

I expect to hear the familiar car horns and engines of Kosita, not the sound of leaves rustling in the wind. I blink the sleep from my eyes as I sit up. "Where are we?"

"Fortuna. Maldana's hidden gem."

"Wha—why?"

"It's my favorite place in the country. Wanted to show you."

"But—they're expecting us at two."

Wesley shrugs, a lazy smile on his lips. "The princess got hungry."

I watch him in disbelief for a moment. He's not a spontaneous person—at least I thought so. I slip on my sandals and climb out of the passenger seat car, a dreamy stare lingering on the village.

When I meet him at the front of the car, he grabs my hand and guides us ahead as if lacing our fingers is completely normal. No hesitation. The path leads to Fortuna's downtown. I feel the salty air on my skin and hear the dancing waves on the other side of the small village below.

"Tourists don't often come here because it's on such a big hill," Wesley explains. "It's difficult for a lot of people."

Less than a block into town, I see how. My feet press into my sandals as we step downhill and I already dread having to climb back up when we leave. I wrap my free hand around Wesley's arm, completely clinging to him.

We pass through the outdoor markets selling trinkets,

clothes, and produce. People smile and nod and my stress dissipates with each second. With more household staff learning I'm princess, it's only a matter of time until it reaches the news. But here, no one knows us. I don't have to worry if my family or the Higher Court catch me looking at Wesley longer than I need to, standing closer than I should. Here, now, I can lean into every touch and wander every gaze.

I push all the princess and royalty stuff from mind. Wesley consumes me entirely, and I've never felt happier because of it. When we reach the town square, a small band plays instrumental music. He tugs my hand, twirling me into a dance with him among the other pairs.

"You're *dancing* with me?" I gasp. "Hell must have frozen over."

He looks offended. "I've danced with you."

"After rejecting me first."

"Because I wanted to do *this*," he says, pressing my hips flush against his—much firmer than our dance in Kosita. He lowers to kiss behind my ear. "And this."

Nerves spark along my core. I can't hide the flirtatious hint in my voice. "What else?"

I shudder at his low chuckle against my neck.

"We're in too public of a place for me to show you."

It's the first time he's entirely unguarded with me. Not just hidden behind trees or in dark kitchens, but out under the sun. I don't know exactly what our future looks like— and two months ago, that would make me panic. All I know for sure is that I want him by my side.

In addition to the hills making Fortuna unfavored by tourists, there are fewer shops than expected. Most of the streets that Wesley and I wander through are residential neighborhoods, but the views are picturesque. I squeal at the German Shepherd puppy up ahead, sitting loyally by his owner's side on a stoop. The owner, out smoking a cigarette, gives me permission to pet the jumping dog who happens to be in its piranha phase.

After ripping myself away before I become a dog thief, we come across a restaurant that sells french fries. Although I'd rate the food a six, petting a dog prior bumps it up to a ten out of ten.

"There's one more thing I want you to see," Wesley says, leading me through a park and down a set of outdoor stairs that turn into a nature trail.

"How did you find this place? Fortuna, I mean."

He shrugs. "I had to travel for some jobs."

Our hands find each other again as we walk in silence until the trail ends at the wide mouth of a cave. The roaring echoes are undeniably those of a waterfall. I tighten my hand around Wesley's as we enter. Mist sprays across my legs, and I smile when I reach the curtain of water spilling into a pool below. Its power rumbles in my chest.

I wander ahead. "This is..."

A dozen words could describe its raw beauty, but I fall speechless. My eyes flutter shut as I take a few deep breaths, the fresh ocean air cleansing my lungs. I turn toward Wesley.

"Can you feel that? In your chest." At his confusion, I step closer and instruct, "Close your eyes," before placing my hand on his heart. "And just breathe."

Eyes still closed, he lifts a brow and speaks in an obvious tone. "I am."

I whack him. "*Meditating* breaths."

"It's hard to focus on anything else with your hand on my chest."

When I remove my hand, he traps it in place and opens

his eyes. "I didn't say to move." He leans down and kisses me softly until I deepen it, that familiar churn of desire returning once he groans. I run my thumb over his stubble before finding the hair at his nape, tangling my fingers.

As stunning as this place is, I wish we weren't here. I need to feel every bit of him.

We pull apart at the sound of people coming closer. Wesley leans his forehead against mine and mutters, "We should get back on the road."

I nod. Back to reality.

The next day, Maia is off with Vanessa all day to meet her pet chickens, and I don't get out of bed until noon.

For god's sake, my bed frame has posts at each corner and is an *extended part* of the floor and ceiling. Not to mention the blissfully soft mattress. How can anyone expect to leave this bed with ease?

It takes me two hours to bathe and get dressed for nothing in between eating the food I ordered. Dad and Ruby have been on another excursion, so I don't have to worry about running into him. I make a list of the things I need to do in the upcoming weeks, including hiring an assistant. It's quite a perfect day.

Until Jack calls me at five o'clock.

"Hello?"

"Princess Nina, good evening. It's Jack Costas. Do you have a minute to talk?"

I hesitate at his formality, so I play it off. "Sure. What's up?"

"With Beck's contract coming to a close in a few weeks, I'd like to ask how he has been as your security detail."

My blood runs cold. Contract? "I-I'm sorry?" I stutter.

"His professionalism, Your Highness."

I wince at my caving stomach. I never knew Wesley had a contract. He's my bodyguard—indefinitely. Is he planning on disappearing in a few weeks just like that? A lump builds in my throat.

"Oh—um. I-I'm really sorry, Jack, but I'm getting another call from someone I've been trying to get in touch with," I say, the lie spilling out smoothly. "Can we pick this up another time?"

"Yes, of course. I will call back another time."

"Thanks, bye." I hang up instantly and call Wesley.

CHAPTER FORTY
WESLEY

"Where are you?" Nina asks before I have a chance to say hello.

I sit up in bed, pausing at her strained tone. "My apartment. What's wrong?"

"Where's your apartment?"

"Uh—Antonia wing. 305. Now answer my question."

"I'll be there in five minutes," she says, and hangs up. I stare at my phone in disbelief before scanning my messy apartment. *Karító.* I stumble off my bed and clean fast enough for my mother to be proud.

The entire time, I try to figure out why Nina sounded stressed and why she demanded to come here. But in a quick, dreadful thought, I realize it's probably about us. Is she going to end it?

Nina is the princess of Maldana. Soon, she'll be queen. I'm not just her bodyguard; I'm a former hitman. The Higher Court would never allow us to be together. I stopped in Fortuna because our time would be up as soon as we returned to the palace and I didn't want to let her go just yet.

Resisting her is more than the fact that my career would fall apart further. The dark memories of my past life have not gone away, and they won't—not anytime soon. She helps me find the good in the world; I see it every time I look at her. Each kiss and touch sends me deeper into a fantasy of a life with her and I'm convincing myself it's possible. But I don't know if I can do that with these memories clawing up my throat every day.

When I answer her knock, Nina pushes the door aside and strides into the apartment. One look at her outfit and I know she's out to kill me. She's wearing a cropped shirt that ties around her neck to expose her shoulders, paired with ass-hugging pants of the same pattern. The urge to touch her has never been so strong.

"Jack called me," she says. "He wanted to know what I thought of you as my security."

I blink, ripping my gaze from her body to find her indignant expression. "Okay..."

She plants her hands on her hips. "Should I tell him you make me feel safe—or what it feels like to have your tongue down my throat?"

"I..."

"You're *leaving*?"

"I—was only contracted to be your security until or if you went public."

She grimaces. "Just like that."

"What am I supposed to do?" I regret the words immediately; I'm still pulling myself away from the thought of kissing her exposed skin.

"Maybe *tell* me!" Nina looks away as tears threaten to fall. The sight snaps me into reality. "I thought we had more time," she says, voice cracking. "I thought you *wanted* more time, I thought—"

"Nina—"

"No," she insists. "At least tell me why it's so easy for you to walk away from this."

Easy.

The simple word sets my chest on fire. I've stared down the barrel of a gun enough times to feel comfortable, yet keeping my hands off Nina this summer has been the bane of my existence.

"Easy?" I echo. "None of this has been fucking easy. You think I wanted to watch another man put his hands all over you this summer? Whisper in your ear? Flirt with you?"

Nina opens her mouth, struggling to gather the words. She doesn't know the torment.

"Being your security is the first ethical job I've had in years so what the hell am I supposed to do when the one person who makes me want to be a better man becomes the same thing that stops me? I am *clawing* my way to being a good person, one who doesn't fall for his client and respects boundaries but you—you control me. You own my every thought, my every fucking desire. I can't *breathe* without knowing you're safe or happy." I let out a breath, lowering onto the edge of the bed and looking up at her. "You own all of me, angel. Each goddamn part."

Nina pushes off the dresser and kneels before me, taking my face in her hands. "I may not have known you then, but I know you now. The man in front of me is good and kind and so thoughtful it hurts. I've learned more about myself and my family in the last few months than I have my whole life. I worry about everything and my mind is in constant chaos. The only place I know peace is anywhere I'm with you... and it kills me that you think I'm keeping you from being a good person. You *are* one."

I smother a defeated sigh, leaning into her hand and muttering, "Because of you."

"It's not something earned or given. You're only seeing more of who you already are. And I want you, Wesley. All of you."

I'm in love with this woman—more than I thought I could. A relationship outside that door might not be possible, but she's right in front of me, willing, wanting. I close the small distance, covering her lips with mine. The tender kiss quickly turns needy and I pull her onto my lap. My groin stiffens at the feel of her straddling me. Nina suddenly shoves me onto my back, a smirk tugging at her lips. I know what she's thinking—because I'm thinking it, too.

Finally.

CHAPTER FORTY-ONE

NINA

I freeze, troubled at the sight.

Is Wesley's bare torso sculpted like an ancient god? Yes. But it's also covered with scars. Almost a dozen are scattered over his ribcage, chest, and shoulders. My fingers brush the ridges of healed wounds, heartache threatening to overtake me at what he went through to get these.

He notices my hesitation. When he reaches to tilt up my chin, I stop him. I lower and press my lips to the long scar beginning at his sternum, planting kisses until it ends above his navel. He shivers.

"Come here," Wesley says, flipping us over and pinning my wrists above my head. He slams his lips onto mine and I arch into him, my final thread of resistance snapping. I wrap my legs around his waist and kiss him hard enough to make up for each lingering moment and longing glance. My belly churns with lust when his teeth clamp around my bottom lip.

"You have no fucking idea how long I've wanted this—to have you underneath me."

It's my turn to shiver as he traces my waistband lightly,

dipping under to grab my bare hip. "No panties?" He groans. "You really know how to bring a man to his knees."

I hold back a smile. "It doesn't look like you're on your knees to me."

He chuckles. "Have some patience."

I squeal when he suddenly yanks me closer to the bottom of the bed by my hips. I watch him peel my clothes off piece by piece, my skin sizzling every time he touches me. There's no agony quite like longing for Wesley. He's the personified version of my passion and lust.

He drinks in the sight of me bare in front of him, and I feel myself getting wetter at the hunger in his eyes. Starting at my ankle, he slowly kisses up my body, speaking between each one.

"I have thought—"

He kisses my calf.

"Dreamed—"

My knee.

"Craved—"

He softly bites my inner thigh.

"Your skin—"

He kisses my lower stomach, sending sparks up my center.

"Your taste—"

I tremble when he drags the tip of his tongue from my navel to between my breasts.

"What you sound like when you take me."

Wesley takes one of my nipples into his mouth, his fingers twirling and pinching the other. I moan as the ache between my legs intensifies, and I bite my lip to keep from whimpering. I need him *now*. If it didn't feel so damn good, I'd push him onto the bed to speed this up.

"Wesley," I whisper in the same desperate way I had that night in the kitchen. "Please."

He looks at me, his expression as salacious as mine. "Please what?"

I nearly flick him in the forehead. Were the past two months of foreplay not enough? I grumble impatiently. "Eat me, fuck me, do *something*."

He laughs, kneeling at the end of the bed and spreading my legs farther apart. I inhale sharply and grip the comforter when his tongue presses against my sensitive core. I let out another moan, my lungs tightening as his finger slides into me.

"So fucking wet," Wesley mutters. His tongue flicks in a perfect rhythm that won't take long to send me over the edge.

"Oh my god," I whimper, my back arching off the mattress when he adds another finger. His free hand shoves me flat and clamps around my breast. He holds my eyes and hand through every twitch and sound I make, watching me fall back as he picks up the pace, wild and greedy. I buck my hips whenever his tongue hits the right spot and his fingers reach the innermost part of me.

I would do anything to bottle up this feeling, to never forget the sight of him between my legs as he works me through an orgasm. I'm not the most experienced person, but I have enough to recognize how fucking phenomenal he is. The fact that it's *Wesley*, the man who holds my heart as if it was designed for him, makes it so much better.

As I catch my breath, he plants soft kisses up to my neck, whispering, "Until watching you come, I didn't think you could be even more beautiful."

Fabric brushes against my leg, and I realize he hasn't even taken his pants off yet.

"Please tell me you have a condom," I whine, wrapping my legs around him. He untangles from me and darts to the linen closet eagerly enough for me to laugh. I scoot to the headboard, noticing the wet spot I left behind. I bite the inside of my cheek. Whoops.

I watch the corded muscles of his back as he rifles through the closet. His phoenix tattoo spreads halfway down, flames encompassing the born-again creature.

Wesley returns with the condom, audibly cursing at the sight of me lounging among the pillows. I usually cower away from this type of scrutiny, but he looks at me like I'm artwork. His gaze falls when I spread my legs. He drops onto the bed, making to crawl toward me until I press my toes into his shoulder.

"Nuh-uh." I gently push him back. "Strip."

He blinks. "What?"

"I said"—I lean closer, my answer defiant—"*strip.*"

Given the fact that I'm entirely naked, it's only fair. When he gets up, I settle into the pillows in preparation for my show. I scan from his bulge up to his eyes staring back at me as he unbuckles his belt. He unzips, and I reach between my legs to rub myself in circles.

Wesley stifles a groan. "You're killing me, angel."

The nickname, his coarse tone—lust stabs at my core again. Arousal coats my fingers as he slides off his pants before following it with his boxers. I bite my lip at the sight of him, large and ready.

I crawl down the bed toward him, rising onto my knees. He pulls me close, and I think back to the day he sat behind me on the moped—how I could feel him against me. My body aches with anticipation as I gently rake my nails across his hairy chest. I want him more now than I did then. He covers my hand with his own, kissing me before pulling my legs out from under me. I fall onto my back with a squeal, already reaching out for him again.

He slides the condom on, lining himself at my entrance as he takes one of my breasts in his mouth and grabs the other. He rocks into me slowly at first, then all at once. The pressure, pleasure, pain—I can't help releasing a strangled moan. I clamp my mouth shut, slightly embarrassed.

"Are you okay?" Wesley asks, a concerned furrow in his brow. "Do you want me to stop?"

I dread even the idea. I shake my head and bring him closer. "Don't you dare."

He chuckles, hooking his elbows under my knees to grasp the back of my neck and keep me in place. "That's my girl."

His rough voice invigorates those three words, only adding pleasure to each thrust. My body tenses with plea-sure as the new angle brings him closer inside me than before.

"Fuck, Wesley, oh my god."

I claw at his arms and fight to memorize the feeling of every inch. Even with his chest flush against mine, it's not close enough. I know he thinks the same; his touch wanders my body without breaking the kiss or rhythm. My breasts, my waist, my hips. His hands are never empty, always filled with some part of me. It makes me feel more vulnerable than ever before. I feel seen, caressed, *worshiped.*

We move in sync, our pent-up lust melting together to make every stroke as euphoric as the last. I tremble at the wet sounds and cling tighter to him.

"Listen to how fucking good we sound together," he whispers.

We shift back into the middle of the bed and Wesley tosses my legs over his shoulders. He moves with intention, precision. Being the subject of that precision sends a warm, silky feeling through my stomach, intensifying at the sound of his grunts and moans. Goosebumps shoot down my legs as I clench around him. The tighter I cross my ankles behind his head, the harder he fucks and the more numb my body gets.

"*Oh, shit, I*—" The words die on my lips as I climax again.

Wesley slows, bracing an elbow beside my head. I run my hands down his body, feeling the sheen of sweat over his skin. I've craved his body, his smell, his taste for months —and I'm devouring the whole fucking meal. There's no one I want more than him.

"How many is that now? Two?" he asks, slightly breathless.

"You're *counting*?"

He looks at me as if I should know this. "Of course. Anything less than three is unacceptable."

I laugh. "Then you're in luck because that was the third."

"Good." He kisses me, and even though my legs feel like jelly, I push him onto his back and straddle him.

Butterflies ripple through my body at the ravenous look in his eyes, and I quickly fix my hair and hope it doesn't look like a rat's nest. Both of us moan as I lower onto him, twitching and rocking my hips to adjust to this full feeling.

Wesley reaches behind me and grips my ass. "Watching you ride me is the best goddamn view in the world."

A smile pulls at my lips. I brace my hands on his chest to ride him faster. His head falls back as he mutters a bunch of curse words in Maldanian. He snatches my hips to take control, his muscles tensing. He groans and thrusts harder into me as he comes, and it's hot enough to make me come, too.

I collapse against his sweaty chest. For moments, we lie together and slowly catch our breaths. His arms close around me and I shut my eyes as the feeling creeps back into my limbs and the world spins a little less.

"We should've done that weeks ago," I mutter.

He chuckles, planting a kiss on my head before discarding the condom to settle in bed with me.

I want this—forever. I want him in bed beside me, smiling, laughing, holding. The world stops when I'm with him, and there's no one I'd rather be frozen in time with.

Once I read Maia's text about coming home late, I silence my phone and set it on the nightstand. Warmth spreads through my belly at the sight of Wesley waiting for me. With his shirt on, I slide into his arms and tangle our legs. He draws circles on my thigh across his waist as his other hand wraps around one of my curls.

His heart beating under my palm, I trace one of the scars on his chest and feel the ridges of puckered skin. I tilt to look up at him.

"You said I'm your first ethical job... what was it before?" I ask, my voice soft.

He pauses, trouble tugging at his face. He opens his mouth to speak, but all he can manage to whisper is, "Another time."

It couldn't have been *that* bad if the head of security assigned him as my bodyguard. I don't press the subject, kissing the spot I'm resting on before closing my eyes.

The evening slips by, accompanied by the unspoken fact that I'm spending the night. Wesley cooks me dinner—if marinara sauce dumped on pasta counts as cooking—and I perch on the countertop to watch him work, his sweatpants hanging low on his hips. I only make it three minutes before wrapping my arms around him from behind. Pressing my lips to his bare skin isn't enough affection. So I clamp one of his meaty muscles with my teeth.

He hisses. "Did you just bite me?"

"Can't help it." I nip him again, a little harder this time. He winces and tosses an arm above to bring me to his chest while the other stirs the sauce.

"You're a…" Wesley trails off in thought. He makes the talking gesture with his fingers. "What is the English word —for the fish that bites? E Maldasso no kaiséitré piranso."

I giggle. "Sì, e piranso stara e piranha. I'm a piranha." I nip his shoulder right by my mouth. I take a better look at the scar—or burn mark, it seems—that I'd bitten. It's in the shape of a diamond, almost deliberate. "What's this one from?"

He glances at it, then tries to shrug off the question. "Something stupid I did with my military buddies. Your Maldanian is getting better," he says with a proud smile, and my stomach tingles from the praise despite knowing he's lying about how he got the mark. He nudges my cheek with his nose, dragging his lips across my skin. "Mi verinìta Maldasso."

My Maldanian queen.

I arch into him on instinct. My body reacts to him as if it's half of a single entity. While we end up eating the entire pot of spaghetti, my appetite for Wesley is insatiable.

CHAPTER FORTY-TWO
NINA

A lawn mower wakes us up at six-thirty in the morning.

With a pathetic whimper, I bury my face in the pillow. "Why?"

I feel Wesley shift as an arm snakes around my waist and pulls me across the bed. "The Antonia wing doesn't have official tenants. No courtesy rules."

His rough morning voice releases a set of butterflies in my stomach. From what I feel against my ass, he's as turned on as I am. As much as I want to go back to sleep, reality is creeping in and I need to leave soon. We lay tangled for another ten minutes as sleep takes its time leaving my body. I drag my finger over a scar on Wesley's forearm in front of me.

Letting myself fall in love with him is the first selfish thing I've done. It puts Jack and the Higher Court and even my family in an awkward position, and I don't care.

I sit up, blinking myself awake and untangling my hair to throw into a bun. I rub the sleep out of my eyes and survey the apartment. Our dinner plates from last night are still on the counter. I've never gone to bed with dishes out like that before.

Wesley stirs, his hand slipping under my shirt—*his* shirt—and squeezes my bare skin, a habit I'm noticing more. He always wants to touch my skin. He sits up and trails kisses from my shoulder to my neck.

"What's going through that beautiful head of yours?" he mutters.

I release a slow sigh, reaching behind me to comb my fingers through his soft hair. My voice stays in a whisper, as if any louder would shatter the night. "It just doesn't feel real."

"What doesn't?"

I turn to him. "This. Us. Now."

Wesley hums before pushing me onto my back. He climbs on top of me and I revel in how comfortable it feels to have him between my legs. He lowers to my neck, pressing a gentle kiss while sliding the shirt above my breasts.

"How about now?"

I chuckle. "No."

He grips my backside, the sudden pressure making me gasp as he kisses my collarbone. "Now?"

I bite my lip to stop from giggling. "No, but you're getting hotter."

His head dips lower. "Then what about…" The same moment he takes my nipple softly between his teeth, his thumb finds the perfect spot between my thighs. "This?" he whispers as he rubs in slow circles. "Does it feel real yet?"

My eyes flutter shut and I arch into him, pleasure rippling up my stomach and down my legs. "Keep doing that and it will."

I feel him laugh. A sharp knock suddenly raps at the door, and our heads snap up.

"Wait here," Wesley says, sliding off the bed and stepping into sweatpants as I cover myself with the blanket. When he checks the peephole, he glances back. "It's your sister."

"*Maia?*"

He barely cracks the door before Maia forces her way into the apartment. She closes the door and immediately faces the corner and says, "Are either of you naked?"

Half yes. I stagger to find my clothes. "Just—stay turned around. How did you know I was here?"

"Your phone location, duh." She huffs impatiently. "Everyone is awake and Dad and Ruby came home early. I heard Dad say he wants to ask you to go to brunch with him so I went to give you a heads-up. And then you weren't answering."

"Fuck. Have I mentioned you're the best sister?" I say, ripping off Wesley's shirt and tossing it to him. My stomach tingles from his unabashed stare at my breasts. I step into my pants and turn for him to fix the back of my shirt for me. When he's done, he wraps his arms around me from behind, burying his face in my neck to plant a quick kiss.

"It wouldn't hurt to mention every so often," Maia says.

"You can look," I tell her, grabbing my phone and stepping into my shoes.

Once Maia steps outside, I perch on my toes and pull Wesley into a kiss. He holds me against him without hesitation, biting my lip to keep me from pulling away. I shove down the urge to slam the door behind Maia so Wesley and I can steal a little more of the night.

"I'll text you later today," I mutter.

His expression is as crestfallen as mine. If only the sun

would rest for a few more hours. "Okay," he whispers with a nod, and I follow my sister into the hallway.

I manage to escape Dad by hopping in the shower before he reaches my room.

We'll have to talk again at some point, but all my mental strength is gone. Not only do I need to help the communications team with our lineage announcement, I also need to tell Raven and pack up my entire life. My stomach aches with grief to leave her—even if she's settled and living with her boyfriend. I'll tell her when I return home.

Despite the grief, my excitement for the future intensifies: living in Maldana, learning about Mom, helping people, and being a princess.

Wesley.

Over the next few days, acting as if I'm not completely in love with him is torturous. I want to hold his hand. I want to look at him longer than a few seconds. I want him beside me during Sunday brunch with Aunt Bev and the family.

I want everyone to know that I can be loved.

Having him entirely is more invigorating than I imagined. It's not just that I feel special because I get to see a side of him he rarely shows; it's the fullness I feel with him. While I love how he *physically* fills me—even the memory gives me chills—Wesley has each part of me in his arms. My sadness, my joy, my affection—he takes it all like it was meant for him.

I manage to carve an hour of "shopping" between meetings. In reality, Wesley and I get french fries and ice cream and put the world on pause for the afternoon. We sneak off to a tiny park and sit under the shade on a bench. There are plenty of things for us to work out and plan, but we fall into a rhythm of silence, followed by a debate of what's better: small dogs or big dogs. I say both. Wesley says big, of course.

"This is kind of our first date," I say, "if you think about it."

He grimaces, tossing an arm behind me while the other strokes my leg draped across his lap. "I can do better than french fries on a park bench."

I peck his lips. "French fries on a park bench with you sounds nothing short of perfect."

Wesley smiles. I'm privileged to have the title of princess. Fancy dinners and opulent clothes are going to be the standard now. Together, we can be real and humble.

He gets up to throw our trash away on the sidewalk behind us, but after nearly a minute, I look back. He's not a slow walker.

"Wes?" I scan the area, but he's not here. I rise to my feet. "Wesley?"

He wouldn't disappear without saying anything. Panic seizes me as I wander for some hint of where he is. When I turn and bump into someone, a man says, "Miss Laffley."

The man is three times my size and has tattoos up his neck. It's at least eighty-five degrees, and he's wearing a suit jacket.

"Come this way and I'll bring you to him," he says, and his calm tone unsettles me.

"Excuse me? How do you know my name?"

"He's not here. Come with me; I'll bring you to him."

"Where is he?"

The man huffs, his patience thinning. He grabs my arm,

firm but gentle—a warning, a sign that he's stronger than me. My heart jumps into my throat. "This can be easy or difficult. Your choice."

All I can think of is Wesley and that he wouldn't leave me. Whoever this person is, I know he did something to him.

"Just tell me where he is," I grit, fighting the scared and frustrated tears pricking at my eyes as I pull against his tightening grip. *Why did I let him touch me?*

He shifts his jacket aside to reveal the gun in his waistband. My blood runs cold and my legs almost weaken. "As I've said. Easy... or difficult."

Who is he? Part of Lo Revínastí? Why did they take Wesley?

I glance around for a hint this is all in my head or for Wesley to pop out from around the corner. But there's nothing. I swallow the lump in my throat. "You'll take me to him?"

"Yes, madam."

I nod. Relief rushes through me when the man releases my arm. He gestures toward a black SUV where the door is already open. I'll be at his mercy the moment I get into the car. I scan around for Wesley again. I could run, hide, and call Jack. But that wouldn't help Wesley. He could be dead by then.

I get into the car.

The man in the driver's seat is smaller than the Big Man. I clutch my crossbody bag to my chest. As soon as Big Man slides into the car behind me, the driver pulls off.

"Where are we going?" I ask, only to be met with silence. "Can you at least tell me your name?"

Nothing. The ride continues and fear continues

gnawing at my core. Is Wesley okay? Did they kill him already? Why do these men want him?

"Give me your phone," Big Man suddenly says.

"I-I'd rather not."

When he reaches into his waistband, I snap, "All right, all right. No need to get all threatening again. Here. You could've at least said please."

He doesn't reply as he rolls down the window and tosses my phone outside.

"Wha—hey, *asshole!*" I shove his shoulder before my good sense reminds me *not* to agitate someone with a gun. "You owe me a new phone!"

All he does is stare at me with a slightly annoyed expression.

Great. I'm definitely going to die.

After ten minutes of driving, the car stops in front of what looks like an office building. It has character, noting its old age, but possesses plenty of modern updates. Big Man opens the door for me and leads us to the elevator. I note the emergency exit in the far-left corner and hope it can be useful later. We take the elevator to the fifth floor. I lock my knees to keep from buckling.

The parting doors reveal a room of cubicles. The personal materials and files on the desks tell me it's an active business, but I can't decipher what kind. When Big Man puts me into an office, I collapse into one of the chairs, massaging my knees. No phone. No Wesley. No idea where I am.

I startle when the door opens behind me. A man strides inside, a pleasant expression on his bearded face. He wears a suit without a jacket, tattoos snaking out from his wrists onto his hands. I can tell he's the boss by how relaxed he is.

"Miss Laffley. I'm quite sorry for the theatrics."

I rise. "Where's Wesley?"

"Mr. Troutbeck is preoccupied. But as soon as we've conducted our business, you can see him again."

I exhale slowly. This isn't Lo Revínastí.

"And who is we?"

The man startles, flicking his head as if annoyed with himself. "Oh—excuse my manners." He extends a hand. "Arlo Serrano."

I gently shake his hand. "How do you know who I am?"

Arlo approaches a minibar and uncaps a glass bottle. "Well, I noticed that Mr. Troutbeck has been something of a... detail for you. A bodyguard. I can tell you're a client of his, but I don't know why."

Perhaps my title could help—offer me protection of a sort. But I shouldn't reveal any information until I see Wesley. I strengthen my voice despite my fear. "I want to see Wesley. *Now.*"

He tilts his head, his expression reluctant. "I've answered *your* question. It's only fair you answer mine. For example, we've done some research, but the only thing curious about you is your birth certificate. There's no name listed under mother, and we can't find any trace of hospital records in your birth city, either. Tell me, why?"

"I don't know," I say truthfully. I don't know why Mom isn't on my certificate or how she managed to keep it hidden. The public might want to see it for proof she's my mom. I make a mental note to ask Aunt Beverly later. If I ever see her again.

"A normal girl," Arlo continues. "A college graduate—congratulations, by the way."

After giving attitude to the man who threw my phone from the window, I ensure to remain somewhat polite with Arlo. I'm keenly aware of my limited knowledge, but he's dangerous. That much I know.

"Thank you."

"And yet you're important enough here to need a security detail."

"I—I'm not at liberty to say."

He nods, sipping what looks like whisky. "I understand."

"What business do you have with Wesley?"

With a pleasant smile, he echoes, "I'm not at liberty to say."

I stare at him as an uneasy silence falls over the room. He's at least middle-aged, but the wrinkles don't deter from his intimidating nature.

My stomach drops when I hear a muffled *"NINA!"*

"Wesley?" I peer through the office's glass wall for a hint of Wesley, but I don't see him. I look at Arlo, my patience vanishing. If he wants to stop me, he'll have to kill me. I yank the door open and hurry toward the voice.

"I wouldn't go that way," Arlo says cryptically. The fact that he's not following me intensifies my fear. This is exactly what he wants me to do.

CHAPTER FORTY-THREE
WESLEY

A pedestrian had bumped my shoulder. Then everything went black.

When I come to, I immediately realize that I was drugged. The prickle in my shoulder confirms it. My blood runs cold at the new environment.

Nina.

I scream her name despite the grogginess. I'm tied to a chair, my wrists bound by zip ties, in a plain room—an office. There's a window behind me, aimed at a brick wall, a desk covered in an array of blades and weapons, and a clear tarp under me. The door in front of me opens, and relief floods my chest when Nina enters.

"Wesley," she whimpers.

No one comes in behind her, so I say, *"Run."*

Confusion crosses her eyes as she tugs at my restraints. "What? I'm not leaving—"

"Stop," I bark. "You have to run *now.*"

The dread prickles back into my body when two men enter. "Too late," the first man says with a glass of brown liquor in hand. I recognize him instantly.

Arlo fucking Serrano. The brother of my dead boss, Santiago Serrano.

It doesn't make sense. They *hated* each other. Santiago discussed making Arlo one of my targets, but never got around to doing it. After the explosion, Arlo absorbed his business. They have no loyalty, and I didn't kill his brother.

"Leave her out of this, Arlo," I grit. Whatever *this* is. My head spins from the aftermath of the tranquilizer and my wrists ache from the zip ties. I should start dissociating, filing through memories and safe spaces for the inevitable pain ahead. But I can't. Not with Nina here.

"You know me! Oh, I'm flattered." He leans down to eye level, his blue eyes clouded by wrinkles staring back at me. In a raspy voice, he says, "It's him, all right."

"Fuck off. Just let her go so you can tell me what the hell you want." I have nothing for him. I worked in silence, made no alliances, and therefore hold no hidden information.

Arlo rises and steps to Nina, who wraps her arms around herself. She shivers when he brushes a curl away from her face. "What do you know about your bodyguard, Miss Laffley?"

She doesn't answer.

"Would you like to know who he is?" he presses. "Who he *really* is?"

My chest caves. I never met him before, but Santiago always labeled his little brother as a drama-seeking pain in the ass.

I want to panic and tell her not to listen to him. But what's the point? I should've known this would happen. I tricked myself into thinking there would be an easier way for her to find out.

Nina still doesn't answer, but it won't stop him. I shut

my eyes and brace for my newfound peace to shatter, knowing she'll never look at me the same.

"A few years ago," Arlo continues, "political deaths among my enemies and associates alike started looking suspiciously... *unsuspicious*. Contract killings were not unheard of or popular. You wanted someone dead, you sent your men to take care of it. But this man... this man murdered without humanity. No one knew his real name; not many knew his face, so everyone called him El Revalté. The Ghost." He downs the remainder of his drink and circles me like a predator. My two worlds are blending and I don't know how to stop them. Nina and the underground. Light and darkness. Shades of grey filter around me and I need to do what I can to get out of here without her hating me in the end.

"The day my brother died, he told me he was El Revalté's boss and contracted him out—on physical records only, if at all. No trace. My brother knew he was going to die that day and wanted to tell me The Ghost's real name. And after a little research, there he was. The Ghost was none other than Wesley Dominik Troutbeck. An army ranger moonlighting at a hitman. It could be a movie."

Serrated dread coils around my throat. Despite being tied to a chair, I feel like I'm slipping and falling into darkness.

My night with Nina was the best of my life even if I had the burdening truth on my shoulders. For the night, she was my salvation. She was *mine*. Mine to please. Mine to love. But the look she gives me now is the exact one I fought to never see. Disbelief, shock, and, worst of all, fear.

"What do you want?" she asks Arlo, and I smother my slight surprise.

He claps a hand on my shoulder, but Nina is the one

who flinches. "I only need a conversation with him. Maximo will make you comfortable right next door if we need you."

"What—no!" she exclaims while being forced out the door by Maximo—who's twice my damn size. I bite my tongue, suppressing the fury building in my chest. Thrashing and yelling won't help either of us.

Arlo sets his empty glass on the desk and moves in front of me. "I understand why you like her."

"If she has so much as a mark or sheds a single drop of blood, I will rip out your throat." My deadpan, almost bored tone throws him off.

He stares, face tight in thought. "I thought you would be scarier than this."

"I'm a man of my word, and your faith in that won't change the outcome. Now ask your goddamn question before I lose my patience."

Arlo crosses his arms. "Who killed Santi?"

"An explosion," I lie.

"I have an eyewitness who swore he was shot. If my brother wasn't shot, he would've gotten out of that building alive."

"What do you care? You took over his company."

"I *care* because our poor mother is distraught beyond belief—and no one kills my brother but me."

He's a businessman; he should know hubris kills.

"If your eyewitness swears he was shot, why didn't they tell you who it was?"

"Died before he could," Arlo says with a shrug, lowering onto a stool with a relaxed demeanor. "And I believe *you* can tell me who shot him."

I'd rather die than give Jack up. He shot my former boss

in cold blood before I lit the fire. Jack isn't only the reason I'm alive; he's the reason I'm free.

"I can't."

Arlo huffs. "I don't care that you snitched on my brother. Thanks to you, I'm a lot richer. I am here because my mother is a pain in my ass and even if you end up dead without telling me what I need to know, I can tell her I did everything I could. So let's wrap this up so I can go on with my week, yeah?"

In the distance, I hear car horns. We haven't left the city at least. Efficiently drugging me required three people at least. If Arlo treats this interrogation as a bump in his day, he has little back-up. But if he heeded my reputation at all, he'd have more.

I level a glare. He revealed everything to Nina out of boredom. He liked watching my life fall apart.

I don't know how I'm getting out of here, but when I do, I'll kill him just for that.

CHAPTER FORTY-FOUR

NINA

Maximo shoves and locks me into an office next door.

A sob rips from my throat. Wesley has killed people. He *hunted* them. My stomach turns as I realize that the same hands that caressed me had taken lives.

Had he strangled someone the way Anton Robert tried with me?

I touch my neck with trembling fingers, shutting my eyes as tears escape.

But all I can picture is how attentive he was to me that night. The necklace, my hair pins, washing my hair, playing a card game.

That's my Wesley.

I trust him. The pleading in his eyes before Maximo took me away was genuine. *He* is genuine. I hold my hand against my stomach and steady my breath.

I can't stay here and let them torture Wesley. The thought of him getting any more scars fills me with rage.

The room has a tiny window and a desk with a jacket

strewn over the arm of a small couch. I scan the room for an idea—anything—that might help us. Arlo said to put me next door, and we only walked about a hundred feet down the hallway. I crank open the window only to see nothing between the ledge and concrete five floors below. With a huff, I shut the window and empty my crossbody bag onto the desk. Hand lotion, hand sanitizer, a lighter, a hair tie, my wallet, and a bracelet. I bought the lighter and bracelet at a souvenir shop; the former is probably more helpful here.

I need a distraction and a way to get to Wesley. I could try to unlock the door with the bobby pin, but I know nothing about picking locks. The lighter could be useful; do I really want to set a fire? I glance around the office again. It's not abandoned; someone works in here at least sporadically. There's a mug, a cup of pens, and a notepad. I yank open the drawers to find sticky notes, more pens, an empty stapler, and—jackpot. Literally. I pull out a bottle of half-empty Jack Daniels whisky. If I go the fire route, this will be essential.

Possible distraction, check.

Now, I need to reach Wesley.

The window isn't an option. Is there an air duct? Hopefully one like the movies, large and sturdy and a direct path to where I need to go.

Yes, but no.

In the upper corner of the room, there's an air duct that looks about as wide as my hips. And not an inch bigger.

"Fuck."

It's not screwed in, so I only have to tug it from the wall after standing on the chair. I perch as high as I can on my toes, straining my ear for any sign of other voices.

"Who was—"

The distant voice, followed by muffled noises, is faint but I know it's Arlo. His extreme rasp is distinct. After slowly pushing the couch in front of the door and the desk under the duct, I tie my hair into a low bun. I climb up high and crawl into the tight space.

I hate letting any part of my skin touch a public chair or wall, and I'm shoving my entire body into a building's air duct that likely hasn't been cleaned in years and has dead bugs—or worse—inside.

A shudder runs through me as the space gets tighter. *Go someplace else. Picture somewhere new.* As I wiggle ahead toward the voices, I squint and pretend I'm under a blanket. A really large fucking blanket. Sparks slice up my core as panic strikes. I can't.

Not here.

I pause and shut my eyes, flicking back to my night with Wesley. My breath staggers in my chest. It was more than the sex. It was the comfort that wrapped around my heart from knowing I'm loved.

But the quick, cutting reminder of what Arlo is doing to Wesley urges me ahead. Anger is a much better motivator.

After ten minutes of wiggling, I finally reach the room where Wesley is. I passed a couple of suspicious... *things* on the way—a dead roach or something alike—but I closed my eyes each time. There's an alcove in the duct that reveals Wesley, Arlo, and Maximo below.

"You want this over with, *I* want this over with. Tell me who killed Santiago."

Wesley says nothing. Maximo winds back and punches him across the face. In the stomach. In the chest. I squeeze my eyes shut and fight the sob threatening to release at the sounds of Wesley's labored breathing.

Behind my eyelids, I see the evening we spent at his

grandparents' house. I see him staring back at me, promising that no one would ever hurt me again. The invasive sounds of flesh punching flesh blur the memories. Wesley coughs, struggling to catch his breath. I hear Arlo chuckle.

"Following you the past month was fun," Arlo says. "Watching you fall in love with the woman you're supposed to protect. Tricking yourself into thinking it could last. You're ex-communicado. A shunned soldier. What was it Santi said to me? Ah." He lowers in front of Wesley. *"He's useful for one thing. Killing who I tell him to.* It's interesting. Everyone says you're the deadliest man there is, but all I watched you do is hold Miss Laffley's purse and look at her like she's the eighth wonder of the world." He leans closer. "Tell me who shot my brother so I don't have to kill her the same way."

Wesley lifts his head and spits in the man's face. Apprehension curls inside me. Maximo drags a blade across Wesley's chest, his agonizing grunts echoing through the room. I clamp a hand over my mouth, gritting my teeth.

This second, nothing is stopping them. I'm powerless, just like I was the night Anton attacked me. My gut twists painfully. No. I refuse to be that person again.

With a steadying breath, I creep back through the ducts. It creaks with every inch. My hands sweat and tremble through the time it takes me to return.

I take long, deep breaths when I reach the office again. My head spins, and I grip the desk to control my breathing. I don't do this stuff. This spy shit. *Arson.* But as I chastise myself, I snatch the trashcan and start shredding and balling up the notebook paper. I dump in every flammable thing I can find.

Not only am I setting fire to a room I'm locked into, but I'll then proceed to crawl through air ducts that I can only pray won't collapse under my weight and trap me in a building I set fire to.

No pressure.

I set the trashcan on the couch so the fire could latch onto something big. I pour the remainder of the Jack Daniels in the can and fling a few drops on the cushions. People could get hurt. People could *die*. The sound of Wesley's pain burns into my mind. The cryptic threat of whether Maximo will kill me is haunting.

What other choice do I have?

I roll up a sheet of paper and set the end on fire. The other items burst into flames when I drop it into the trashcan. No time to waste. I crawl back into the duct with the sounds of crackling following me. By the time I return to Wesley, the fire alarm goes off. I cry out at the echoing siren piercing my eardrums. Maximo and Arlo leave to investigate.

After twisting at an awkward angle, I kick the grate from the wall and slide through, my skin painfully scraping against the edges. I drop and push back to land on my butt as air pushes back into my lungs. The alarm continues blaring. I scramble to my feet and snatch a knife from the table, slicing it through the binds around Wesley's wrists. Tears well in my eyes when I lower in front of his bloodied and bruised body.

"Wesley," I plead, dropping the weapon and taking his face in both hands. "Wake up." I brush over his swollen brow, my heart pounding in my throat.

His eyes flutter as he comes to. "Wha—Nina? What happened?"

"I had to do something."

Wesley pinches the bridge of his nose as he gets a hold of himself. "No, you should've run—"

"It's done now." I hand him the knife. "Get us out of here."

CHAPTER FORTY-FIVE

WESLEY

I thought Nina pulled the fire alarm, but I pause at the burning stench.

I cut a look at her. "Did you start a fire?"

She shrugs. "Maybe."

I get up and start gathering all of the weapons I can fit on my person. The .22 caliber handgun has four bullets. There's no time to apologize or beg for forgiveness. I'm certain Arlo already left out of caution, but his men will be infiltrating any second to kill me—*us*.

"Do you trust me?" I ask Nina.

She blinks. "What? Yes."

"Listen to me." I take her arm and lead her toward the corner of the room. "Then I need you to do *everything* I say, no questions asked, no arguing, no hesitation. Can you do that?"

Fright fills her eyes, but she nods. I have to wade through this problem in limbo—something I've never done before. I shouldn't turn on auto-pilot and kill my way out. Not only do I want to escape with fewer bodies because of Nina, but for myself. I don't want it to be my first instinct, but it has to be for now. The most important thing is getting her out of here.

Still, the less she sees, the better.

"Crouch down," I order, footsteps gathering outside the door. At least three, maybe four people. When she does, I hand her a knife. The alarm smothers the footsteps, but I feel the vibrations. "Stay here and close your eyes no matter what you hear."

"What—"

"No questions asked. Keep them closed *no matter* what you hear."

The door opens, and I point and shoot before even turning to the first assailant. The bullet hits his stomach. As he falls, I walk forward and shoot the second assailant in the head. I send a knife into the heart of the first one, eliminating him entirely.

I lunge at the door where a third man steps in, gun in hand. I snatch his wrist, yanking him closer and pressing the gun under his chin before pulling the trigger. My head buzzes from the sound. I shove his body toward the next assailant entering and use that distraction to take him out with my last bullet to the head.

The fifth and final assailant barrels into the room and I manage to push his hands up the second before he pulls the trigger. I hear the bullet strike the ceiling as I take a knife from my pocket to stab him in the gut.

When he doubles over, I meet him in the middle by plunging the blade under his jaw.

Arlo could've given me a challenge, at the very least.

I trade guns before hurrying to Nina, whose eyes are still closed. She flinches when I come close, her grip on the knife tightening.

"It's me; it's okay. Keep your eyes closed." I guide her up

with a hand over her eyes as we wade through the bloody surroundings. "Just a little longer."

I remove my hand once we're out of the room.

"Here!" she exclaims, running to the emergency exit. "This leads out front."

We rush down the stairs. Pure adrenaline keeps the pain from crippling me. My eyebrow and chest throb. It's a good thing I wore black today or my shirt would show every drop of blood. Not that the sliced fabric over my heart ruins it enough.

Arlo might be calling reinforcements; we need to get underground fast. When the stairwell dumps us onto the street, I pull Nina into the alley. Firetruck sirens blare in the distance, getting closer with each second.

"Where are we going?" she asks, and I don't answer; I'm still figuring it out.

Maximo appears from behind the dumpster, and I manage to grab his shirt collar before he can tackle me. We crash into the brick wall and I hear Nina gasp as pain erupts from the wound in my chest.

"RUN!" I yell to her before his fist collides with my face, sending flashes of white across my vision. I land an uppercut and a punch to the kidney that would knock over most. But Maximo, befittingly named after Maldana's god of war, is a freakishly large man who gets me on the ground far too easily. I grapple with him above me, receiving two more punches until his head suddenly jerks aside, blood spattering onto my face as he's bludgeoned by an object.

Stunned, I nearly get trapped beneath his unconscious body. Nina stands to my right, panting, with a metal pipe in hand. Her hair is frizzy but her jaw is tight.

"I told you to run," I say.

She drops the weapon and offers a hand to help me up.

"I will do everything you say—except leave you behind." She stares at Maximo's limp body as blood spills from the wound. "Is he dead?"

"Brain damage? Yes. Kill him? No." *Maybe.* But that won't make her feel better. At her shaken expression, I snatch his arm and reveal his tattoo of a snake wrapped around a cross. "Look. This tattoo means he either works or used to work with Vitalis. They're human traffickers."

They're the organization that Santiago did business with, the reason I went to the authorities.

She inhales a sharp breath and defiantly says, "I hope I killed him."

CHAPTER FORTY-SIX

NINA

We speed-walk through the streets, sticking to alleys where we can. My heart has been in my throat for the last five minutes. Wesley has his arm around me, his head bowed.

"Can you tell me where we're going now?" I ask as he guides us through a cramped outdoor market.

"We have to get underground, but there are more people following us."

A pang of fright echoes through me. I want this to *end*. "Are you sure?"

"Positive." He glances over his shoulder while we turn a corner. "Just stay calm."

I hold him tighter. "Easier said than done."

This is a market I'd peruse for souvenirs for Raven or unique dresses for myself. Never in a thousand years would I think I'd escape a group of murderous criminals while under the arm of the hitman-turned-bodyguard I fell in love with. I'm ready to wake up in my bed at any moment.

When we reach an intersection, Wesley suddenly shoves me as a man lurches into the space between us. The crowd opens up as he defends himself from the attacker. I frantically search for someone, something, *anything* that might help.

People look at me both frightened and confused, but I grab a mango from a fruit stand and chuck it at the man attacking Wesley. It hits him in the ribs, distracting him for a fraction of a second that Wesley uses to get the upper hand.

But before I can run toward him, someone grabs a fistful of my hair and yanks me back hard enough to tumble a few feet away. My knee scrapes on the concrete as I land. Behind the man who threw me, I spot another one headed for Wesley.

"Wesley, look out!" I scream.

I crawl back as the assailant in front of me walks closer, but an elderly woman with a headscarf slaps him and starts reprimanding him in Maldanian. He stares at her, baffled. An old man steps up to him with a baseball bat in hand, also scolding him in very quick Maldanian. The only word I can understand is *woman*.

A few more people step up with the same attitude. I watch in astonishment as a young woman helps me to my feet and gestures for me to go.

Wesley.

I sprint around the crowd of disapproving elders toward Wesley, who staggers to his feet. "Are you okay?" I ask, steadying him and glancing at the two writhing men on the ground.

"Come on."

I jog behind him out of the market, my panic worsening with each limping step he takes. "Do you need a break?"

He only shakes his head as we turn down a populated

alleyway. He approaches a homeless man among a cart of foraged items. "We need to see Adonis."

The homeless man, with a hood over his head despite the heat, brushes us off. "Ne sémero pino tu milas di."

I don't know what you're talking about.

Wesley catches his arm before he leaves, revealing the mark below his collarbone for a few seconds. The man rethinks his decision, and when he leads us through the alley, I realize that the mark was Wesley's burn scar—a brand. Fear threatens to coil around my limbs and lock them in place. How horrific of a business was he in where they *branded* him?

I hesitate to follow the man down into a cellar, so I clutch Wesley's hand as darkness closes around us. The damp, musty stench of garbage sticks to my skin.

But after unlocking a door, we step into a hallway that's the complete opposite of where we came from. Sconces flank the dimly lit corridor. Its walls are clean and the rug beneath my feet looks expensive. The musty smell lingers, but it's manageable. We approach a warehouse-like room with a large rectangular table in the center. Few people scatter around as if hanging out.

The homeless man—who might not be homeless after all—approaches another and bows his head to speak. This one is middle-aged with jeans and a plain T-shirt on. Tattoos spiral up his arms. He looks at Wesley and me, taking in our appearance.

"As I live and breathe."

Wesley squeezes my hand before whispering, "Wait here." He approaches the man. "Adonis."

"What can I do for you?"

"Shelter. Just for the night."

"Shelter from who?"

"Arlo Serrano," Wesley says, and offers nothing more until Adonis doesn't reply. "He wants information he believes I can provide. We only need a phone to make a call and a place to stay for the night. I'm not asking for any weapons."

"You want me to get involved in the affairs of a Serrano." He chuckles. "You're a rat."

"No, I'm just a man who hates being lied to."

A rat? Arlo didn't mention anything like this. It dawns on me there's still a lot I don't know about Wesley, and it's unsettling. Adonis crosses his arms, raking a gaze over me. My feet ache, I probably have blood on me, and I'm scared to look at my hair.

"Who is she?"

"My client. I'm her bodyguard."

"Who is important enough to be *your* client?"

Wesley meets my gaze, hesitating. If he thinks the truth can help us, then so be it. The world finding out who gave birth to me seems like such a small concern after standing near death so violently in the last couple of hours. I give him a definitive nod.

"The firstborn daughter of the late Queen Ophelia."

Adonis barely reacts. "The queen had no children."

"No. She had two daughters who grew up in the United States."

I would've assumed that he'd need proof, or at least would put up some type of argument because of my race. Perhaps Wesley is important enough in this business where his word is enough.

"It looks like we have royalty in our midst," Adonis says with a slight smile. "Everyone knows the rules here. No harm will come to you." He steps closer to me, and I resist cowering from the mesmerized glint in his black eyes. "I hope you will remember the mercy I've granted you here, Your Highness."

My voice is small. "I will. Thank you."

Relief starts to prickle through me as we wade toward our room for the night, but a woman cuts off our path. I feel disgusting, covered in dirt, blood, and dust, and my patience is thinning.

"It really is you," the woman says, leaning against the wall with her arms crossed, black hair draped over a shoulder.

Wesley sighs. "Daria."

"I thought I would never see you again."

My skin prickles. *Ex-girlfriend?*

"If it was up to me, you wouldn't," he says.

Maybe not.

"I'll pretend that doesn't hurt." Daria pouts. "You're in town on business?"

"No."

She hesitates as if expecting elaboration. This time, he doesn't offer it. She clears her throat, eyes sharpening. "You got out. You should've run halfway across the world."

"Maldana is my home."

She scoffs. "Then it's no wonder you're back."

"I'm not back," he grits. "What are you even doing here? You hate Kosita."

"Maybe I was hoping you'd return." From her lustful stare at him, my suspicions are confirmed. They had a relationship. Daria slowly assesses me, and I try not to squirm or hide behind Wesley.

"Who's this? You haven't introduced me to your friend."

Every now and again, I might question myself or envy another woman's style or figure, but this woman downright frightens me. There isn't a single hair out of place and I'm sure she could kill me without chipping her nail polish.

"She's *very* beautiful," Daria purrs, reaching out as if to touch one of my loose curls. "Hi—"

Wesley snatches her wrist, its painful grip making her wince and rip away. She sends him a glare. "Fine. Message received."

He leads us away from her without another word. But when I peek over my shoulder, I spot her studying me from head to toe, her expression tight.

CHAPTER FORTY-SEVEN

NINA

A plaque outside our room for the night reads *Presidential Suite*, and the interior lives up to the name. The expensive, sleek design is all black.

It's good to know princess privilege extends underground.

Someone drops by with a cart, and Wesley accepts it as if he'd been waiting. It has a stack of clothes, socks, a first aid kit, some canned food, and a phone.

I hold up the last item. "A phone?"

"A burner," Wesley says. "I'll be able to call Jack and arrange for a pick-up first thing in the morning."

Life outside of the last few hours falls in on me. My family must be worried sick. I hand him the phone. "Can you do that now? And make sure he tells my family that I said I'm okay?"

As he makes the call, I head into the bathroom to unpack the first aid bag. To my right is a walk-in shower with glass walls. I shiver at what atrocities might have been done to afford designs like that.

I grimace at my reflection. I need a shower. Dirt

smudges along my arms, legs, and face. I tame my frizzy hair by redoing a bun, this one at the crown of my head. I clean the tiny scrape on my knee, marveling at the fact that it's the only wound I got out of this tumultuous day.

"Is everything okay? What did Jack say?" I ask when Wesley appears behind me. I watch him through the mirror. "Did you tell him to talk to my family?"

"Of course. We set a time and place to meet tomorrow morning. Six a.m."

"Why can't we go now?"

"It's getting dark, and Arlo expected us to come here, so he probably has his people outside."

"If he knew we were coming here, then why didn't we go somewhere else?" I wail, and I clamp my mouth shut when he looks at his torn shirt. I can't focus. "Shit, right. That's the whole reason I unpacked this thing. Take your shirt off."

"Don't worry about me; I'll take care of it." He brushes me off and reaches for the gauze.

I smack his hand away. "It's not up to you. Shirt, off."

He sighs, too exhausted to argue with me as he tugs it over his head. Bruises blossom up and down his body. "Yes, ma'am."

He takes a few painkillers as I wash my hands. I fill the spray bottle with water to clean the blood around the two gashes on his torso—one on his chest and the other on his ribs. He winces when I peel off a piece of fabric that stuck to the open wound.

I crinkle my nose. "Sorry."

He shakes his head. "No, it's okay. I'm fine."

He has two slits in his body and a face of bruises and cuts. He's not fine. I use a gentler touch, savoring the feel of his coarse chest hair under my fingertips. The thought of

Daria, or any other woman, seeing Wesley naked or sleeping with him makes my stomach twist. I clear my throat.

"Daria was your girlfriend?"

He blinks as if surprised. "I, uh—if you could call it that."

My face warms. "Friends with benefits, then."

"That's not what I—"

"It's okay," I interject, masking the slight tremor in my voice as I move to the cut on his ribcage. "I get it—she's stunning. Deadly, too, by the looks of it... That's your type?"

Maybe I was just a bump along the way. There's a whole new side to him, a violent one, and what if I don't fit? What if he remembers the thrill and doesn't want me anymore? He stiffens as I flush the open skin with water. Droplets slip down his waist and I pretend that desire isn't curling inside me.

"You're my type," he argues, his hand brushing my hip. "Only you."

"Even though I'm not some bad ass who knows how to kill a man in twenty different ways?" I lean down to softly blow on the wound.

Wesley releases a sharp, shuddering breath. *"Fuck,"* he mumbles, and I smirk at the goosebumps pouring over his skin. He tightens his grip. "I don't know, angel. You've already killed me a hundred times."

Butterflies break free in my chest. He grazes my chin with his finger, prodding me to look at him. Warmth prickles through me at the mere sight of his face. Even with a cut on his brow, a bruised cheek, and a bruised eye, he's handsome beyond reason. His deep-set eyes, thick brows, feather-soft hair, his scruff. *I'm so in love with him.*

"As long as you don't hate me," he says softly, "I'm not going anywhere."

His direct demeanor knocks me into reality. I shiver as if doused with cold water. Arlo's words replay in my mind.

This man murdered without humanity.

I inhale shakily. "Answer my questions, then. No arguing. No hesitation. Can you do that?" I ask, echoing what he said to me earlier. It's a subtle challenge. *I trusted you. Now it's your turn.*

"Yes," he whispers.

I open my mouth, but no words come out. Once I ask this question, it'll never be the same. "I—were you... were you an assassin?"

His Adam's apple bobs as his breath hitches. "Yes."

It's chilling to admit that it doesn't truly frighten me. If Wesley is supposedly a bad person, what does that make Arlo? What does it make the people who branded him?

I brush my finger over the diamond mark on his shoulder. "Why did they brand you?"

He hesitates. "Contract killings and organized crime in southern Europe have been starting to work together more. Adonis owns the underground and tries to stay neutral. It's a place where business can be conducted without violence. There's no fighting of any kind, and this mark is that oath."

"Why'd you... quit?"

Do assassins put in their two-week notice? I'll keep the second question to myself despite my growing curiosity.

"My boss—he lied to me, so I turned him in."

"What did he lie about?"

"He said he was only trafficking weapons. He wasn't," Wesley explains. I stare at him, waiting for the end of that sentence. "Girls. He was trafficking young girls."

I blanch and take an unconscious step back. "What? And you—"

"Turned him in," Wesley insists. "Gathered enough intel to put him in jail."

"But now he's dead—and Arlo wants to know who did it. Do you know who?"

He shakes his head. "Don't ask me that."

Plausible deniability. I don't argue. There's no ethical dilemma of whether he killed women, not after meeting Daria. "Did you... did you ever kill kids?"

"*No,*" he snaps. "Never."

I shrink under his glare. "Don't look at me like that! I have no idea how this works."

"It's why I wanted to be the one to—" He cuts himself off with a sigh. His gaze lowers. "That's not the part of me I want you to know."

Wesley has given me so much of himself, and I see everything he is and can be, but he's hanging on by a thread. He's trying to get us out of here and protect me from more than physical violence.

I shift closer. "Last question." Unlike my sister, I'm not one for confrontation. But I need to know. "Are you in love with me?"

Desperation fills his eyes. "More than you know."

I swallow the emotion lodging in my throat and close the distance between us, capturing his lips. Despite his rough exterior, his kiss is soft. I shiver when his hand slides to the back of my neck. A territorial feeling rushes into me. This is my Wesley. Gentle, passionate, *mine*. He doesn't belong to Daria or this line of business—only me.

I slip my fingers down his chest to his belt. Before I can unbuckle it, he stops me.

"Wait," he whispers, breathless.

"What's wrong?"

"I—we can't."

I blink. "What?"

"We can't," he repeats.

I check his bandages, ensuring it hasn't bled through and the tape is secure. "Does it hurt?"

"No, it's not that... Your, uh—your adrenaline, it's starting to crash." He takes my hand, and I notice that it's trembling. In fact, my entire body is tense. I roll my neck, exhaling in satisfaction at the crack. He kisses my fingers. "Today was a lot. Your emotions are heightened; I don't want to take advantage of you."

Today, I saw things I never thought I would. I've been out of my element for months, but Wesley is the one decision I've always been sure of. I tighten my hold. "Yesterday, today, tomorrow. Adrenaline or not, it doesn't matter—I'll still want you."

He sighs, touching my forehead with his. He squeezes my hip. "I'm trying to be a gentleman."

The rejection stings, but I tamp down the feeling and step away. "Fine," I quip, holding his gaze as I unbutton my shorts. "While *you* be a gentleman"—I slide them off before pulling my T-shirt over my head—"*I'm* taking a hot shower."

I smirk at how hard he's trying not to break eye contact. I move to turn on the shower, his heated gaze burning my skin. It only takes seconds for the water to warm up. After stripping my bra and underwear—a bit slower than necessary—I step into the walk-in shower. Sex aside, the water and steam ease my aching body. I release an involuntary sigh. Behind me, Wesley remains in the same spot I left him.

I peek around the corner and point to the wrapped bar of soap next to him. "Can you hand me that?"

"Uh—yeah." He snaps into reality, unwrapping it before bringing it to me. He leans on the edge of the glass wall and watches as I scrub my skin. He bites his lip, gaze frozen. "I don't know what I did to deserve such a perfect view like this."

My stomach prickles. Wesley is the first man I feel comfortable being completely naked around. I'm not in a rush to divert his attention. Each part of my body, literally and figuratively, is seen, loved, and worshiped by Wesley.

I lean in as if to kiss him, pressing my breast against his arm. "No one's asking you to be a gentleman."

He captures my lips roughly, his tongue prodding and teeth nipping. I giggle as he struggles to get off his shoes and pants as quickly as possible.

"Wait!" With a hand on his shoulder, I stop him from entering. I wince, chiding myself for not thinking this through. "Your bandages. They shouldn't get wet."

"Fuck the bandages. I've waited too long for you." He backs me against the wall, connecting our lips as the water sprays on us.

I pull from this kiss and lift a stern finger. *"Don't get my hair wet."*

CHAPTER FORTY-EIGHT
WESLEY

Sleep won't come to me tonight.

The gun I swiped from one of Arlo's mercenaries sits on the nightstand with six bullets inside. I wanted to have it prepared in my hand all night, but Nina's uncomfortable with a gun in the bed.

Rolled into a burrito, she sleeps soundly beside me. She twitches and whimpers, telling me she's dreaming. When she cries, *"Stop,"* I know it's a nightmare.

"Nina," I whisper, a soft hand on her arm.

She flinches awake, rolling into my ready arms once she remembers where we are.

"Nightmare?"

She nods into my neck. "Do they ever stop?"

I smother an exasperated smile, pressing a kiss to her head. "If they do, you'll be the first person I tell."

I feel her sigh and snuggle closer. My body warms as she kisses my throat. It doesn't take long for her to fall back asleep and for me to resume staring at the door. Even now, with the woman I love in my arms, the peace doesn't feel permanent. I'm not convinced someone won't bust into the room and try to take her from me.

No one attacks us on our route to meet Jack.

We don't come across any of Arlo's men—that we know of. I find no signs of being followed. He expected us to go to Adonis; it's why he sent three of his people to take us out in the market. For some reason, Nina and I were unbothered the moment we stepped foot above ground.

Daria.

The name hits me fast and sharp. She pounced seconds after I spoke with Adonis. She must have overheard and snitched. I hate that I'm surprised; nothing but frigid steel lies under her skin.

She probably sold him information about what she overheard. Arlo likely wanted to see where we go, if it's true. After that, she'll have earned some of his trust. It's not enough for her to be a snitch; everything is a game to her.

Nina's family folds her into a sobbing hug the moment she steps out of the car. She gives me a knowing look over Maia's shoulder as I walk inside with Jack.

"Who do you think told him?" Jack asks.

"My money's on Colin. Most likely to get caught and fold in interrogation."

Colin was another hitman who helped get Santiago in return for when I got him out of a conundrum in Barcelona. Never cared much for him.

Mason, Gregory, and Silas are waiting in Jack's office for the meeting, all of our phones collected and bodies scanned for wires.

"I need to speak with you alone first," I tell Jack. There's a lot to debrief, but I have to tell him about Nina and me. As the others leave, I rub my hands together, exhaling a long breath. My stomach growls. The canned food for dinner last night didn't cut it. I ache for a proper meal.

"What is it?"

"Nina and I slept together," I deadpan. No time to sugarcoat.

Jack blinks, confused. "No, you didn't."

"Sir—"

"No," he interjects, "you *didn't*. Because you respect me, Beck. You remembered that I put *my* new job at risk to get you this position and you didn't do the number one thing I told you *not* to do."

"It's more than that. I'm in love with her."

He grimaces as if insulted. "That makes no fucking difference!"

"It makes every difference. I wouldn't tell you if it was a one-time thing." I step closer. "When I say that I love her, that also means there isn't anything I won't do to keep her safe. Arlo could have killed her because he wants answers from me on something you did."

Jack blanches. "What are you saying?"

Guilt starts to build inside of me. He put a lot on the line to help me after I closed one of his years-long investigations within two months.

And then I slept with my client and the future queen of Maldana. I hate the feeling of betraying him, but Nina being hurt—or worse—is a deal-breaker.

"Arlo knows how I feel about her," I explain, "and if he finds a way to use her as leverage, *there isn't anything I won't do to keep her safe.*"

CHAPTER FORTY-NINE

NINA

I take another shower once returning to the palace.

My family's emotions and relief weren't a comfort. After being attacked by Anton, their concern for me doubled, and now it tripled. My stomach twists; I don't like being the source of any distress.

With my hair and body washed, I lower onto one of the steps leading to the bed and tuck my knees to my chest. For what feels like the first in a while, I'm alone. I inhale a deep breath and shut my eyes. No lawnmowers, cars, planes, or voices. It's quiet.

I drop my head. Memories flash across the back of my eyelids of Wesley being cut and punched. His painful groans. His black-and-blue face. My chest wrenches from those few seconds I tried to wake him up.

And Arlo is coming back for him.

I've done everything for my family. If not for Dad, I wouldn't have quit volleyball, picked a five-year program and worked myself into the ground, or even gone to school in-state. I could've fought for those things, but Dad's will to argue was always stronger than mine. I know Maia didn't ask me to be the peacekeeper; keeping our little family flowing easily has always been my job. Dad made sure of that.

I quickly step into my sneakers and head toward the voices in the sitting room of this wing. My parents, Maia, and Aunt Beverly suddenly cut their discussion short, perking once I appear in the threshold.

"How do you feel?" Ruby asks.

"Fine," I say. "Do any of you know where Wesley is? I need to talk to him."

Aunt Beverly rises, her knee-length dress swishing around her. "Mr. Troutbeck is in a meeting with Jack."

"Where?"

She stiffens. "It's best to let our security team handle this matter."

"I still have to speak to him."

Dad gets up and walks toward me. He runs a hand over his troubled demeanor. "From what I see, this is danger-ous... You should be staying as far away from him as possible."

My lungs tighten. "Him?"

"It," he corrects, his gaze falling. "You should stay away from *it*."

I can only imagine what they were discussing before I walked in. They made judgments based on a file of informa-tion about Wesley. But that doesn't show what he's truly like.

"I understand you're upset," Aunt Beverly says, "but these protocols are to keep you safe. It's our understanding that this problem concerns your bodyguard, not you."

Tears of frustration prick my eyes. "*This problem,*" I grit, "became mine the second I watched the man I love beaten and nearly killed. You expect me to walk away?"

"If it's—"

"No," I cut off Dad. "I'm done making decisions based on how it might affect you or this family." I look between him and my aunt. "You two might be okay with ignoring the people you love, but I'm not."

I spin on my heel and head down the corridor, ignoring their calls for me.

It doesn't take me too long to locate Wesley. I jump in on the security team meeting, sitting between him and Jack.

Jack recounts yesterday's events based on Wesley's information, and I confirm every frightening detail. I don't leave once we move on to discussing Arlo's business and influence, and all except Wesley appear surprised or even unsettled by my continued presence, Mason included.

"Your Highness," Jack says, "we will send for you when we come up with a notable idea. You should rest after such a long day."

I won't let him, or anyone, discredit my seat at the table. I set the fire that got us out. I nearly killed someone. I'm the princess and eventual queen of this goddamn country. I earned my spot here.

"Thank you for your concern, but I'm staying." I look around. "I know you all think I'm naive—"

"We don't think you're naive at all," Jack says.

"Fine, then however much credit you give me, *give me more.*"

A quiet moment passes over the group as if considering whether they want to argue this. They don't.

Wesley speaks up. "We need to offer him something he wants even more than who killed Santiago."

"A blind eye," I suggest. "We're bound with the police and military, correct? They investigate everything regarding the Elias family, including me. What if we give him a get-out-of-jail-free card?"

He shakes his head. "That's not enough."

"If we emphasize how big of a charge kidnapping the princess is," Mason says, leaning back in his seat with crossed arms.

Jack waves a hand. "He can argue he didn't know at the time. It'll get thrown out."

"Kidnap is kidnap," he stresses.

"Yes, but kidnapping a royal family member is the threatening charge, which can get thrown out. It's not strong enough."

"There's no love or loyalty between Arlo and his brother," Wesley pipes. "He didn't necessarily believe my reputation and was ill-prepared. Now that the princess and I bested him and left a mess, he'll be gunning for us out of pride."

Silas presses his elbows onto the table. "But you said he left you alone on your way to the rendezvous. How much does this affect Her Majesty's safety?"

I blink, realizing that *Her Majesty* is me.

"I think one of my old associates saw us underground and wanted in on the action," Wesley says.

Old associate. We spoke to no one other than the homeless man, Adonis, and—Daria. I bite the inside of my cheek. I might respect her if she didn't put Wesley and me in more danger.

"Is there a reason we can't arrest him for everything else he's done?" I ask.

"It's a waste of our court system's time and money," Jack explains. "He has enough lawyers to drag it out for years. Meanwhile, he'll make bail and continue business as usual."

"The police have an investigation started on him, though?" asks Gregory.

"Yes. We could kick this to them, but it doesn't solve the fact that we're waiting for Arlo to green-light Beck."

I mask my distress. The meeting goes on for another hour until we stop to eat. My family keeps their distance, almost as if they don't know how to act around me. It's the first time I made a decision wholly for myself, and I force down the guilt. In spite of being princess and starting a career in service for others, Wesley is the one thing in my life I won't compromise on.

CHAPTER FIFTY

WESLEY

By four o'clock, I convince Nina to eat dinner and rest. She agrees only if I spend the night with her—which I'll never turn down.

When the rest of the team is off-duty, I sit with Jack on his office patio.

"As much as I hate to admit it," he says, taking a drag of his cigarette, "it makes sense."

"What does?"

"You and the princess. I can see why during the meeting." He releases a sharp breath, shaking his head at himself.

I cough over my surprise, surveying the perfectly landscaped garden in front of me. The citronella candle on the end table crackles. "I didn't mean for it to happen."

He snorts. "No one ever does."

"What I said earlier—"

"It's okay," he interrupts, twisting his wedding band. "I'd do the same."

It wouldn't feel right to sacrifice Jack—to let Arlo live and cause this chaos. "I was going to say that I can't picture myself giving you up. Arlo will be dead just for touching Nina."

He chokes out a sardonic laugh and mutters, *"Jesus."*

I sometimes forget how straight-and-narrow Jack is even though he's the one who shot Santiago in cold blood. Silence falls over us as we pass the cigarette back and forth. I make a note to brush my teeth before seeing Nina. She hates the smell.

"The only way out of this involves something illegal," I say.

"You could go into hiding."

I shake my head and return his cigarette. "Nina would kill me."

"Then disappear. I can get you out on a plane tonight."

After what happened today, I would leave in a heartbeat if it meant keeping her safe. She shouldn't go through that again, but her defiance is groundbreaking and I have no desire to test it. The way Maximo's head snapped aside when Nina cracked it with a metal pipe and said, *"I hope I killed him,"* afterward left me slightly shaken. I've seen much worse, but I've been thinking of her as fragile when I shouldn't.

"Nah, I can't do that to her," I say lowly.

"Then what are you thinking?"

The only thing Arlo might want more than his brother's shooter is a profitable business deal. As much as I dread the possibility of doing this, I don't see another way. I'm not sure if he would be dumb enough to green-light the princess of a country, but he'll definitely put a hit on me. He has the tenacity of a stubborn child and would burn the world just to get what he wants, even if it bites him in the ass by shelling out a million-dollar bounty on my head.

"A deal. I... take out one of his opponents."

"Are you sure?"

"I don't see another way. We spent the entire day trying to come up with a solution. There's nothing else."

Jack huffs, putting out the cigarette before rising. "I'll use my clearance to pull his records. See what we can offer."

I'm finally fighting for something—for someone. My tiny world—once filled with dread, blood, and darkness—has grown and I don't want my old life anymore. This would be my last underground job. The thought of going back under claws at my chest.

I hope Nina will still love me by the end of it. I *need* her to.

I'll be fine. I'll survive. As long as Nina is safe. It would ruin me beyond redemption if she was harmed because of this. Being tethered to her is the release I didn't realize how desperately I needed. She unlocked part of me I forgot existed.

Jack and I spend an hour reviewing the information, and we conclude that Jose Rivera is Arlo's biggest competitor. Neither is the biggest drug supplier in southern Europe. If Arlo wants to be the biggest, Rivera is the next obstacle.

I call Adonis and request to conduct business with Arlo at his compound, but he declines outright on the grounds that his neutrality is compromised by letting Nina and me seek refuge. Instead, he offers to pass along a message about where to meet, and Jack and I agree on the location where Arlo had interrogated me. The building Nina set on fire.

Next, we schedule the royal guard to be on standby tomorrow at noon. Last, I turn to my boss and say, "I need to borrow your car."

"For what?"

"Contingencies."

Jack hesitates, considering me for a moment before releasing a breath and tossing over his keys. "Don't wreck my baby."

"Don't plan to."

I drive to my safe deposit box downtown to grab my emergency bag. After double-checking that all of my equipment, paperwork, and cash are inside, I head to the apartment of my old roommate, Noah, who instantly informs me that my room has already been rented out. I almost pity the new person.

I offer Noah five hundred euros to park around the corner from a building—where I'm meeting Arlo—and to bring me the car if I call. If I call, he has to find another way to get home.

"Just like that?" he asks.

"Two-fifty now, two-fifty after. I might not need you, though."

"Will I still get the other two-fifty?"

I nod.

"And all I have to do is sit in a car and wait for your call —maybe."

"I'll text you exactly where to park and exactly where to drive to, should I call you. You sit there and do *nothing*. You call no one. You talk to no one. You don't look through the car. I'll know if you do *any* of those things and there will be hell to pay. Understood?"

Now it's his turn to nod.

"Good. Arrive at the east side of the palace tomorrow morning at ten o'clock and call me. I'll get you through." My phone dings with a text from Nina.

"The *palace*?" Noah echoes.

NINA

Are you coming?

I have a surprise.

I slap the money into Noah's palm and leave without another word. Anticipation thrums through me on the drive back, followed by a pang of guilt. I don't want to lie to Nina—I respect her. Everything fell apart in the first place because *I* was lied to. She deserves better than that, but I would rather her be safe and hate me than in danger and love me.

As I head to Nina's room, I throw back some pain pills for my wounds. It won't leave a permanent scar, but I'll be damned if it doesn't hurt.

"It's open!" she calls when I knock on her door.

I enter to find her stretched across a beige tufted sofa, wearing a short silk robe. She grins at me, twirling her finger around the curly phone cord as she listens to whoever is on the other line. Damn. How can I view her as anything other than an angel? She's other-fucking-worldly.

I drop my bag of clothes by the door and cross the room, my gaze locked on her bare skin.

"I know," she says into the phone as I lower beside her and drape her legs across my lap. "Ruby, I'll be okay... Yeah, but this is *my* decision..."

I stroke her calf at the sight of her troubled demeanor, pressing my lips to her knee, her thigh. This is what I want —to come home to her every day. Her good days, bad days, I want all of it. While continuing to stroke her leg, I slouch down to lean my head against the back of the sofa.

Nina huffs. "No, this isn't to get back at him. This is the *opposite* of that... You've stayed out of my fights with him up until now. Why do you suddenly care? ... That's not what I meant." Her head falls back in annoyance. "Yeah, I know I'm being selfish. That's the whole point... Listen, can we just try this again tomorrow? ... All right... Okay... Love you, too... Good night."

With a long sigh, she hangs up the phone behind her.

"I don't want to cause a rift in your family," I say, although there's no way in hell I'm giving her up.

She attempts a smile. "There was a rift long before you showed up."

"Still. I don't want to make it worse."

She combs her fingers through my hair, watching me dreamily. "It's less about you and more about me doing what makes me happy, no matter how they feel. They'll get over it and learn to accept the man I'm in love with."

I lift a brow. "You love me." Half a statement. Half a question. I know that she does, but she hasn't told me outright the way I told her.

A smile pulls at Nina's lips. She climbs onto my lap, her robe slipping from her shoulder to reveal the lacy bra underneath. My erection grows as I glide my thumb over her nipple peeking through.

"Wesley Dominik Troutbeck," she begins, gripping my hair to force my gaze to hers, "I am completely and madly in love with you. I don't care what your job used to be. I know who you are, and I love you in your darkness as much as I love you in your light."

This woman brings me to earth and puts me in a new dimension at the same time. She's my home, salvation, and an extension of my soul. I brush away a lock of her hair, caressing her cheek before covering her mouth with mine.

"I really am the luckiest man on earth," I say against her lips. I slip my hand under the silk, hooking a finger in the panties over her hip. "Is this the surprise?"

Nina nods, her cheeks turning pink. She wore this for me, and the thought only makes me harder. I tug on the string at her waist. The robe falls over her soft skin and I nearly salivate at her full breasts in front of me. I grit my teeth, my body tensing with need. I lightly slap her ass.

"Get on the bed. I want to unwrap my present."

CHAPTER FIFTY-ONE

NINA

There's no bliss like waking up beside Wesley. Flipping around in bed and finding him there is all the coffee I need.

Not really, but he's already as important to my mornings as coffee. And that says something.

We savor the little time we have before meeting Arlo at noon, and I make sure Wesley changes his bandages and takes ibuprofen.

I was surprised to hear that he was going to give Arlo what he wanted alongside information about Santiago's hidden assets. I wanted to be in the room with Wesley. He wanted me to stay at the palace. I compromised by taking a spot in one of the surveillance vans out front.

I step into a pair of denim shorts with a T-shirt from my high school volleyball team before tying my hair into a bun at the crown of my head.

"Are you really going?" Maia asks, arms crossed as she stands in the middle of my room.

Wesley left over an hour ago and I have to meet Jack at

his office in ten minutes. I lower onto the divan to lace my sneakers.

"I have to."

"No, you don't."

"Maia, *please*," I snap. "This is hard enough as it is and I don't need you or Dad or Ruby making it worse!"

She deflates, dropping her arms. "Then I'm coming, too."

"Why?"

"Because if shit hits the fan, I'll be there to help you."

I survey her ripped jeans and flowy shirt. I chuckle, rising to my feet with my hands on my hips. "And what would you do?"

Maia rolls her eyes and reaches into her back pocket. She flicks open a switchblade at least six inches long. "Slice and dice, duh."

I choke out a laugh, shoving her shoulder to walk out the door with me. "You'd be proud of me. I treated some dude's head like a baseball with a metal pipe."

Despite my repulsed shiver, I don't regret hitting Maximo. He would have killed Wesley.

Maia blanches. "Holy shit."

"He was a big guy!" I argue.

"How big?" she asks, seemingly unconvinced.

"*Twice* the size of Wesley."

She winces. "Damn."

My heart thunders. I don't understand how people can deal with these high-stress situations on a regular basis. After the past few days, I'm ready to sleep for a week.

I sit with Jack in the van, watching Wesley head into the

partially burned-down building. I'm grateful it didn't entirely collapse. As awful as these people are, I don't truly want to hurt anyone.

I resist bouncing my knee as I hold the headphones to my ear, listening to Wesley's breaths through the microphone.

"I underestimated you," Arlo says. "I admit I thought the stories were bogus."

"Nobody's perfect," Wesley says with a sniff.

"Name one reason I shouldn't submit this contract."

"Jose Rivera."

"What about him?" Arlo asks.

"I'll take him out for you and we call it even."

I lift my head. *What?*

He laughs. "Just like that, huh? The man lives in a fortress."

My stomach caves. I look at Jack, hoping that he's panicked, too, but he listens intently, his head lowered and brow furrowed.

"What is he doing?" I ask.

"Making a deal."

"I thought he was giving Arlo what he wanted," I say. Why would Wesley offer to kill someone for him? My panic deepens as they list further details of the deal. "If he does this, how do we know Arlo won't hold it over his head and ask for more?"

"It's a business deal." Jack's reply is curt, as if I'm bothering him.

"Will it make Arlo stronger?"

Jack doesn't answer. Fury simmers under my skin. Wesley wants to get out of that world—and Arlo Serrano is dragging him back under. When I become queen, I want Wesley at my side, and Arlo will figure out a way to hold proof of this over his head in exchange for more jobs—more *killings.*

We were supposed to do this together. Instead, Wesley *lied* to me and took a completely different route.

I shove Jack's shoulder, my hands shaking with anxiety and anger. "Hey! *Will this make his business stronger?*"

"*Yes!*"

"We're setting ourselves up to get *fucked* in the future," I bark, jumping out of the van before I can second-guess myself. There's no way Wesley will do a job for Arlo, not when he's trying to change. He could get seriously hurt or killed. What if he has to call in a favor to get out alive? Then he's indebted to another mercenary who will call on him in the future. Call me paranoid, but it would be the perfect opportunity for everything to go wrong.

"Your Highness, no!" Jack yells as I run into the building. I hear his footsteps behind me, but it's too late.

I need to offer something—*fast.*

Or nothing at all.

Who does Arlo think he is? *Look at the big picture.*

"No!" I yell, stopping in the wide-open area between the lobby elevators. Arlo's men startle and aim their guns, so I lift my hands in surrender. It's a good thing Wesley all but wrestled to put me into a bulletproof vest. I ignore the simmering look he gives me.

I drop my arms and say to Arlo, "This ends now."

Wesley shifts toward me. "Nina—"

"The *only* way this works is if we do it together," I snap, my voice hushed. I bite back my hurt and focus on the task at hand.

"I understand why you're so brave, Miss Laffley. You have the royal guard behind you," he says, and I glance around for Daria. She's the one who snitched, but she's not even here.

"He's not doing any jobs for you."

"Is that so?" He chuckles. "What is your offer?"

"There's no offer. Walk away or become an enemy of the royal institution and I spend my career taking you down."

His chuckle turns into full-bellied laughter. He glances at the six people behind him. I keep a strong face in the spite of the ridicule. Arlo steps closer to me. "You don't have the guts. It'll be a bloodbath and your conscience can't handle that."

"Can't it?" I challenge, matching his step so there's a foot between us. "You can blame this fire on whoever keeps a bottle of Jack in their desk. Couldn't have set it without them. And how's Maximo? I hope his recovery is smooth." I lower my voice. "There might be death in this path, but think long and hard about who will be standing by the end of it. A centuries-old monarch, or your little business?"

Arlo's jaw ticks, and I control my features as much as possible. Truthfully, the furious sense of betrayal from Wesley keeps me from cowering.

Just when I think Arlo is going to back down, he lunges, yanking my arm and pulling a gun.

I land against him, my back to his chest, as cool metal presses against my head. My defenses crumble at the sight of Wesley's panicked eyes and my body tingles with anxiety. Shit, shit, shit.

"Can't take me down if you're dead," Arlo says into my ear, his breath fanning my skin as his hand wraps around my throat. My chest tightens, and if fear hadn't clogged my throat, I'd vomit.

"Don't do this," Wesley threatens. "You said yourself you underestimated me."

"I think I will bring her with me." I shudder at the kiss Arlo plants on my temple. "For now." He presses the barrel of the gun under my chin, and I hate the whimper that escapes as he drags me through the emergency exit.

After discarding my bulletproof vest, Arlo shoves me through the open door of a waiting SUV. Indignation sparks up my core, but I shouldn't be violent—not yet at least. He climbs in behind me and slams the door. The driver peels off and I struggle to catch my breath. I clutch the door to steady my spinning head.

"Where to?" the driver asks when the narrow alley dumps us onto a main road.

"Drive around the city. We need to lose Revalté. I bet he's chasing us like a dog right now." A wicked smile spreads across Arlo's face. He turns to me, the gun still pointed. "You almost won."

I'm at his mercy, no matter the red-hot anger boiling under my skin. While he has the gun and strength, I notice the nervous tick in his eyes. He was going to give in.

I look out the window for the fifteen minutes of driving, fighting to ignore the fact that a deadly weapon is pointed at me. My emotions pile inside me so high that goosebumps cover my skin. I wish I hadn't ambushed the meeting like that. I wish Wesley trusted me enough to have a conversation about our options.

The car pulls in front of a luxury apartment building. A blond man, not much older than I am, opens my door, and I'm faced with another gun. "You scream, you run, you die."

I only manage a nod as he and numerous other men guide me through the lobby. I inhale slowly. At least I won't be locked in a dark basement.

I watch everything. The dust in the corner of the elevator. The defective button for the third floor. The way Arlo's ring looks a size too small. I don't know if I'm searching for a way out or a distraction from what's happening.

I'm led through a lavish apartment into a windowless room with two sofas and a coffee table between them. The blond man shoves me onto one of the sofas. I notice the minibar next to the door and hear the distant voices of others in the apartment.

"I won't leave you alone this time. I learned my lesson." Arlo lowers across from me. "Are you thirsty?"

I shake my head.

He snaps his fingers for the same blond man to pour a glass of liquor. Arlo lights a fat cigar, puffing smoke around his face.

"I don't understand why my brother didn't kill him years ago," he says in Maldanian.

"Too obsessed with money," the blond one replies, leaning on the doorframe.

From the way the two of them look at me, they don't know I understand Maldanian. I can decipher the bones of their discussion, and having to translate in my head keeps me from being reactive and giving myself away.

"Morality threatens loyalty, Pavlos. We all know that," Arlo says, voice gravelly as he takes a long drag of the cigar. He stares at me, his gaze hungry, vengeful, and curious. "The Ghost is coming for us because we took his whore." He flicks ashes onto the expensive carpet. "And if we don't get her out of here, all of us are dead."

"We can put her on a plane."

Terror thrums through me. I want to say I'm appearing fearful so he lets his guard down, but I'm not acting.

"Call Suchko," he says. "We can give her to him. See

how fast it can happen. And get Daria on the phone." He leans forward, elbows on his knees as he switches to English. "You're awfully quiet. You had a lot to say back there. Cat got your tongue?"

Despite my shaking limbs, I don't break eye contact.

I'm just watching you chase your tail.

I clamp my mouth shut, forcing the words in. He doesn't get the satisfaction of a response.

CHAPTER FIFTY-TWO

WESLEY

I wasn't fast enough.

I watched him lunge. I watched as he held a gun to Nina's head and wrapped a hand around her throat. Arlo would have backed down if she hadn't taken that step forward.

Now he has her and everything I've fought to protect is at risk.

If I wasn't ravaged by fear and vengeance, I'd be furious at her. I run out of the building, already dialing Noah's number, to find Jack and the royal guard pulling up.

"Do you know where he might go?" Jack asks.

I ignore the question and hold the phone to my ear. "Bring the car."

"Now?" Noah stutters.

"Now!"

"There's—police or something—"

"Get as far as you can. I'll meet you."

Jack watches me hang up. "Who the hell was that?"

Before I can answer, someone screams, "BECK!"

I perk, scanning the sidewalk to see Nina's sister

barreling toward me with Mason in tow. I'm not surprised she was waiting on the outskirts. "Maia?"

"Where the *fuck* is my sister?" she asks fiercely, shoving me with enough force to send me back a few steps. "You said you'd look out for her and Mason tells me she was taken?"

Mason puts his hand on her arm. "Your High—"

"I'm getting her back—I need you to trust me, all right?" My phone buzzes with a call from Noah. I start walking away, but Maia follows closely with Jack and Mason not far behind.

"*Trust* you? Do you know where they might be going? What are you—"

"Where do you think you're going?" Jack scolds.

I ignore them and spot Noah from outside the royal guard's perimeter. He steps out of the gray R8 Audi and I take his spot, flipping into reverse without answering a single question.

I hold the phone to my ear. "Where do you want to meet?"

"That's not how you greet people," Daria tsks. "We talked about this."

"Considering you're a narcissist with control issues, I'm assuming you won't tell me where Arlo took Nina over the phone. *Where are you?*"

She chuckles. "Niko Elias Park. Under the northeast bridge."

I step on the gas as she hangs up.

I was never in love with Daria; she was far too embedded in the underground. Her priorities were always on the next job, anything to get her ahead.

I drive into the park the furthest I can. It's a cloudless, sweltering day, meaning most people are inside. Locals, at least. Tourists continue traipsing. I twist a silencer on a .9 millimeter as I head to the bridge, my chest burning. Every second that Arlo has Nina is another step toward my becoming El Revalté again. I wanted to keep my two worlds as far apart as possible. But I can't leave El Revalté behind yet.

"Tell me where he's taking her," I call while walking into the tunnel.

Daria turns to me with a huff. "Is she really worth—"

Without stopping, I cut her off with a bullet to her knee. Her howls echo. Before she collapses, I catch her with my forearm against her throat, shoving her back into the brick wall. I press the gun between her ribs lest she reach into her pockets. She releases a strangled sound, clawing her manicured fingers at my shoulders.

I keep a stony gaze as panic fills her eyes. She knows I don't hurt women and intended to take advantage of that.

All bets are off when it comes to Nina.

"When I remove my arm, you're going to tell me where Arlo is taking her. If you don't, then I will do this"—I increase pressure on her trachea, hearing it crunch—"and watch you die."

She looks as if she doesn't recognize me. *Good.* I release just enough pressure for her to speak. Her strained breath is almost pathetic. "He's—moving her from... the Magnolia in th-thirty min—"

Thirty minutes. The Magnolia is almost ten away.

I drop her to the ground and head back to where I came from. She'll warn Arlo within minutes, and then he'll take Nina somewhere else. Somewhere unattainable. So I aim at Daria's head and pull the trigger.

My phone rings nonstop, each one ignored.

I check all building exits and find a black SUV out front, confirming where they'll be leaving. The only rooftop with tactical advantage is across the street and three buildings down. It should give me four hundred yards. It's a buzz-door apartment building where the roof has a wall perimeter.

I check my timer. Thirteen more minutes.

The wound on my chest throbs with my pounding heart. I unzip the duffle bag, pull out a Remington 700, and load in a few .308 rounds before sliding the bolt forward and locking it. I prop the rifle on the ledge and peek through the reticle at the front entrance. Four hundred yards confirmed. I adjust the scope. Two left. One down.

My phone rings again. I answer it without looking. "Jack."

"It's about damn time," he growls. "What are you doing in Milagro?"

He's been tracking me. Hopefully that means he's not far behind, but I couldn't risk him and the guard making a scene by infiltrating. Those get bloody.

"She's being moved from Magnolia apartments in eight minutes. Come quietly."

"Wait—"

I hang up and slip my phone into my pocket. I settle into the weight of the gun in my arms, its familiarity reminding me of a life I no longer want.

CHAPTER FIFTY-THREE
NINA

Arlo leaves the room.

Pavlos takes his spot, his eyes studying every bit of my figure. I squirm when he stops on my legs. He notices and smirks. The closest weapon is the bottle of alcohol on the minibar. I uncross my ankles in case I need to lunge for it.

Arlo reenters the room and claps his hands once. "I hope your bags are packed!"

My blood runs cold, poisoned with dread. I know Wesley is planning something; he won't stop until I'm home safe.

I only hope that it happens before I'm flown into another country.

Pavlos grins as he takes a zip tie from his pocket. He stands in front of me, closer than necessary, as he binds my wrists. He hauls me up as we head toward the elevators.

Don't get into the car.

No matter what, I need to fight. I could die, but I'd rather fight here than in a foreign country. Arlo drapes a suit jacket over my bound wrists before we walk through the lobby.

"Same rules, princess," Pavlos says. "You scream, you run, you die."

Fuck that.

He grips my arm tight as we walk outside. The heat smacks me in the face as I notice the car's open door in front of me. Deep breath. Time to fight.

Fssss-pop!

Something warm splatters my face. Pavlos's hold on me loosens as he drops to the ground, blood pouring from the hole in his head. My ears start ringing, muffling the shouts.

Pop! Pop-pop-pop!

I turn in time to see Arlo grabbing me, a gun to my head, as the royal guard approaches, armed with weapons. Someone leads Jack, who clutches his bloody arm, behind a van that pulls up. I spot another dead body—one of Arlo's men. I shake the jacket from the wrists as Arlo tries to back us into the building, only to find the doors shut and locked. He bangs the glass and curses, still using me as a shield.

My entire body vibrates and the buzzing hasn't subsided. I can't decipher the shouting. I can't do anything with my wrists bound and an arm wrapped around my chest. How is this happening so fast? Time moves at increased, warped speed—and I'm stuck in slow motion.

Arlo drags us a few feet down the sidewalk, and I look at Pavlos's body again. The bullet wound is on the left side of his head, but the royal guard approached from the right.

Wesley.

It has to be.

The thought pushes the world back into my mind just enough to move. Arlo still cowers behind me, shouting threats and demands. I brace my legs and pour all my strength into shoving us back against the brick wall. The ricochet from his gunshot helps, and I knock the wind out of him enough to loosen his hold. I instantly drop to the ground and curl into a ball, knowing what's next.

A whizzing sound hisses through the air, followed by wet gurgling. I scramble out of the way the moment before Arlo's body falls, and my stomach lurches at the sight. The ringing in my ears gets even stronger as the world cuts to a halt again. I can't rip my eyes from the torn hole in Arlo's throat. Blood oozes out, drop by drop. His mouth is open. His eyes are vacant. Hands close around my arms to lift me, but my limbs have lost all feeling again. I don't know who's holding me, but he drags me away from...

Chaos.

An ambulance opens its rear doors, and whoever carries me—Silas—sets me on the edge. He slices my zip ties and frees my wrists. I shut my eyes as the buzzing pierces my head. The paramedic steadies me, asking questions as she searches for signs of injury. I can't hear her over the ringing. She clamps her mouth shut when she realizes I won't answer.

What the fuck just happened?

"NINA!"

I startle, looking up to find Wesley. Energy slams back into my body, and I sprint to him. He captures me in his arms, reaching up to lock his hand on the back of my neck. A sob scratches from my throat as warmth floods me. I dig my face into his neck.

"Thank god," he cries in a whisper.

I clench his shirt, the tears finally breaking free amidst the chaos of ambulances and police. He hugs me almost too tightly, but the feeling of his chest against mine calms my heartbeat.

"I'm sorry," he says into my neck. "I'm so sorry. I never should've lied."

I want to apologize, too, but words get stuck in my throat. When I pull away to breathe, he checks me for wounds.

"Are you okay? They didn't hurt you, right?"

I nod. Wesley studies my face, brushing away drops of blood with his thumb. Blood that's not mine. I shudder, pulling him to ride with me to the hospital. The paramedic tries asking me questions again. I answer, but that doesn't mean my hands have stopped shaking.

When she starts yelling at the driver about the traffic, I lean on Wesley's shoulder. "I'm sorry, too," I say, my voice cracking.

"Don't be," he says gently, kissing my head.

There's so much to say, and I say nothing at all. I froze *again*. I didn't move fast enough, *twice*, to keep from Arlo grabbing me. Silas had to drag me to safety.

Seconds after I sit on the edge of the hospital bed in a private room, my family rushes inside. My heart drops when Wesley leaves the room, but I catch his eyes. He nods, as if inferring he'll be right outside.

Despite everything, I lean on Dad's chest as he hugs me, feeling the thump of his heart. Maia holds my hand. Ruby strokes my back. I not only cry because of what I saw, but of feeling loved by my family.

In the silence, my stomach grumbles loudly. Maia snorts, and we break out into fragile laughter as the nurse steps into the room for my examination.

"We'll go find you some food? A meal?" Ruby suggests.

I nod. "Okay."

Dad and Ruby leave for the cafeteria while Maia

promises to sit outside the room. Before the nurse can start, I ask, "Uh, is it okay if my boyfriend is in here with me?"

The nurse blinks, surprised. "Oh—of course."

She peeks out the doorway, and Wesley soon follows her inside. This woman isn't a threat, but I want him close by. He sits in a chair as she runs me through some tests. My heartbeat has long settled, but my hands are just starting to calm.

"I'll be back in a few minutes," she says, handing me a bag of crackers and a water bottle.

I set them aside, unable to eat yet. Wesley stands beside me, stroking my back. To think we were curled up, cozy in bed, just this morning.

"Was that you?" I ask suddenly. "Who... who shot them."

I know the answer. Perhaps knowing and hearing it will somehow make a difference—make it easier. He tucks some of my frizz behind my ear and says, "You're safe. That's all that matters."

His face tenses with anguish, and my heart breaks with guilt at his internal torment. The goal was for Wesley to *not* kill anyone.

"I didn't mean for this to happen."

"What?" he stammers. "This wasn't your fault. Not in the slightest."

"I know, but—"

"No, Nina. None of that. I don't regret what I did, and neither should you."

I lean my head on his chest, easing into his arms. I'm still struggling to register what happened today. It all happened so fast that I didn't remember how to move until three people were already shot.

But it's over. Relief rushes into me when I realize that it's *done*.

I take a giant sleeping pill that night.

Wesley stays with me in case I have nightmares, but my slumber is so deep that time moves from hours into minutes. When I wake, my body is too heavy to move itself. I groan.

Footsteps pad through the room. A weight dips on the bed. "Morning, sleepyhead."

My bonnet is suddenly shifted from my eyes and I find Wesley staring back at me.

"What time is it?" I grumble, nowhere nearly as sexy as his morning voice.

"Eleven."

I groan again. Late. For me, at least. I flip onto my back, smelling aftershave and noticing he's dressed for the day. I rub the sleep from my eyes. "Where are you going?"

"A debrief and then a hearing."

"A hearing?" I echo. "Should I be worried?"

At the end of the day, Wesley killed multiple people. A tiny smile pulls at his lips. "No. Will you be okay for a few hours?"

"Yeah, I'll be fine." I reach out and brush my fingers over his chest, feeling the bandage beneath his shirt. "How bad does it hurt?"

He shrugs. "Not much." He kisses me before getting to his feet. "It's a good thing you woke up now. I already ordered you breakfast. Should be here any moment."

I extend my body in a stretch, my arms above me. "French toast?"

"Of course."

After Wesley leaves and I stuff my face with french toast, Dad knocks on my door. It's relatively normal between us for the first time in what feels like months. We talk about our plans for moving from America to Maldana. And for a few minutes, we even talk about Mom and how I feel closer to her. Anger threatens to simmer underneath my skin, a reminder that it shouldn't have taken almost twenty years to happen. But it's manageable.

My phone dings with a text.

WESLEY

How was breakfast?

It's a simple question, but I still blush at the thoughtfulness.

Delicious. I might fall into a food coma.

At least wait until I get back.

"Everything okay?" Dad asks.

"Oh—yeah," I perk, setting my phone down. "Just Wesley checking in on me."

He releases a long breath. "Your bodyguard, huh?" he says, leaning back on the sofa and pausing to find the words. "He's a frightening man."

"Not to me."

"He's a *murderer*, Nina," he snaps, and I fall silent. The memory of blood pouring from Arlo's open throat flashes across my mind. That was Wesley. The vision will haunt me forever, but I can't bring myself to blame or hate him for it. It wouldn't feel natural.

Dad softens, his tone almost pleading. "I... He killed those men."

Stiff silence wedges between us. I shrink, wrapping my arms around my middle. "What do you want me to say, Dad? That I love him in spite of that? Because I do, and I'm *not* convincing you to understand my reasoning."

In other words, I'm tired of arguing with him.

"He killed for me," I add, my voice quiet. "Wouldn't you want your daughter to be in love with someone who would kill to keep her safe?"

Dad might not have pictured me falling in love with a former assassin, but it's a good thing it's not up to him. He lifts his hands in surrender before touching my wrist.

"I'm grateful for him," he admits. "You're right; he saved my little girl. I just *worry*, Nina. All I ever do is worry about you and your sister. I want you girls to have everything you ever wished for."

I shrug, fighting the prick behind my eyes. "All I *want* is a dad who's... who's *there*—one who loves me for being his daughter and not what I can do for him."

My voice cracks and the tears come, anyway. He scoots closer to wrap his arms around me, and I curl against his chest, shedding soft tears. I cling to my father, inhaling the scent of the cherry almond lotion he always wears. We stay like this for minutes, and I finally know what it feels like for him to see where I'm coming from. He doesn't try to correct me.

For the first time, he's there for me.

"The Court wants him gone," Dad says quietly.

I pull from the hug, wiping my face. "Who—Wesley? That's what they told you?"

He nods. "They're having a meeting about it in an hour."

"That's bullshit," I sneer before I can think twice about cursing in front of my dad. "Mom left so she could be with someone she loved and wanted a future with. What would she say if they were trying to do exactly what drove her away?"

His eyes glisten with unshed tears. I'm sure this reminds him of everything that happened with Mom all those years ago.

"Then we should tell them that."

CHAPTER FIFTY-FOUR
WESLEY

Nina doesn't realize that she's the reason I'm not being charged.

Not only because I was protecting the future queen, but because she mentioned Suchko when she told the royal guard—and the police commissioner—everything that happened.

Suchko, the biggest product supplier and business partner of Vitalis.

Vitalis, who specializes in human trafficking.

I should've shot Arlo the second I saw him at the meeting. The princess of Maldana almost being sold into human trafficking warranted such deadly force, according to the head of the royal guard, the police commissioner, and a Supreme Court judge. Regardless, the hours of pouring over the salvaged records of my crimes leave a heavy pit in my stomach.

The fact that those were a small portion of everything I've done only makes it worse.

The effects of the past few days break me down at last. Exhaustion steals my energy.

Nina. Her name echoes through my heart as I walk down the corridor. Just a few minutes of being with her, holding her, and I'll start to feel better.

I spot Maia exiting her bedroom as I turn the corner. She pauses, cocking a hip. "I asked you to look out for my sister—not fall in love with her."

"Apologies, but to be fair, it happened long before our conversation."

She smirks. "Good answer." Her bracelets chime together as she crosses her arms. "Do I call you Wesley now?"

"Wesley is fine, yes."

Awkwardness lingers around us, but Maia's the type to feel most comfortable in an awkward situation. "I trust you with her," she says sweetly. Then, in the same tone, she adds, "Break that trust and I'll break your neck."

I can't help the chuckle breaking free from my chest. "Understood."

"And she's not in there," Maia calls as I approach Nina's bedroom door. "She's in the throne room."

After another five-minute walk, I stride into the room with a long path lined with pillars. I spot Nina standing in front of the throne at the other end.

Once I get closer, I say, "This view is the reason I call you *angel.*"

She looks over her shoulder. The windows behind the throne reach the ceiling, the evening sun illuminating her figure. "What view?"

I wrap my arms around her from behind, burying my

face in her hair. "When you watch the sky or sunset, the light outlines you." I kiss her neck. "Angel. Mi angeli."

I feel her tense as she blushes. She holds onto me, shifting her head to connect our lips.

"I had a meeting with the Higher Court today," she mutters.

I hum. "No doubt they want me gone. Bad publicity."

Nina shakes her head, attempting a smile as she meets my gaze. Her eyes glisten in the light. "It's taken care of, so don't worry."

I lift my brows. "As in..."

"As in they can't tell me who to love. Your records will be sealed and you'll make as many public engagements as you want."

"Which is none."

She chuckles. "I know. And another thing. Jack told me about the task force for Lo Revínastí. I want you to lead it."

My eyes widen. That's not what I expected her to say.

"The job isn't meant for anyone else," she presses. "We both know that."

I hadn't had time to consider work after this, but I nod and say, "Okay." It will keep me close to Nina and I'll be doing something I'm good at: hunting.

When I notice her watching the throne, I say, "You can sit there, you know."

"But there's a rope."

She points to the velvet rope that prohibits further entry. With a scoff, I unhook the latch and gesture toward the expensive chair.

"Your Highness."

She rolls her eyes, but a smile spreads across her lips. She takes my outstretched hand, walking up the dais before wiping her palms on her pink floral dress.

I slide my hands into my pockets, watching her. The golden hour glows against her brown skin as she pulls her soft curls to one shoulder. Lastly, she smooths the dress beneath her as she sits on the decadent throne, her movements graceful and delicate.

Mi verinìta Maldasso.

I might be biased, but the throne was made for her. Royalty. Princess. Queen. Nina was meant for this. When she meets my eyes, an incredulous grin flies onto her face and she clamps her hands over her mouth.

"How does it feel?" I ask.

"Overwhelming." She huffs, flopping back into the million-dollar seat. After a moment, she blurts, "Take me somewhere."

"Like where?"

"Anywhere—as long as it's just us. Everything is about to get a whole lot crazier and I want to go somewhere with you first. We can leave tomorrow."

"Hm." Excitement thrums through me at the idea of having her all to myself for days on end. There's one city I've always wanted to visit. "Rome?"

Nina grins. "Rome is perfect."

EPILOGUE
NINA

TWO YEARS LATER

I hunch over the bathroom counter, tears dripping from my eyes.

This is something I've wanted—something we've *both* wanted—yet fear strangles me until I can't breathe. Stella won't tell anyone she bought me the test; my assistant prioritizes discretion over everything. But I desperately wish I had *someone*.

Like my mom.

Not Ruby. Even though Dad and I have been slowly fixing our relationship, I'm still distant from my stepmother.

I drop to the floor, my back against the cabinet and my knees against my chest. *I want my mom.* I want my mom to hug me and say it's going to be okay and I want my mom to tell me that, no, pushing a baby out from between my legs *isn't* going to hurt.

None of those things will happen.

I stare at the broken towel rack dangling on the wall.

Wesley told me he was going to fix it. He'd been gone for nearly three weeks and it broke during one of our many moments of reconnecting.

But now, all I can do is watch that damn rack hanging on for dear life. *Just hold on.* I shut my eyes, tears streaming down either side of my cheeks, and let my head fall back. There's so much to be scared of.

I'm not happy. Not yet. I want this baby—Wesley does, too. We've been talking about it for months, but at the first hint of reality, I feel myself shutting down. What does that say about my future as a mom?

I wrap my arms tighter around my knees, hoping to disappear. But a shock of panic jolts up my spine at the thought of crushing my baby.

"I'm sorry, I'm sorry," I tearfully whisper as I touch my stomach, my legs now crossed under me.

I take three long, deep breaths and stagger to my feet. My reflection is a mess; frizzy hair, tear-stained cheeks, red eyes. Wesley can sniff out my bad mood from a mile away, so I wash my face, put in a few eye drops, and add some oil to my curls.

I need to pull myself together. Once the four positive tests are hidden, I head into the kitchen. Our chef only works when Wesley is home and I need to busy my hands, so I pull out a red bell pepper, a knife, and a cutting board.

Yes, I'm scared of what's to come from this baby, but my life hasn't been calm since I first arrived in Maldana. I barrel through it headfirst; Wesley is always the one to slow me down. He handles the disappointment from my communications office when I need to cancel or postpone an engagement because of burnout. I'm a people pleaser; my husband isn't.

I think back through our tumultuous two years together

and how we deal with so much on a daily basis. There's always something in the works, something big happening every two or three months. But we find pockets of time just for us.

After the summer we fell in love, we ran off to Rome for three weeks when it was supposed to be three days.

I flew home to see Raven and pack up my things only to return to my identity being leaked in Maldana. The stress kept me in bed for days, and Wesley took care of me. But I adjusted, and the public welcomed us. Everything changed. The news, although huge in Europe, wasn't much on a global scale—meaning I could live a relatively normal life when I visited America.

We flew Wesley's family to Kosita, who bear-hugged me on sight. With Vanessa's permission and encouragement, Wesley and I moved into the house in Antina. I started working as princess—my first year was essentially a trial—and it looked bad at some points, but Wesley was there for me through it all. Once my approval ratings jumped to eighty percent, the Higher Court started discussing my coronation for queen.

And Wesley proposed.

And, despite him wanting a trip to the courthouse on a Sunday afternoon, we planned a wedding.

And a coronation.

And eight months later, here we are. Pregnant.

In the impending chaos, my stomach suddenly lurches to overshadow my fear. I want Wesley right now. He's the only one who can talk me through this.

It feels like my heart triples in size when I hear the front door open. I'm still nervous to bits, but a sense of ease washes over me when my husband calls, "Babe?"

"In here!"

He was teaching combat classes today, so he wore a uniform of camo pants and a black T-shirt. The sight reminds me of how I got pregnant in the first place. I drop the knife and reach up to knot my arms around his neck. Wesley pulls me flush against him, capturing my mouth with his. Butterflies swarm my body as I inhale his scent—sandalwood cologne mixed with sweat.

"Long day?" I mutter.

He melts into me. "Always."

I kiss him again, and again, and again. When he pulls back to see my face, his brows instantly knit. His thumb grazes under my eye. "Have you been crying?"

"What? No." I recoil, turning around so my husband's frame pins me in place. "Are you hungry?" I ask before he can speak further. "I can stir fry these if you want." I resume slicing the pepper with a slim sense of pride that my hands are steady.

"I want you to tell me what's wrong," he says, hands caressing my hips.

"Nothing," I chirp.

"I know when my wife is upset. Your eyes are red and you hate cooking."

I stop slicing. Damn, he's right. When my tense shoulders ease, he steps back. My heart thunders as I consider how to say it. *Hey, remember when we broke the towel rack?* No, he'll instantly think I'm reminding him to fix it, even though I should. *Remember how we talked about wanting a kid to spoil for Christmas this year? Well, what about—*

No. Too long.

Fuck it.

I whirl around and blurt, "I'm pregnant."

"You're—" He blinks.

I nod. "Pregnant. Us. Well, not you, since you're a man, but me. Pregnant."

After a moment, he glances away and whispers, "Shit."

My stomach drops. *Shit?* I wait for him to continue, but he doesn't. Instead, he digs into his pocket to fish out his phone.

"What—" I cut myself off at the sight of his trembling hands.

I've never seen Wesley shake before.

"I need to call Silas—no, Mason—to start setting up interviews," he says, swiping the screen. "We'll have to pick female security because after what happened with us, we know it's a possibility—and we need to upgrade our current system." He shakes his head and searches around. "Shit—where's a notepad?"

I blanch as he zooms to the junk drawer to pull out a Post-It note and scrambles for a pen. A fucking *pen*.

"*Wesley.*" The crack in my voice makes him stop. "I tell you I'm pregnant and you're—talking about security?"

He meets my gaze, his panic melting into guilt. "Fuck." He closes the distance in a second, kissing me even deeper than he had when he first walked in. "I'm happy," he insists. "God, I'm so happy. But holy shit I'm terrified."

"I am, too, but you're—"

He slides his hands through my curls as if anchoring himself to me. "Losing my mind?"

My nerves dim, and I guide us to the closest chair at the kitchen table. I slide onto his lap, and my husband silently drops his head into the crook of my neck. With one arm secured around me, his free hand caresses my stomach. I thread my fingers through his hair, gently scratching his head in the way I know calms him.

I thought I would be the one who needs comfort, and even though he's anxious, I know I'm giving my child an amazing father.

Which is why my heart breaks when I hear his strained whisper. "I've done horrible things, angel. What if our baby gets the worst parts of me?"

I tug his hair so he meets my gaze. My tone fills with conviction. "And what if they get the best?"

The corner of his lips quirks ever so slightly. "You're the best part of me."

My chest warms, but I hate that the darkness of his past continues clouding the way he sees himself. "You're going to be an incredible father to our child." I kiss his stubbled cheek, down to his jaw. "Imagine they get your random pockets of humor, your never-ending need to protect the people you love, your work ethic."

His hold around me tightens. "Your kindness," he chimes in. "Your brains."

I brush a lock of hair from his forehead. "Your looks."

He stares incredulously. "Me? My child will have a queen for a mother."

"And a hero for a father."

The tension in his face withers, replaced by adoration. "We're going to be parents," he says softly.

For moments, we hold each other's gazes in emotional disbelief. "I love you," I whisper, brushing a finger over his bottom lip.

"I love you, too." He leans forward to kiss my mouth before pressing his lips to my jaw, my neck, then my collarbone. "You are everything to me, angel. My home, my salvation, the breath in my lungs. And if I died tomorrow, I'd become the breath in yours. I promise to find you in every lifetime and tell you I love you over and over." He touches my stomach, and I notice the tremor in his hand. He speaks gently, as if the words are delicate and unprotected. "Our baby is one of the many ways to show that I love you."

Tears prick my eyes. This is what I longed for—and I wish I waited until he was home to take the pregnancy test. "I'm so lucky to be loved by you."

He shakes his head. "It's not luck, it's fate. Plain and simple."

"Then what are my chances of you taking me upstairs?" I ask, running a hand down his chest as I press a kiss behind his ear. A yelp escapes me as he flies from the chair with a grunt, lifting me with him.

"Anything my wife wants," he says, aware that I love it when he calls me that.

No one in the universe can love me the way Wesley does. Most often, he knows what I need before I do—and vice versa. We move in harmony, catering to each other's ebb and flow. Even though he feels threaded into my very existence, we choose to be together every day.

I strip my tank top as he carries me upstairs, his hands locked where my ass meets my thighs. He instantly nuzzles his face between my breasts in a way that makes me laugh.

I always feared that this life of royal expectations and prying media would chase him away and end our relationship before it could truly begin. But he's never let it cloud our relationship even once. I've always been his main focus.

Time slips by as Wesley guides my body through climax after climax. The euphoric rush is familiar and intoxicating; it grabs hold of us until we're left sweaty and panting, our bodies tangled under the sheets. I wiggle the feeling back into my toes.

Honestly, it's a miracle it took more than two years for him to get me pregnant.

I press kisses against his neck and inhale his scent like a vacuum. Tingles dance up my center and wrap around my heart, utterly enamored with this man. My love for him is endless.

I peek up at him. "I hope it's a girl."

He pulls back to see me, brushing a curl from my face. "I want a healthy baby."

I level a glare. Of course that's the priority, but he has a preference. I know he does.

"I want a boy," he admits with a huff. "I grew up with women. I need a boy."

I laugh. "Let's brainstorm some names."

"Already?" He caresses my waist as I climb on top of him. "We still need to get you to the doctor for a formal check-up."

I nudge him. "C'mon, just for fun."

"All right, all right." He shifts among the pillows and hums in thought. "Uh—Kai."

I crinkle my nose. "Pass. Um... Lola."

Wesley shakes his head so violently that a small lock of hair trips onto his forehead. "Absolutely not."

"What—Lola's cute!"

"Lola sounds like a girl who disobeys her parents."

"I disagree, but fine. Lola's out."

"What about... Julian?"

I squint. "Like—King Julian from the Madagascar movies?"

He chuckles. "Okay, we'll pass on that."

I huff, sliding off him and settling at his side. He slings his arm across my body. "Hmmm, Sadie," I offer.

"*Sadie?*" Wesley echoes with disdain in his voice. He whistles suddenly as if calling a dog, the sound cracking through the calm. "*Sadie, come! Come here, girl!*"

I break out into laughter. Okay, Sadie *is* kind of a dog name, but whatever. "We'll think of something."

Wesley's hand slips under my shirt, caressing my lower stomach. I feel him kiss the top of my head.

"I'm gonna get fat," I blurt, staring at his hand. I'll blow up like a balloon soon enough.

"*Pregnant,*" he corrects.

"Same thing."

My body is going to change, and even though it's daunting, I'm okay with it. My husband will go above and beyond to make sure I feel beautiful. But the media is going to rip me apart. They'll study each shift, the way my body holds the baby weight and how long until I bounce back. I want to avoid telling the public I'm pregnant for as long as possible.

I don't care much about how I tell Dad and Ruby. My relationship with my father might have improved, but we lack closeness. Ruby, too. If anything, Ruby and I grew apart as Dad and I grew slightly closer. But through it all, Maia and I haven't wavered. I'm still motherly as hell to her, but it's easier with Wesley around. He can talk sense into her when I become a broken record.

She worried me during our first year as royalty. She partied a lot and even hooked up with Roman at one point. We finally got her botanical garden up and running outside of the city, and she's poured all of her focus into its laboratory. It's become her pride and joy, and the media has noticed that by finally backing off of her.

Even so, something is still going on with her. She knows I suspect something and has been keeping somewhat distant. We still talk just about every day, but I feel her pulling. I hope this news will bring us closer again.

"What are you thinking about?" Wesley asks, his voice gentle.

I heave a sigh and look up at him behind me. "How are we gonna tell Maia?"

Keep turning the page for the first chapter of Maia's book,
Royal Pain!

MALDANIAN DICTIONARY

ciao - *hello/goodbye*

bueni - *good*

buenimara - *good morning*

buenitera - *good afternoon*

bueninera - *good evening/night*

cómi stara? - *how are you?*

stari bueni - *I'm good*

parafóré - *please*

gracea - *thank you*

sperí - *wait*

ne - *no*

sì - *yes*

ke - *and*

pino - *what*

no - *we*

e - *a*

tu - *you*
    tusé - *you* (plural)

mi - *my*

di - *from/of*

gi - *with*

kest - *most*

epi - *for*

numerí - *name*

osé - *which*

mucho - *very much*

fimare - *hunger/hungry*

tora - *cake/pastry*

pomke - *apple*

niassa/niasso - *grandmother/grandfather*

revalté - *ghost*

prosítentto - *be careful*

sto - *very*

piranso - *piranha*

panímorísi - *beautiful*

pígo - *little*

opis - *like*

angeli - *angel*

ponte - *long*

siporí - *can I/I can*

milla - *hair*

pielli - *skin*

cranéos - *skulls*

caporer - *to pet/caress*

parné - *dog*

sou - *who*

mianna - *woman*

estaf - *this*

ya/stara - *to be*

eni - *here*

íma - *it's*

niávo - *I work*

cópente - *true/real*

revínastí - *revolution*

vi - *live*

maldasso - *maldanian*

milar - *to speak*

Amerikí - *America*

veni - *to come*

le - *she*

kesmáris - *stubborn*

lordi - *flower*

comagri - *to cook*

bueni kara - enjoy (your food)

mondélo - *world*

sémero - *I know*

seremísa - *serenity/peace*

tósché - *touch*

kaiséitré - *to call/to say*

verinìta - *queen*

ten staran sto panímorísi - *you (plural) are very beautiful*

tofalimente - *of course*

ACKNOWLEDGMENTS

First, I thank Anne Hathaway and Audrey Hepburn. These two queens inspired an era of my life that I wrote *Roaming Holiday* in honor of.

I want to thank my ever-so-perfect husky for just existing.

I want to thank my betas for being wonderfully patient with me. Amina, Kacey, Jennifer, Marina, Hailey, and Rosana: thank you thank you thank you for your feedback and critiques. You helped so much!

Ellie Blackbourne, thank you for helping me through my doubtful moments. I'm so grateful you're my bestie!

Emily, thank you for being the best sister I could ask for.

My family, thank you for always supporting me and showing up. I'm endlessly grateful.

The *Roaming Holiday* cheerleaders over on Instagram, thank you *so* much for all of your kind words and messages. I want you all to genuinely know how much you helped me.

Josh, thank you for being the reason I write romance.

Royal
Pain

ONE
MAIA

"Yes, I'm a nightmare, nothing new."

I toss the tabloid magazine across the backseat of the car, a knot of anger twisting my gut from that stupid headline. I glance over my shoulder. "Why do you even have this?"

My best friend stiffens as she climbs into the car behind me, and I regret not masking the clip in my tone. "I stole it," Lyla says, "from a guy in a cafe when he wasn't looking."

"Wait—" I choke out a laugh, my agitation disappearing. Leave it to Lyla to steal a magazine before someone can read about my many disappointments as deemed by the media. I shouldn't be surprised.

She smirks. "You know I got you."

At least the tabloids stopped calling me a witch because of all the healing crystal jewelry I used to wear. My team convinced me to dilute my hippie style since it led to rumors I worship the devil, and I'm sure it didn't help that I dressed up as a witch for Halloween that year.

Not a good look for the princess of Maldana.

The car pulls from the curb and I kick my heels off,

dropping my head back with a groan. "Remind me why we went to that stupid breakfast."

"For money."

I grimace and shut my eyes for a sliver of sleep. Stuffing my feet into heels and putting on a full face of makeup before eight a.m. feels like a crime, not to mention objectifying since we're only looking pretty so the donors want to keep giving us their money. I can't screw it up the way I have so often before. Art galleries, green corporations, universities—they're the few businesses clean enough for donations, and we need to keep the garden in their best interest. At least Dr. Pagoda was there to do most of the heavy lifting. She's way more diplomatic and educated than I am.

I reach for the cloth bag on the floor and take out my padded piggy slippers. They give my feet a fuzzy embrace after hours of tight heels. Twenty minutes later, the car pulls through the security gates of Felicity Gardens.

"Just a few reports and then movies at your house?" Lyla says. I don't know why she has to confirm it, considering it's been our routine every Friday for the past five or six months.

"As long as we watch *The Proposal*."

Her eyes brighten as she shimmies her chest. "I say yes to anything Ryan Reynolds."

"Are you kidding? I'm watching for Sandy B."

We both laugh. My head of security opens the door before I have a chance to finish putting my shoes back on, so I stick with my slippers. I usually beat him to it and insist on doing it myself, but Mason is a by-the-book kind of guy. Always has been.

"Pick me up at three?" I say as I climb out of the car. I

normally drive myself to work, but Mason picked me up for the event this morning.

"You got it."

He helps Lyla out behind me before leaving us. She stares at the retreating car until I force her around. "Will you stop?" I say with a laugh. "He's not going to date you."

"But he's so sexy," she whines, dropping her head against my shoulder. "I'm not saying we need to date. Just hook up."

I shake my head. I've explained it a dozen times, but she won't accept how loyal Mason is to his wife, even though she died. He still hasn't revealed much and I keep trying to pry him open like a stubborn clam. All I managed to squeeze out of him was that his wife's sister had taken custody of his kids after her death. He's still such a mystery —and it low-key drives me crazy. But I know what it's like to have your privacy stripped, so I don't push him like I used to.

It nearly broke my heart when he resigned as my body-guard a year and a half ago. Even though he's head of my security and oversees certain events, Zeke accompanies me in public. Mason needs to stay out of the public eye because of his government history, and it makes sense.

We step inside the building and before I can head to the closet holding my spare clothes, I spot a figure in the waiting room ahead. Lyla catches me lingering and follows my stare.

"And who the hell is *that*?" she whispers. "Damn, he's fine."

Lyla needs a man for a night—or a better vibrator. Although yes, this man is fine as hell, I know exactly who he is and he's no one good. Still wearing my fitted, knee-length black dress and piggy slippers, I stomp over to the waiting room.

"What are you doing here?" I ask, then instantly bite my tongue as his eyes land on me. Dammit, he's even prettier in person.

He outstretches a hand. "Hi, I'm the new donor. I'll be shadowing for a bit. My name's—"

"I know who you are. Thank you, but we pass on your donation."

There's not a chance in hell we'll accept money from him. Not from a man whose company displaced thousands of families. Not from a man whose company destroys acres upon acres of land for mining.

I haven't found a single redeeming quality about Tristan Farrugia.

Okay, fine. He's a chiseled specimen of human perfection and it makes him so much more hate-able. His dark eyes are framed by unfairly long lashes and his skin is a smooth tawny shade. He's dressed impeccably in a white dress shirt and black slacks. But no amount of good looks can make me forget what Space Technologies has done. Just last month, I signed a public letter urging Maldana to raise the minimum wage. The company that lobbied against it? Space Tech.

He's the definition of a handsome devil.

"I'm afraid it's too late for that," Mr. Farrugia says.

"Excuse me?"

He watches me with pity and I want to slap the look off his face. More importantly, I need to know what the hell he's talking about. "Bridget! Where's Bridget?" I call, searching for the financial director. I turn down a hallway and head straight into her mind-numbingly bland office. "You did *not* accept a donation from Space Tech."

She rises from her seat, lips pursed. She really tried to sneak this by me. "I did. Our funds were quickly—"

"Does Dr. Pagoda know about it? Does the *queen*? Let's start there."

"Well, once the—"

"It's a yes or no question."

Her face hardens. "No."

I let out a harsh breath, flexing my hands to try to grasp this level of absurdity from a coworker. This was the *first* thing she was taught in this role. *The most important thing.*

"Every single penny donated to an official royalty project must go through the queen. Do you even understand the hypocrisy of a botanical garden accepting money from one of the world's worst polluters?"

Mr. Farrugia—whom I hadn't known followed me in here—steps into view with a halting hand. "Now, those statistics—"

"Back off!"

"Your Majesty!" Bridget exclaims, horrified that I spoke to a CEO like that. "Money doesn't grow on trees. We have to be realistic if we want to keep this place up and running."

I don't trust a single billionaire. *No one* can obtain that much money without stepping on the necks of others.

"This garden's existence hinges on our ethics. The queen has worked tirelessly to show this country we will not accept a penny of political donations or perceived political donations. You want to help our budget? Congratulations, you just increased it by eighty thousand a year."

She blanches. "I—Your Majesty, with all due respect, Dr. Pagoda—"

"We both know Dr. Pagoda doesn't bother with any of the garden's administrative work. Your things should be out of here by the end of the day."

ABOUT THE AUTHOR

Marina Hill is a multifaceted author of books from romance to historical fiction with an eventual path into fantasy. With over a dozen publications of short stories, her work has been hailed as fun comfort reads while managing to discuss important topics. A New Jersey native, Marina spends her days working around books and her nights writing them.

Also by Marina Hill

Little Writer
Fumbled Love
Royal Pain

CONNECT WITH ME!

Instagram
@marinahill.docx

Website
themarinahill.com

If you enjoyed *Roaming Holiday*, please consider leaving a review on your platform of choice! Reviews help authors tremendously.